Bring
me
Home

For my readers.

Note to Reader

Music is an important part of this series. Some chapters in this book begin with a musical note. The musical note indicates there is a song on the *Bring Me Home* playlist that pertains to or is mentioned in that chapter. Please feel free to open the playlist on a computer or mobile device and listen as you read.

The playlist is available on YouTube at:
http://bit.ly/bmhplaylist

The playlist is available on Spotify at:
http://bit.ly/bmhplaylists

CHAPTER ONE

Claire

IN THE LAST five weeks, I've read the letter I received from my mother's rapist twice; the first time was before I knew who the letter was from and the second time was to make sure I wasn't seeing things. Yes, my mother's rapist sent me a letter. And yes, that is how I refer to my father. This doesn't change the fact that, for five weeks, I've been carrying that man's letter around with me everywhere I go.

Even now, as I stroll across the driveway toward my old home, the letter is folded and tucked into the bottom of my purse. As I approach the door, I still get an urge to knock, even though such niceties are no longer necessary. Jackie, the best foster mother a girl could ask for, gave me a house key two weeks ago.

This is my home.

I open the door slowly, still slightly afraid that I'm

going to run into Chris, though I planned this visit for a Thursday evening instead of a weekend because I knew he wouldn't be here. I step inside and close the door softly before I make my way to the kitchen. Dropping my purse on the breakfast bar, I immediately head for the fridge to grab a bottle of water. As I close the refrigerator door, someone clears their throat behind me.

Turning around, I find Rachel standing on the other side of the breakfast bar. Her dark hair is pulled up into a messy ponytail, but she still manages to look perfectly pulled together. She never blinks as we stare at each other for a moment.

"Chris said you weren't going to my birthday party next week," she says, and her glare softens a little.

Rachel can be abrasive and she sometimes takes the phrase "honesty is the best policy" to the extreme, but she's also intensely emotional and sensitive. She used to play piano with Chris's band occasionally, but she just writes music now. She plays beautifully and actually taught me a couple of songs when Chris and I were still together.

"I'm not sure it's a good idea for me to hang out with you guys right now."

I don't tell her that my therapist actually encouraged me to go to the party when I told him Chris had invited me. I don't want to be one of those people who constantly says stuff like, "My shrink doesn't think it's a good idea." The problem is, I catch myself thinking these kinds of things all day long. My therapist is adamant that I shouldn't shut out the people I love in my attempt to get my head straight, but I'm terrified that everyone is secretly judging me for what I did to Chris.

Rachel and I were never best friends. It was always understood that Jake was her best friend and Chris was mine. Sometimes we got along great and sometimes we tolerated each other. I don't feel obligated to go to her birthday party, but the hurt look on her face makes me feel like I may be becoming too detached in my quest to find myself.

"I know you think you're doing what's best for you," Rachel says, "but Chris is right, you need—" Jackie walks in and Rachel immediately stops speaking.

Jackie looks radiant as ever; her short, dark hair and makeup are impeccable. As I watch my foster mother approach me for a hug, I can't help but hope that she will find someone to share her life with. She's always putting everyone else's needs before her own.

She holds her arms open and beckons me. "Bring it home."

I wrap my arms around her curvy waist and nestle my face into her shoulder. Closing my eyes, I inhale the crisp, floral scent of her perfume. This is the scent I've come to associate with love. Just the idea of having Jackie back in my life makes my throat ache.

I haven't called Jackie "Mom" since the first and only

time I did so five weeks ago. I have this stupid idea that if I say it too often, it will lose some of its impact. When I told my therapist, Dr. Goldberg, that I was still having trouble calling her Mom, he asked if I felt guilty for loving Jackie as if she were my mother. I didn't have an answer for that.

I let go of Jackie and she looks me over for a moment, taking in my baby-blue UNC hoodie and faded skinny jeans with the hole in the right knee. I'm not wearing a lot of makeup today and my blonde hair is pulled into a messy ponytail that doesn't look deliberately messy like Rachel's.

"You look beautiful," she says with a smile. "Are you ready to go?"

"Go where? I thought we were having dinner at home tonight."

I turn to Rachel and she's trying not to smile. "We're taking you out."

Jackie raises her eyebrows. "Is that okay? I know it's a school night for you, but we've been dying to take you to this new restaurant downtown. It's classy and the waiters are gorgeous. Rachel and I have gone to ogle them three times since they opened up a few weeks ago."

The idea that Jackie and Rachel have been hanging out without me makes me a little jealous. But right now I'm more suspicious of this change of plans. Jackie isn't shy when it comes to men, so ogling waiters sounds like something she would find entertaining. She chooses to stay single because she insists serious relationships are more trouble than they're worth at her age. I've always had a strong suspicion that she avoids relationships because she's afraid of being devastated the way she was when Chris's father left.

"I'm not dressed to go out to a classy restaurant. Anyway, why are you two so eager to take me out tonight?" I open my bottle of water and take a long swig.

Jackie and Rachel glance at each other before Rachel replies. "It was my idea. I wanted to take you out to ask you something."

"Okay, now I'm even more confused. Why don't you just ask me now?"

Rachel sighs, looking slightly annoyed that I don't want to play along with this suspenseful dinner date she has planned for the three of us. "Claire, you know I don't have a whole lot of girlfriends. And I haven't spoken to my sister in three years. You're the closest thing I have to a sister."

A sister.

My eyes dart toward my purse on the breakfast bar. I've only read that letter twice, but I remember every single word.

Claire,

You may not recognize my name. Your mother did a good job of protecting you from her past. Henry Wilkins at Northstar Bank contacted me recently. He informed me that you refused the trust fund your mother set up for you before her death. I hope you will reconsider your position on this, as that money is rightfully yours.

I also hope you can find it in your heart to forgive me for my transgressions and that you won't hold my past against your half-sister. Nichelle just turned seventeen last week and she's very eager to meet you.

I hope this letter finds you well.

Your father,

Phil

Rachel rounds the breakfast bar toward Jackie and me then holds out her hand. I spot the giant rock on her finger right away and I'm instantly reminded of the two rings sitting on top of my bedside table in the dorm.

"Jake and I are getting married. I was hoping you'd be my maid of honor."

I try not to let her see the panic I'm feeling inside. The idea of being Rachel's maid of honor scares the shit out of me. Ninety percent of the time, Rachel is awesome, but it's that ten percent that makes me want to run screaming out of this house.

"Congratulations," I say as I reach out to give her a hug. I let go quickly and she eyes me, awaiting my answer. "Are you sure you want *me* to be your maid of honor? I'm so busy with school right now and it's not like I live around the corner. I don't know if I'll be much help to you."

"It's not going to be a huge wedding," she says, and her

lips curl into a giddy smile. "We've been together too long for this to be a huge deal. We're getting married in Vegas on New Year's Eve. I just don't want to stand up there on my own while Jake has his two best friends next to him. My sister won't be coming and since you and Chris broke up, the only girls I've had around are Tristan's skanks." She looks down as she speaks the next three words. "I've missed you."

"New Year's Eve is in seven weeks."

"You'll be on break, won't you?"

Before I can reply, my phone starts ringing in my purse. I pull it out and see Chris's name. I'm tempted to let it ring, but answering it will give me some time to think of an appropriate response to Rachel's request.

"Hello?"

"Claire, is Rachel there?"

He sounds annoyed and impatient, as if he's in a hurry.

"Yeah, she's right here."

"Give her the phone, please."

I hold the phone out to Rachel and she looks confused. "It's Chris. He wants to talk to you."

She rolls her eyes as she takes the phone from me. "What?" She purses her lips as she listens. "I wasn't trying to avoid you. I left my phone at home." She starts tapping her foot as she listens some more. "Whatever, Chris. It's my wedding and I can do whatever the fuck I want."

She hands me the phone and I can hear the distant

sound of Chris's voice coming through the speaker as I hold it at arm's length. Rachel turns on her heel and marches out of the kitchen. I slowly bring the phone to my ear.

"Chris?"

"Don't listen to her. You don't have to be in her wedding. It's not your problem that she can't maintain a single female relationship."

"It's fine. I'll be on break."

"No, it's not fine. I know you're trying to get yourself figured out. Don't let her guilt you into doing anything for her if you're not ready."

"Chris, I swear I'm fine."

I'm not really fine. In the last three months, I've learned that my mother committed suicide; my father raped my mother and contributed to a trust fund in my name; Chris learned I gave up our daughter for adoption without his knowledge; and five weeks ago I was given two rings, one from each of the two most important men in my life. I am definitely not fine, but I'm better than I was five weeks ago and I should be even better in seven weeks—I hope.

"Shit. I wish I would have known she was going to ambush you. I wouldn't have left."

I don't say anything because I'm actually glad he's not here. I've only seen Chris once since the night I found out that Abigail's parents don't want us in her life; the night I lost her for the second time.

"I'm fine. Are you on your way home?"

He's silent for a moment. "Xander and I have one more conference call in a few minutes then I'll be on my way. Are you going to be there?"

"No. I'm going out to dinner with your mom then I'm heading back to the dorm."

The silence between us is filled with all the things we haven't said to each other since the night I rejected his marriage proposal five weeks ago.

"Are you coming over for Thanksgiving next week?"

There's a note of desperation in his voice that makes me want to forget my Thanksgiving plans to be with him. "I can't. I already promised Senia I'd go to her parents' house."

I want to add that I will definitely be there for Christmas next month, but December 25th seems so far away and insignificant right now.

"Tell Senia I said hi."

"I will."

There's a brief pause where I feel like both of us are holding our breath, trying not to blurt out something we'll regret.

"Have fun at dinner. I guess we'll talk later."

I end the call and finally notice Jackie. She's staring at me with that knowing look; the look of a mother who, without a single word spoken, can see and feel her child's pain. I bite my lip as I try not to let her see what is so plainly obvious.

CHAPTER TWO

Adam

YOU NEVER KNOW you're making a mistake until it's too late. Sometimes we know we're taking a risk, but we always hope for the best. We hope that our mistakes will be forgiven, or at least forgotten. We hope that our mistakes will teach us something. Sometimes, unfortunately, mistakes are just mistakes that can't be undone or forgotten.

I got the feeling that Claire was hiding something from me when I took her to the UNC vs. North Carolina State football game two weeks ago. We've spoken on the phone a few times a week since the night I surprised her at Cora's, but our conversations are short and weighed down by this feeling that we're both holding back. I want to ask her when she's going to talk about the ring I gave her and I'm sure there are things she wants to talk to me about, but instead we speak as if we haven't explored the depths of each other physically and emotionally. Like we're strangers.

We met at the stadium two weeks ago in Raleigh, like some kind of fucking blind date or casual lunch with a friend. The walk across the parking lot and through the stadium to our seats was excruciatingly silent. I couldn't even bring myself to tell a joke to break the ice. Something has shifted between us and it's more than just the stench of the sweaty guy seated in front of us.

The whole time we were waiting for the game to begin, I just wanted to reach across and grab her hand, to touch her skin.

"Dr. Goldberg talked to me about his kids the other day," she said as she tapped her foot nervously. "I think he was trying to make me feel comfortable, but I kept thinking about how he was trying to make me feel comfortable and that made me feel uncomfortable."

"You sound like a nut."

"Yeah, that's kind of why I'm in therapy."

She flashes me a weak smile and I have to look away. "How was your Halloween?"

Small talk?

She turns her head to glare at me. "Really?"

I shrug because I don't really know what else to do at this point. This friendly "date" is not going the way I had planned.

"What the fuck are we doing here?" I ask. "I mean, why are we doing this?"

She stares at her hands in her lap. "I don't know," she whispers. "Because I'm fucked up. Because most days I'm hanging on by a thread and I don't want that thread to snap."

She bites her lip and I finally reach across and grab her hand. The snack peddler arrives at our row and she immediately lets go. I order us both a hot dog. As soon as he's gone, she breathes a deep sigh and takes a tiny nibble from her food.

"You can talk to me, Claire. That's what I'm here for."

"Have you talked to your dad?"

She doesn't want to talk. Fine.

"I told you not to worry about my dad. He'll get over me quitting eventually."

"But what about your trust fund? How much did these tickets cost?"

"It's just money. It's not going to make me happy. Being with you is what makes me happy."

A painful nervousness settles in my stomach as I speak these words, as if saying this aloud has made me doubt whether it's actually true. Claire *does* make me happy, usually. But I'm definitely not happy right now.

She's silent as I stare at the hot dog she's barely touched. Our last meal together was pizza, shared just moments before she admitted to having sex with Chris while I was in Hawaii. Claire and I were broken up at the time, which was the main factor in my decision to forgive her. I fucked up letting her go. And as sick as it makes me to admit it, I know she would never have been with Chris if I hadn't broken up with her. I'm the one who pushed her away.

But I'm determined to fix the mess I made. I just wish the mess inside Claire's head were something I could repair. The only person who can fix that is Claire, but now I'm torn between giving her the space she needs to do that and the fear that I'll lose her *again* if I give her too much space.

"I work with a woman named Maddie," I begin. "She told me that her husband comes home every night and turns on ESPN for three hours, then they eat a late dinner, shower, and go to sleep. That's been their routine for almost twenty years."

She looks up at me with interest. I haven't really spoken to Claire about my new job yet. I've been side-stepping her questions every time she asks me about it. I don't want to tell her that I hate this new job. Greg Wyatt, the president of Wyatt & Jones Architects, promised me the same level position I held while working with my dad at Parker Construction. I didn't expect to get a lead architect position, but they've had me doing entry-level drafting that any asshole fresh out of college or technical school can do.

"I asked Maddie if she thinks the routine is what keeps her and her husband together," I continue. "She told me that what keeps them together is the fact that during the three hours he watches ESPN she's shopping online."

Claire squints at me. "Where are you going with this?"

"What I'm trying to tell you is that familiarity is good, it's comfortable, but sometimes we can get *too* comfortable. Sometimes, we make stupid decisions because we get complacent."

"Adam, are you saying I've made stupid decisions or are you trying to tell me that you broke up with me because you got complacent?"

"I'm trying to tell you that sometimes you have to go outside your comfort zone to find true happiness."

She closes her eyes and takes a deep breath through her nose. I know that look. She wants to meditate. She used to do this a lot when we first started dating, before I found out about Abigail.

"I feel like we've both taken ten steps back since I went to Hawaii. I just want you to know that I'm ready to move forward."

"I'm not ready. I'm nowhere near ready. Do you know what Dr. Goldberg diagnosed me with? Besides depression, I've been suffering from PTSD for the past five months. I need you to give me some time to get my head straight. Please."

A man stops at our row and eyeballs the seats to my right before he scoots past us with two large cups of beer. He spills a little on Claire's jeans and I try not to get annoyed.

"I'm so sorry. I'll get you some napkins," he says as he

moves back toward the aisle.

"It's fine," Claire insists, throwing her hand up to stop him. "Really, I'm fine. Go ahead and sit down. The game's starting soon."

The man smiles at her and I feel a tremor of jealousy reverberating through my chest. He steals a few more glances at her before he sits two seats away from me. I don't notice Claire staring at me until I tear my eyes away from him.

"Are you mad because he spilled a little beer on my leg?"

"I'm just worried about you."

She shakes her head because she knows I'm lying.

"Fine. Yes, I can't stand the way he was looking at you."

She reaches under her seat to grab her purse. "Maybe this was a bad idea."

"You're leaving?"

My phone vibrates in my pocket as she slides her purse over her shoulder. "Wait a sec. I have to get this in case it's Greg."

I pull my phone out of my pocket and the name flashing on the screen makes my heart stop: Lindsay Harris.

Fuck.

I glance at Claire to see if she noticed the name and she's looking right at my screen. I hit the ignore button and tuck the phone back into my pocket, but it's too late. Why

empty steel bowls and toward the back of the shop. When I enter my mom's tiny office, she's leaning back in her chair with her eyes closed.

"Mom? Are you okay?"

She jumps a little and lays her hand flat on the desk to steady herself. "Jesus, Chris!"

"Why are you sleeping in your office? Didn't you sleep last night?"

She shakes her head as she arranges a messy pile of papers into a neat pile on her desk. "No, I didn't. I'm worried about Claire."

"Please don't do this to yourself. She's working things out right now. We need to give her some time and space to do that." I reach my hand out to her and she grabs it so I can pull her up from the chair. "When she's ready, she'll come back. She just got a little lost."

My mom's face scrunches up as if she's in physical pain then she wraps her arms around me. "I don't want her to be lost. I just want her to come home."

I rub her back as she sobs into my shoulder. "I have some good news. Do you want to hear it?"

"God, yes." She lets go of me and wipes her face as she steps out of her office and into the kitchen area.

I lean back on the edge of the worktable and smile. "I might be able to do the album and the tour without leaving Claire. I talked to Gene at Arista and he said he's going to try to get the production team to fly out to Raleigh next week."

Asking Gene Hadley, rock star producer at Arista Records, to fly the production team out to a tiny studio in Raleigh was not easy. I try not to be an over demanding artist. But staying in Raleigh is too important for me to worry what anyone, even Gene, think about this decision.

My mom's jaw drops. "I think that's the best news I've ever heard."

"Good. As soon as I hear back from Gene, I'm going to surprise Claire with the news." I heave a deep sigh as I think of all the things that can go right and wrong when I deliver this news to her. "I miss her so much."

"You said it: when she's ready she'll come back."

I nod my head, though I'm not entirely sure if that's true. "I know. Well, I just wanted to give you the good news and to ask you a favor. Can you call Rachel and convince her to tell Claire she doesn't have to be in the wedding? She's not answering my calls."

My mom shakes her head as she grabs a large, steel bowl from a shelf. "Chris, sweetheart, you have to let Claire make her own decisions. If she wants to be in the wedding, let her be in the wedding."

"But she doesn't want to be in the wedding. I heard it in her voice."

"She doesn't want to let Rachel down. I saw it in her *face*. Let her do something nice for somebody else. It's good for her."

I try not to roll my eyes as I push away from the table. "I'm going to pick up Tristan. Do you need anything before I go?"

"Where are you going with him?"

"We're going to a friend's house. Why?"

"A girl?"

"No, not a girl. We're going to Billy's house. You remember Billy? He came over three weeks ago to pick up some pedals." She eyes me suspiciously. "Mom, I'm not going to do anything stupid. I'll be back by six at the latest. Tristan and I have to practice in case we start recording next week." I kiss her cheek as she pries open a large plastic tub of flour. "I'll see you later."

"Wait a minute," she calls out when I'm halfway across the kitchen. "What's going on with the baby?"

My mom hasn't been able to say Abigail's name. I think she feels that speaking her name aloud will make her more real and more difficult to let go.

"I can't say. I'm not bringing you or Claire into this until I get it figured out. I don't want to get your hopes up. But I'm working on it. I'm not giving up."

She nods and I head out of the kitchen quickly before she can question me anymore. The subject of Abby is not something I like to discuss with anyone. Ever since my dad left, I've never really been the type of person to talk about my problems unless it's to try to find a solution. And there's no solution when your parent up and abandons you. The only person I've ever bared my soul to is Claire, but this isn't something I can talk to her about yet. I need to give her some time to heal and I need to figure out what's going to happen with the post-adoption agreement before I discuss anything with her. Until then, I'll pretend to be strong, even though the truth is that I feel like more than half of my heart is missing.

I wave at Melina as I pass her on the way out of the store. The smell of downtown Raleigh is an unpleasant jolt compared to the sweet smell of the bakery.

The truth is, Tasha, my adoption lawyer, and I are still trying to figure out a plan to approach Abigail's parents again. I'm not giving up on my daughter. And I'm trying really hard not to blame Claire for Abigail's parents backing out of the open adoption agreement. I know that if Claire has a chance to see Abigail, to hold her, it will heal her; the way holding Abby's hand in the hospital changed something inside me. But I won't discuss this with Claire unless we have an agreement in place or a visit scheduled. I want nothing less than yearly visitations.

Tasha already drew up a new agreement that I plan to present to the Jensens myself. It details the visitation and communication rights and what I'm willing to do to secure those. I just hope that the things I'm willing to sacrifice are enough.

CHAPTER FOUR

Claire

FROM THE TIME my mother died when I was seven to the day I arrived on Jackie's doorstep when I was fifteen, I was convinced I was invisible. Like Schrödinger's cat, I only existed when someone observed me. But the way Chris and Jackie *saw* me changed everything. I wasn't a nuisance or a paycheck. I was a real person who didn't need to cause trouble to be noticed and respected. Chris and Jackie changed everything, and by *everything* I mean *me*.

Dr. Goldberg and I sit across the desk from each other. I'm trying not to tap my foot impatiently as he writes notes in his file regarding everything I just told him about my years in the foster care system—well, almost everything. Only Chris knows everything that happened before I came to live with him and Jackie. Chris was always there when I needed to talk about heavy subjects, like the day he came to my dorm six weeks ago to comfort me when he found out about my mother's suicide. Now I have Dr. Goldberg to talk to, but I can't even bring myself to tell him about the letter I've been carrying around in my purse for five weeks.

Right now, the only person who knows about the letter is Senia, and she insists that I need to respond. She thinks I need to meet my sister, Nichelle. Though Senia's never said it, I think she's just as worried as I am that Nichelle is in danger of being violated by her father the same way my mother was. Preventing something like that from happening is not a responsibility I ever thought I'd have placed on my shoulders. My soul is already buckling under the weight of my own responsibilities. But Senia is right. I need to meet Nichelle. I need to look in her eyes and see for myself that she hasn't been broken the way my mother was.

"How did you feel when you were told your mother's death may have been a suicide?" Dr. Goldberg asks.

His face is kind and relaxed and his slightly messy crown of black curls combined with the brown sweater he wears makes *me* feel relaxed.

"I felt like I had just been told that my mother never loved me."

"Do you still feel that way?" he asks as he continues to jot down notes.

"Sometimes." He pauses for a moment and I take a deep breath before I continue. "My mother was raped."

"By her uncle?"

"No, her uncle's son also raped her when she was seventeen."

He looks up from his notepad curiously. "Seventeen? That would have been three years after the alleged molestation by her uncle ceased?"

I hate that he always says *alleged* molestation. It makes me feel like we're in a courtroom instead of an office.

"Yes. He's my father."

I'm having second thoughts now. I don't know if I can trust him enough to tell him about the letter. What if he insists on calling child protective services? Not that it would matter. If there's anything I learned in the foster care system, it's that CPS rarely takes preemptive action. They're almost always too late.

The look Goldberg gives me is meant to be sympathetic, I suppose, but I sense a bit of betrayal, as if he's upset that I didn't tell him about my father sooner. That's when I realize I can't tell him about the letter. I have to tell Chris first.

If there's anyone who will understand what I'm feeling right now, it's Chris. He hasn't seen or spoken to his father since he was six.

I get up from my chair suddenly and slide my purse strap onto my shoulder. "I have to go now."

"Don't forget to call Janine to schedule your next appointment."

I smile as I scurry out of the office, eager to get away

from this building. Our dorm in Spencer Hall is clear across campus and I still have a ton of reading to do for Professor Coldwater's class—not that I'm looking forward to reading about divorce and stepfamilies.

By the time I make it into the dorm, Senia is already sitting on her bed with her laptop open and her earbuds in place. She smiles at me and goes back to doing whatever she was doing. I let my backpack drop on the floor then set my purse down on the desk. I dig my hand into the bottom of the purse and pull out the letter from my father.

The neat handwriting on the outside makes me anxious. I think I saw or read somewhere that serial killers often have very messy or very neat handwriting. I don't think my father is a serial killer, but maybe the same handwriting analysis applies to serial rapists.

My heart pounds as I slide my phone out of my pocket and dial Chris's number. He picks up on the second ring.

"Hey, babe."

He still calls me babe even though I rejected his marriage proposal. It doesn't even bother me anymore. It really got on my nerves when he did it while I was with Adam, but now... it just feels natural.

"Chris, I have to tell you something."

There's a pause as he probably tries to decide whether he wants to know what I'm about to tell him.

"Are you okay?"

"I'm fine. Well, no, not really. I... I got a letter from

my father five weeks ago and I think I may need to go to California to meet him."

There's a rustling noise as he moves then, "Hey! I'm gonna take this outside. I'll be right back," he says to someone.

"Where are you?"

"I'm with Xander and Tristan. We're scoping out a studio in Chapel Hill."

"I'll let you go if you're busy."

"I'm never too busy for you. So, wait a minute, you got a letter from your father? The one who raped your mom?"

"Yes."

"Fuck."

"Exactly. What am I supposed to do? He has another daughter, four years younger than me, the same age as my mom when he raped her. I can't just ignore that."

He sighs and I dig my nails into the palm of my hand as I wait for his response. "Claire, I think we may have found a studio here in Chapel Hill," he says, as if I didn't just tell him my half-sister is living with a rapist. "I made a deal with Arista Records that this album would be acoustic so that we'd have a higher chance of finding a studio in this area. Most of the studios are only equipped for acoustic recordings. I did that for you, so I could be close to you while I'm recording. I want to be here for you."

"You don't have to do that, Chris. I told you that you should go to L.A."

"I don't want to go to L.A. And the deal is already done, for the most part. We just have to find a studio now. But my point is, I want to take you to California to meet your dad and your sister, but I need a couple of weeks to record."

"That's it? I thought you were going to tell me I'm crazy for even thinking of meeting him." I sit down in the desk chair as the tension in my shoulders begins to ease a little. "I can wait a few weeks. I *have* to wait. Winter Break doesn't start for another five weeks."

"Well, I guess we'll be kissing under the mistletoe in California."

"Shut up."

He chuckles and I wish I were there to see him smile.

"Are you okay?" he asks. "I have to get back in there before Xander goes into full bitch-mode."

"I'm fine. Go handle your business."

"Hey!" he calls out before I can hang up.

"What?"

"Have a good Thanksgiving with Senia."

My chest floods with warmth that spreads through my entire body. "Thanks. Give your mom a hug for me."

"I'll let you do that next time you come over. Goodnight, babe."

"Goodnight."

I can hardly breathe. I want to curl up in bed and forget about my father and the two rings on my nightstand. I want to wake up five weeks from now, in California, where the only thing that matters is meeting my sister.

I have a little sister.

It's funny how having someone else to look after changes your entire outlook on life. I never got to feel that with Abigail. To go to sleep one night with your child nestled inside you and wake up the next with no evidence your child ever existed is like waking up in a nightmare that never ends. As much as I want to feel like nothing has changed between Chris and me, everything has changed. And by *everything* I mean *me*.

CHAPTER FIVE

Adam

THE FIRST TIME Lindsay called me, after not having spoken to her for over eight months, I think time stopped along with my heart. My first thought, when I heard her voice, was that the DNA test results had been botched. I was certain that she was calling to tell me that I'm the father of her child. Instead, she wanted to know if I'd heard from Nathan, which made me laugh. She told me she hadn't heard from him in a few days and to please let her know if I heard from him. The second time she called, during the football game, it took everything in me not to answer the phone and lose my shit.

Instead, what I discovered is that the true father of her child, the guy she left me for eight months ago, has pretty much abandoned her. After the competition in California, where Nathan Jennings qualified to go to the ASP qualifier in Australia, Lindsay claims that Nathan began acting strange. Then he insisted he needed to go back to California for another competition, which is when Lindsay realized what I've known since I met Nathan Jennings over six years ago: he's full of shit. And he's not ready to be a father.

I don't believe in karma, but if I did, I would most certainly say that this is Lindsay getting payback for what she did to me. But I don't believe in karma. And, having gone through it myself, I actually feel sympathetic.

Of course, I may be sympathetic, but I'm not stupid.

As she steps out of the rear unit of the small duplex, where she and Nathan lived together before he decided to ditch her three weeks ago, I can't help but wonder if something stronger than sympathy has pulled me back here.

She smiles at the baby she's cradling in her arms as she locks the door. Kaia. A Hawaiian name meaning "the sea or restful place." Those are both things I used to associate with Lindsay. She was the only girl I'd been with who wasn't a professional surfer and still loved the ocean as much as I do—until I met Claire. And my relationship with Lindsay was comfortable, restful, until the last three or four months when everything fell apart.

She looks through the windshield at me and I'm tempted to go help her with the car seat and the diaper bag she's carrying along with the baby, but I'm afraid. It feels like something only Nathan should do, but that's just stupid. A friend can help another friend carry a fucking car seat. I scramble out of the car and scurry over to help her.

"Actually, can you take Kaia? I need to strap the car seat in," Lindsay says.

I stare at the baby for a moment. This is the second time I've taken Lindsay and Kaia to the hospital. Two weeks ago, I took them to the emergency room for some type of stomach virus that had Kaia vomiting for over twenty-four hours. Today, it's just for vaccinations. Lindsay claims she's trying to find a roommate to help her out with the other half of the rent now that Nathan is gone. She doesn't want to move in with her parents in Carolina Beach. I don't want to jump to conclusions, but I have a feeling she's hoping I'll offer to help her out.

This duplex isn't far from the apartment Lindsay and I shared during our senior year at Duke. Lindsay isn't a terrible person, but she did some pretty terrible things the last few months we were together. I still haven't forgiven her, though I'm not quite sure how to tell her that without making her feel like she's totally alone.

"Hello? Adam?"

"Sorry. Yeah, I'll take her."

I reach for the baby, who's wrapped tightly in a soft lilac blanket and fast asleep.

"Support her head with your hand," Lindsay says.

I ignore the fact that I accidentally graze her breast with my hand as I take the baby into my arms. She's so soft and warm. I try not to look awkward as I hold her against my chest. She has Lindsay's golden-blonde hair and the most delicate little fingers. The faint shadow of hair on her brow twitches and I wonder whether she's dreaming and what she's dreaming about.

"Are you ready?" Lindsay asks.

Something about the way she asks this question makes me think she means something else. As if she's asking whether I'm ready to forgive her and accept this routine of helping her out until she gets a car. The answer to both of those is *definitely not.*

"Yeah, let's go."

Lindsay has never had a problem holding a conversation. She chatters nonstop on the way to the clinic about how her mother, Lillian, is still living with her "asshole" stepfather in Carolina Beach even though he's cheated on her more times than she can remember. One thing I never understood about Lindsay was why she always got upset over things she couldn't change. Or, maybe I'm just too accepting of things that should be changed.

"Why do you still visit her if it upsets you so much?" I ask as I pull into the clinic parking lot.

"Adam, I've told you this a million times. She deserves better. I'm not going to give up on my mom, but I refuse to live with them."

"You need to learn to let that stuff go."

"Oh, really? And when was the last time you spoke to your dad?"

"That's not the same. My dad and I have totally different issues."

"Yeah, I've heard that before."

"Anyway, that's beside the point. You're going to have to get over your hatred of your stepdad if you don't get a job and a roommate soon."

She draws in a long stuttered breath as she turns to look out the window.

"I didn't mean that the way it sounded."

"It's fine," she says, still gazing out the window. "I know I must seem like a total loser to you now; getting pregnant before graduation and letting Nathan convince me to wait to get a job until the baby was born."

"You're not a loser. I don't think that." I pull my truck into a parking space and glance over my shoulder at the car seat as I kill the engine. "But you can't start feeling sorry for yourself and depending on me to dig you out of this. You ripped my heart out and pretty much ruined my life."

"I apologized for what I did to you. And I'm not the one who made you beat the crap out of Nathan."

"I don't want to talk about that right now. The point is that you can't depend on me. I'm not the person I was when we were together. I've moved on." She finally turns to face me and the hurt in her eyes makes my stomach twist. "I'll help you out with this stuff for the baby, but you need to get a car or a bus pass or *something* soon. I can't keep doing this."

She looks like she's about to cry, but she quickly composes herself and climbs down out of the truck. I hurry over to her side to help her get the baby out of the car seat since the truck is raised. Kaia wakes up when I pull her out of her car seat. She scrunches her eyes and stretches her arms as her mouth opens wide as if she's about to start wailing, but she doesn't. I hand her over to Lindsay and she has a smile on her face.

"What are you smiling at?"

She shakes her head. I'm pretty certain she saw the panic on my face as I anticipated Kaia's screams.

"Nothing," she whispers as she takes Kaia in her arms.

As I watch her kiss Kaia's forehead and comfort her, I'm reminded of the time when I assumed that Lindsay and I would be getting married and raising a child together. It's funny how nothing really turns out the way we expect it to, no matter how certain the future seems. I guess we need to keep adjusting our dreams to fit reality, because life is not going to cooperate. Maybe this makes me a defeatist, but I'd prefer to think of myself as a realist.

As we walk toward the clinic, my phone vibrates in my pocket. I pull it out and smile instantly when I see a good-morning text from Claire.

"Is that her?"

I look up from the screen and quickly pull open the door for Lindsay to enter the clinic. "Yes. And her name is Claire."

And she's the most beautifully broken girl I've ever met.

Chapter Six

CHRIS

ONCE THE STUDIO was booked, the only thing left for me to do was to reschedule the physical therapy for my leg. I can't do that shit right now. The screws holding the rod in my shin make my knee hurt like a bitch, but no one will ever hear me complain about it—especially not Tristan or Jake.

I enter the control room at Reverb Room and immediately set down my guitar on the floor, propped against the control desk. I sit on the edge of the desk and try not to make it obvious that I'm doing this to rest my leg. Tristan is sitting in the desk chair with his back to the controls and Jake is on the other side of the glass partition, in the main room, setting up his drums.

"Gene and the sound tech are late. Xander snuck off to the lobby to stuff his fat face with donuts," he says, glancing at my leg when I attempt to bend the knee a little.

All this walking around, checking out studios this past weekend, has fucked me up. I've only had the cast off for two and a half weeks. I should be lying in bed with my leg elevated, but I need to get this record finished. My first self-titled album. Sometimes I don't even recognize my life anymore.

"Did they say how long it would be until they get here?"

Tristan shrugs. "I think they'll be here any minute. Hey, do you have the phone number for Claire's friend, Celia, or whatever the fuck her name is?"

"I'm not giving you her number. I don't need you fucking shit up for me with Claire."

"All right. I know her name. It's Senia. Can I have her number now? I want to apologize." I narrow my eyes at him and he raises his eyebrows. "What? I was a dick to her. I want to make things right in case she goes to Rachel's wedding with Claire."

"Did you run out of girls to fuck or something?"

He runs his hand through his brown shoulder-length hair and grins. "Yeah, you of all people should know that will never happen."

"What the fuck does that mean?"

"Nothing. Just give me the fucking number."

"Fuck you. I'm gonna go wait in the isolation room."

I make sure to walk without a limp as I leave the

control room and make my way across the main room, past where Jake is setting up, then into the soundproof isolation room where I'll do the voice recordings for each track. Once I get in the room, I shut the door and climb carefully onto the stool under the microphone.

I pull my phone out of my back pocket and see I have three texts: one from Jake and two from random numbers I don't recognize. I deleted all the girls' numbers I had saved in the address book in my phone when Claire and I got back together for those five days. Since then, I get occasional texts from numbers I don't recognize. I usually just delete them, but this last message piques my interest.

Unknown: *We're willing to meet next week if your girlfriend promises not to upset Abigail.*

This is not a random girl and this is not at all what I expected. Abby's parents have never given me their phone number and they have refused to respond to my adoption lawyer, Tasha Singer's, messages for the last four weeks. I'm beginning to think that maybe it's Tasha who has rubbed them the wrong way and not Claire and me.

I just hope Claire won't be upset that I lied to them and said we were back together. I thought it might increase our chances of getting a meeting with them if we appeared to be united and *stable*, like we're doing this as much for our love of each other as our love for Abby. This is definitely true for me. Just the idea that Claire may not feel the same way makes me sick.

Glancing into the main room, I see Jake has finished setting up his drums and the studio manager is in there helping Tristan get ready. The sound tech is probably here. I'll have to call Claire later. But, for now, I can't pass up this opportunity. I have to respond to this text.

Me: *Next week is great. I promise everything will go smoothly. Thanks for this opportunity. I'll be in touch. Chris*

I then shoot off another text to Claire.

Me: *I have good news. You're going to get to see Abby next week. What day/time works for you?*

The studio manager, Jerry, signals to me through the glass. I'm not sure if he's asking me to test the mic, but I have to wait for Claire's response first.

Claire: *Really? I don't even know what to say. How did you make this happen?*

Me: *I promise there was no money involved. I did it because I love you and Abby.*

There's another pause and I watch anxiously as Jerry approaches the isolation room. He pops his head in and his bushy mustache wiggles when he raises his eyebrows.

"There a problem with the mic?"

"Nope. Just need a couple of minutes. I'm almost ready."

He glances at the phone in my hand and nods before he leaves the room.

Claire: *Any time after 4 pm M–Th & after 6 on Fri. Weekends open. Thank u so much. U just made me so happy.*

I grin as I imagine her sitting in class with a smile on her face. Nothing makes me happier than Claire's smile. I think seeing her smile while holding Abby might cause me to reach some kind of happiness overload. It will be difficult to see Abby go home with Brian and Lynette Jensen, but it will be worth it to know that Claire will finally get to feel what I felt. Who knows? Maybe then, both of us will be able to move on and find peace knowing that Abby is in good hands. Maybe then, we'll find strength in each other, knowing that we were both willing to do whatever it took to make each other's dreams come true.

CHAPTER SEVEN

Claire

LOVE IS NOT black and white. It's not even gray. Love is every shade of color in the spectrum, changing with every ray of light given and stolen. Sometimes you forget how much you love someone, until you realize their smile is like a spotlight shined on your heart.

I love Senia like a sister, and the affection and gratitude I feel for her family is just as strong. They took care of me when I needed a place to hide. While I was pregnant with Abigail, they gave me a home at a time when I was certain I'd never have a home again. The smiles they greet me with as I arrive at Senia's parents' house warm my insides.

"*Mi niña!*" Senia's mother Nancy cries as she greets me, her arms wide open.

"Hi, Nancy." I laugh and she hugs and shakes me like a ragdoll. "I missed you."

"Oh, baby, we missed you, too," she says as she lets me go. "Are you hungry? The turkey's not ready yet, but we have some tamales on the stove."

Senia looks at her mom incredulously. "Hello? Do I even exist?"

"Oh, shut up, Senia. Your thighs don't need any more tamales," Nancy says, and she winks at me.

Senia rolls her eyes. "Come with me," she says to me as she nods toward the stairs. "I have to show you something."

We make our way through the maze of relatives and old-world décor up to the second floor. Senia slams her bedroom door shut behind us as we enter the room. I recognize the fruity scent in her bedroom, where I practically hid under the covers for six months.

Senia pulls her phone out the front pocket of her jeans and hands it to me before she leaps onto her bed.

"What the fuck does that mean?" she says as I read the text message she has open on the screen.

Tristan: *Happy Thanksgiving, Senia. Hope you're spending it with the ones you love.*

I look up from the screen and Senia is lying down with her head propped up on one hand while she pats the bed for me to sit down. I sit on the edge of the bed and lay the phone down next to me.

"How did Tristan get your number? And why do you have it programmed in your address book?"

"He texted me a couple of days ago just to say hi. I ignored the text, but I saved his number."

"Because?"

"Just in case."

"In case you want to be treated like dirt?"

"We don't all have two hot guys fighting over us." I try to stand, but she grabs my arm to stop me. "Hey, I'm sorry. I'm just feeling weak."

"Did Eddie call you again?" She nods and the anger I felt when Senia's cheating ex-boyfriend called her last week returns. "You don't need to be with an asshole. You are beautiful and smart—"

"And I give a mean bj."

"Exactly. You don't need a guy who'll fuck anything with legs. You deserve a guy who'll worship you."

"So you think Tristan's just looking for a fuck?"

I don't even answer because this question is ridiculous.

"Do you think Chris gave him my number? How did he get my number?"

"I don't know, but if it was Chris, I'm going to have a talk with him about that."

"No, don't get mad at him. I'll take care of Tristan. I'll text him a picture of my bunion. He'll never text me again."

I try not to laugh because, sadly, I know Tristan is too persistent to be deterred by a picture of her gnarly bunion.

Standing from the bed, I make my way to the dresser where Senia has a photo of the two of us framed in a pink "Best Friends Forever" picture frame. It was taken last Thanksgiving when her uncle took us to his house in Carolina Beach. I was four months pregnant, so I wore a big T-shirt to hide my bulge and hardly spoke to anyone the whole weekend, afraid they'd hear the betrayal in my voice.

"I'm going to see Abigail on Monday," I say as I pretend to be interested in the other framed pictures on her dresser.

"What? How did this happen? Oh, my goodness, Claire! Are you sure this is what you want?"

She leaps off the bed and rushes to my side.

I pause a moment before I look up into her eyes and respond firmly. "I need to see her, even if it's just this once. I don't know if I can even explain to you the ache I feel inside. It's excruciating and it consumes me, day and night. I just want to see her."

"You don't think it might make it worse?"

"I don't know, but this is not the kind of thing I want to play it safe with. This is my daughter. I've never seen her and I already feel like I might die without her. I just need to see her, at least once. I need to know that she's real. I need to see this beautiful person that Chris and I created." I pause to wipe the tears from my face. "I don't know if you can understand that, but that's how I feel. It's what I need."

She stares at me for a moment and her big brown eyes

shine as if she's hatching a devious plan inside her twisted mind. "Claire, I've known you long enough to know that you wouldn't do this unless it was right for you. You have some kind of weird radar for that shit. I also think that I may have misjudged Chris."

"Are you being serious?"

"Yes, I was pissed about the fact that he never got in touch with you all those months you were living here, but I think I just realized something and I'm sorry I didn't realize it sooner." She pauses as she takes a breath and steels herself to speak whatever words she's about to say. "I think you needed Adam to show you how much you still love Chris."

That is not at all what I expected her to say and I'm actually a little pissed. "I don't think so."

"I'm sorry. I don't mean to say that Adam was a stepping-stone."

"I don't want to hear this. Can we just go downstairs?"

She nods and hangs her head apologetically, but I'm still upset with her. I clench my jaw to keep from uttering an angry retort. Adam was *not* a stepping-stone.

I pull my phone out of my pocket and follow Senia out of the bedroom. I open my message app and look at the last text I received from Adam.

Adam: *I'll be in Carolina Beach with family tomorrow, but first I'm stopping by Cora's. I'll be thinking of you.*

I'm not sure if he remembers telling me that Lindsay's family lives in Carolina Beach, but I know that his dad and mom live in Wilmington. I guess he's probably referring to another relative. He has a million aunts, uncles, and cousins. I just wish I didn't have this awful feeling in the pit of my stomach every time I think of this text.

I don't think Adam would ever lie to me, but I get the feeling there's something he's not telling me. When I asked him why Lindsay called him while we were at the football game, he told me that she needed a ride to the emergency room and her boyfriend was out of town. I didn't ask him what was wrong with her because something about the way he said it so abruptly made me feel like he didn't want to talk about it.

Adam has never wanted to talk about Lindsay, and I never pushed him to because I didn't really want to talk about Chris either. But things have changed. If we're supposed to be trying to work things out, we should be offering ourselves to each other completely. Instead, we're having awkward dates and awkward conversations that go nowhere.

Thanksgiving dinner is served buffet-style at Senia's house, and the buffet line snakes through the kitchen as everyone grabs food from all the dishes on the counter. Thanksgiving went from being my least favorite holiday to my favorite holiday after I moved in with Jackie and Chris.

Jackie is the best cook and baker in the world, so the extra five to ten pounds I inevitably gained during the holidays were always worth it. Nancy's a great cook, too, but she doesn't cook the same foods Jackie does; the foods I've come to associate with love and family.

I heap mashed potatoes, turkey, Nancy's famous roast pork, a corn on the cob, and some pumpkin pie onto my plate then I follow Senia to the stairs where we eat with our plates on our knees because there aren't enough chairs at the table for us.

"Claire, long time no see."

Looking up from my half-eaten plate of food, I find Senia's cousin Nico. He's carrying his baby boy, whose name I can't recall at the moment. Nico's wife was pregnant at the same time as I was when I lived with Senia. They all knew I was going to give up my baby. Senia had told them all so they wouldn't ask me about baby names and gender and all that stuff.

Nico's baby was born the month before Abigail, which would make him about eight months old now. He's pinching the button on the front of Nico's shirt between his tiny fingers and just the sight of it takes my breath away. I want to run upstairs, but that's something I would have done a month ago. I have to learn to face this kind of stuff.

"Hi, Nico. The baby's so big now." My voice is shaky, and the sympathetic look on Nico's face tells me this didn't go unnoticed.

"Yeah, little Benny's been sucking down too much pumpkin juice. He swears he's going on a diet after the holidays."

He kisses Benny's forehead and I nearly lose it as I imagine Chris holding Abigail and what that would have been like. I guess I'll find out next week.

"He's beautiful," I whisper. "Just perfect."

"I'm sorry. I didn't mean to upset you," he says.

Senia tries to take my plate, but I hold tightly to it. "You can go upstairs," she whispers. "I'll tell everyone you weren't feeling well."

"I'm fine," I say as I stand and put my plate on the step I was just sitting on and turn to Nico. "May I hold him?"

A smile tugs at the corner of Nico's mouth as he hands Benny to me. Benny's eyebrows shoot up, surprised to be handed off to a stranger, but as soon as I have his soft little body in my arms, he smiles at me. He reaches for my face and I grab his hand to lay a soft kiss on his chubby fingers.

"You're so beautiful," I tell him as his fingers curl around my thumb and he shakes it like a rattle.

He might as well be shaking my soul, because I feel as if all my thoughts have settled into place. Something shifts inside me and I realize that I have no more doubts about seeing Abby. I'm going to meet my daughter. And even if it's the last time I ever see or touch her, it will still be the happiest, most honest moment of my life.

CHAPTER EIGHT

Adam

THE THREE-HOUR drive from Durham to Carolina Beach is much less excruciating than I thought it would be with Lindsay sitting in the passenger seat. I promised to give her a ride to her parents' house for Thanksgiving since Cora's apartment and my parents' house are just ten minutes away. I didn't expect to feel this strange comfort inside me, knowing that Lindsay and Kaia won't be spending the holiday alone.

"I tried calling Nathan again this morning, but I didn't have the energy to leave another voicemail," she says as we pull onto the highway. "Kaia was fussing all night and she didn't even have a fever. I'm so tired."

I don't say anything about Nathan, even though I really just want to badmouth that little gold-toothed motherfucker. I always knew Lindsay would regret leaving me for him, but I never expected him to pull some shit like this after the act he put on in Hawaii. Maybe it wasn't an act. Maybe he just found someone in California who he connected with. Or maybe he just realized that he's not ready to be a father. Whatever the case is, I can't help but feel obligated to help Lindsay through this.

"You should ask your mom to watch Kaia for a little while today so you can take a nap."

"I don't trust my mom with Kaia. She'll probably give her an eating disorder by the time I wake up from my nap."

Lindsay's mom is a nutritionist. When she wasn't telling her clients what to eat, she was busy making Lindsay feel like she shouldn't eat. Lindsay told me about her bout with anorexia during her freshman year at Duke. I didn't meet her until our sophomore year, but she showed me pictures from the months leading up to her hospitalization and it was not pretty. When we lived together, I would catch her throwing away entire meals in the garbage then piling more trash on top of the food so I wouldn't notice.

She seems to be healthy now. Maybe it's a result of the pregnancy, but I find myself stealing glances at her legs and chest as I drive. As much as I don't want to, I keep imagining what she looks like underneath those skin-tight jeans and that soft, cream-colored sweater.

"Were you just ogling my tits?" she asks.

I snap my eyes back to the road. "No. I'm…" *Fuck. There's no way to deny that.* "You've… grown."

She laughs as she crosses her arms over her chest. "Yeah, it's called breast milk."

"You breastfeed her?"

For some reason, this takes me by surprise. The thought of it gives me a strange feeling inside, a feeling I don't want to give in to. A feeling that can only be described as admiration.

"Uh, yes. It's better for her and she's never fussy or gassy, except for last night."

A soft whimpering comes from the backseat where Kaia is lying in her car seat, but the whimpering quickly turns into a rattling cry for attention.

"Should we pull over?" I ask. I don't want to have to listen to that for the next two to three hours.

"She's probably hungry. She'd been asleep for a couple of hours when you picked us up. I should have just sat in the back with her. Yes, please pull over."

I pull my truck onto the shoulder of the highway and Lindsay hops out. She climbs into the backseat and, for a brief panicky moment, I'm afraid she's going to pull out her breast to feed Kaia right in front of me. Instead, she reaches down and lifts the diaper bag off the floor then retrieves a bottle of milk from an insulated pouch. She smiles as she pulls Kaia out of the car seat and cradles her in her arms. Kaia stops crying before the bottle even touches her lips.

I spin around in my seat as I watch in awe. The Lindsay I knew eight months ago barely knew how to take care of herself. Now she holds the life of another human being in her hands.

"You seem to know what you're doing."

She kisses Kaia's fuzzy head then looks up at me, her eyes full of uncertainty. "I don't know what I'm doing, Adam. All I know is I'm probably going to be doing this alone for a very long time."

As soon as she makes this sad statement, Kaia turns her face away from the bottle and begins to wail again.

"Shit. Not again," Lindsay says as she grabs a cloth out of the diaper bag and wipes the milk from Kaia's cheek.

She looks up at me as the baby continues to cry and I feel like she's expecting me to say or do something.

"What?"

"Can you please turn around?"

"Oh, yeah, sorry."

I can't see what she's doing, but I can see it all happening in my mind. Almost instantly, Kaia's fussing is replaced by a very distinct sucking noise. I get a strange urge to call or text Claire, anything to help me not think the things I'm thinking about Lindsay right now.

A joke. That's what this situation needs.

"Hey, what does a nosy pepper do?"

"What? Another joke?"

"He gets jalapeño business."

She laughs so hard that Kaia lets out a startled yelp. I turn around instinctively and quickly turn back when I glimpse Lindsay's breast.

"Shit! Sorry."

"What the hell?" she cries as she continues to laugh. "It's not like you've never seen my tits."

I reach for my keys in the ignition, desperate to start the car and drive far away from this embarrassing moment.

"Are you almost done?" I ask, trying not to sound too anxious.

"Adam, relax. It's just a breast. I'm feeding my child. Get over it."

I take my hand off the keys and close my eyes as I lean back, scared that I might be tempted to look in the rearview mirror. I need to get the fuck out of this truck, or I need to get Lindsay the hell out of here.

"I'll be right back," I mutter as I grab my phone out of the cup holder and hop out of the truck.

I step in front of the truck and quickly dial Claire's number. She picks up on the first ring.

"Hey."

Just the sound of her voice eases my anxiety. "Hey."

"Are you okay?"

"Yeah, I was just thinking about you. Are you at Senia's?"

"Yeah. We just finished eating. They're about to turn on the karaoke machine."

I smile at the thought of Claire singing. I caught her singing a Rihanna song in the shower once and it was adorable. God, I fucking miss her.

"What are you going to sing?"

"I don't know. I was thinking of singing something from the *Grease* soundtrack."

"'Summer Lovin'?" She's silent after I say this, which makes me think I must have said something wrong. "Are you okay?"

She sighs into the phone. "I'm fine. Actually, I'm really happy."

"Why are you so happy?"

"I'm finally going to see Abigail on Monday."

My mind immediately flashes to what I saw in the backseat of the truck just now. There's no doubt that Lindsay loves Kaia with all her heart. You could see it in the expression on her face as she soothed her. I want Claire to feel that bond with Abigail, but I also want to spare her the pain of having that bond broken if Abigail's parents don't agree to further visitation.

"Are you sure that's what you want?"

She's silent for a moment before she sucks in a sharp breath and responds. "Yes, Adam, this is what I want. I'm not going to fall apart if this is the last time I see her. For fuck's sake, I've endured worse. I know I made the right decision giving her up, even if it wasn't the right decision for me. It was the right decision for her. Please stop questioning me. It makes me feel like you have no faith in my ability to make a sound decision."

"I just don't want to see you get hurt."

"And I appreciate that, but give me some credit. I'm beginning to think—"

She stops before finishing this sentence and I'm suddenly aware of the whooshing sound of cars rushing past me on the highway. "What are you beginning to think?"

"Nothing. I have to get back to the festivities before Senia comes looking for me."

"Claire?"

"Yes."

"I have some things I want to talk to you about when you have more time. Can you call me after you see Abigail? I want to make sure you're okay to talk."

"Yeah, I'll call you. Is everything okay?"

I pause as I take a deep breath that reeks of exhaust. "Everything's fine. Have a good Thanksgiving. I'll call you later to say goodnight."

"Okay," she whispers before she hangs up.

I want to blurt out that I love her. It's something I had gotten so used to saying every time we said goodbye, but everything has changed. I'm beginning to think the love I felt for Claire was more desire than love. I have a strong *desire* for Claire to be happy, even if that means she's happy without me.

CHAPTER NINE

CHRIS

MONDAY IS A day most people dread. When you're an entertainer, you don't work normal hours, so Monday feels just like any other day. Unless, of course, Monday happens to be the day you finally get to hold your daughter in your arms after knowing of her existence for three and a half months. Unless Monday is the day you get to watch the person you love more than life have their one wish granted. Then, Monday becomes the day your life changes. I can only hope this isn't the last Monday I ever wake up with this much hope.

I'm sitting on the sofa with my guitar when the front door opens. Though I'm nervous as hell, I can't help but smile as Claire enters the house without knocking or ringing the doorbell.

I lay my guitar on the sofa and stand carefully. "Are you

ready to go?" I ask.

Her gaze slides over me, taking in my clothing. Her eyes widen as she stares at my mouth.

"Where's your lip ring?"

"I took it out."

"Why?"

"Because I'm trying to make a good impression."

"You're wearing a suit?"

"You have to admit it looks good on me."

"Well, there's no denying that, but you look like you're about to walk down a runway or into a boardroom for an important meeting."

"This *is* an important meeting, babe. I don't want to fuck it up."

She looks down at her outfit, a black blazer over a teal dress, and ankle boots. "We don't look like we belong together."

I step toward her, making sure she doesn't notice the discomfort in my leg, and stop just a few inches away from her. She doesn't flinch as I reach for her face.

"You look beautiful," I say as I sweep a soft lock of hair behind her ear. "And *very* responsible."

"Shut up."

I laugh as she shoves my chest. "Come on, let's get out of here before we're late."

Once we're settled inside my mom's Volvo, my mind flashes back to the last time we did this. To say I was devastated after Abigail's parents cancelled our first scheduled meeting would be a hell of an understatement. I almost expect my phone to ring at any moment with the news that they've cancelled again.

As I pull the car out of the driveway, I notice Claire's hands shaking in her lap. I glance at her face and the muscle in her jaw twitches as she clenches her teeth.

"You okay?"

She nods quickly.

I reach across and take her hand in mine. Instantly, the trembling stops. She takes a deep breath and closes her eyes.

"Chris, you know I don't pray, but I want to pray right now. I want to pray that Abigail will feel how much I love her when I hold her. Is that stupid?"

"Not at all. I want the same. I keep dreading that the second I hold her in my arms she'll start crying."

Just speaking these words aloud fills me with both relief and dread. I squeeze her hand as I continue toward downtown, toward the three people in this world who possess the power both to bring Claire and me closer together and to tear us apart. I pull my hand away and from the corner of my eye I can see Claire looking at me.

"What's wrong?" she asks in a small voice.

I wait until I'm stopped at a red light to face her. "I'm afraid."

"Afraid of what?"

"Afraid that I'm too happy right now. I'm afraid that holding Abby will make me happier than I've ever felt and I'm afraid of what will happen if that's taken away from me forever. I'm afraid of being too angry to forgive you."

Her mouths falls open, stunned as she tries to catch her breath. "Oh... I don't know what to say."

"I'm not trying to make you feel bad, I'm just being honest. I'm afraid of what this will do to us. As happy as I am to see Abby, I know that I'm not guaranteed another second beyond today with her. With you... I don't want to lose you."

I turn right onto the street where the Jensens' lawyer's office is located. I glance at Claire every few seconds, waiting for her response, but she just stares straight ahead in a daze.

"Claire, I love you," I say as I reach for her hand again. "But all that matters right now is Abby. Let's go meet our baby and worry about the rest later. Deal?"

She turns to me and smiles weakly. "Deal."

The parking lot is almost completely empty. It's nearly 7 p.m. on a Monday. Most people have gone home for the day while Claire and I are just finding our way home. We make our way up to the seventh floor, to the offices of Hirschberg, Leidenbach, & Associates. The whole building oozes money and, though I've got plenty of that, I feel uncomfortable knowing Claire is probably intimidated by the atmosphere.

"I need to tell you something," I say as we walk down the seventh-floor corridor toward a set of tall, glass double-doors. "I stretched the truth a little and told the Jensens we're back together."

She smiles, not looking the slightest bit annoyed. "I'm so happy right now, my heart is about to jump out of my chest. I don't think anything you tell me will upset me."

I grab her hand and she laughs as I pull her close enough to feel the warmth of her body against mine. Bringing my lips to her ear, I whisper, "When we *are* back together, I'll help you *study* every day."

Her hand slides over my chest and she shoves me away. "Still not mad."

I lean over and kiss her cheekbone. She smiles and shakes her head as I reach for the handle on the tall glass door.

"After you, babe."

"Thank you."

The receptionist looks up from her computer screen as we enter the lobby and I quickly grab Claire's hand to let her know I'm not available. Claire doesn't look at me, but I glimpse a barely-there smile on her face from the corner of my eye. It's nice to be admired just about everywhere I go, but I don't need anyone but Claire's admiration anymore. It took a while to figure that out, but I'm not about to fuck that up again.

"We're here to see Ira Hirschberg," I say to the

receptionist, not bothering to introduce Claire or myself.

She fiddles with the braid draped over her shoulder for a moment, then she dials an extension and speaks into her headset. "Chris Knight is here to see you."

She glances at Claire as she waits for a response, so I take the opportunity to lean over and lay a soft kiss on Claire's temple.

Claire turns to me so our noses are almost touching. "Take it easy. This is a law office, not a bedroom."

I lean over to whisper in her ear. "I'm just trying to give you what you want. And right now, you want everyone here to know we're madly in love."

A man with curly salt-and-pepper hair and thick bifocals comes out to greet us. "Come on in," he says in a gravelly voice as he holds open the door to the back office area. "The Jensens just arrived, so this is perfect timing. I'm Ira Hirschberg. You can call me Ira."

We shake hands and as soon as we step through the doorway, I relax a little when I see a few messy desks. We pass through a corridor of cubicles until we reach a glass wall, beyond which I glimpse Brian, Lynette, and Abigail Jensen. God, it kills me that she doesn't have my last name.

Ira opens the door for us again—a humble lawyer is always a good sign—and I wait for Claire as she hesitantly steps into the conference room. She claps her hand over her mouth at the sight of Abigail and I know this is going to be more difficult than I ever imagined it would be.

"Oh, my God," she whispers through her fingers. "Oh, my God."

I place my hand on the small of her back to guide her forward, but she's rooted in place. "Claire, babe, are you okay?"

She bites her lip and nods slowly as she steps forward. I can see the hesitation on Lynette and Brian's faces as we approach. Brian is holding Abby as she stands unsteadily on the conference table. His eyes are focused completely on her, as if he doesn't want to acknowledge our presence.

"Honey?" Lynette says to get Brian's attention.

Lynette looks me up and down a few times. She seems a bit dazed by the suit. Brian scoops Abby off the table and into his arms then turns to face us.

"We're going to be right outside," he says in a deep, rumbling growl.

Ira looks back and forth between Brian and me. "I have to stay in here, if you don't mind."

"That's fine. Thank you so much for allowing us this visit," I say to Brian and he nods as he hands Abby over to me.

She reaches for Brian as he steps away and my heart aches as I realize she doesn't know me or want me.

"It's okay, baby girl," Brian says as he leads Lynette out of the conference room.

It's as if these words flip a switch inside Abby and she turns to look at me. Her soft blonde hair curls up around her ears and neck and her body is so squishy and warm in my arms. I want to squeeze her tightly and never let her go.

Her wispy eyebrows shoot up, like she's surprised to see me. I smile at her and her eyes widen.

"It's okay, princess."

She still looks uncertain as her gaze shifts back and forth between Claire and me. Her upper lip curls up and I'm afraid this is it—she's going to cry. So I do the only thing I know how to do. Because this is my daughter, I know there is one thing that is likely to comfort her.

I sing the chorus of "Sleepyhead" to Abigail and her gaze is locked on my lips as I sing, as if she's mesmerized. Her fingers curl around my tie and I can't help but smile as she yanks it.

"Hiding with the stars. Put your dreams to bed." I tap her nose as I whisper the last line of the chorus and, suddenly, she smiles.

And time stops.

I never got to see Abby's smile when she was lying in the hospital bed two months ago. The way her lips curl up, showing me the same smile I've seen on Claire's face a million times, makes me want to live in this moment forever.

CHAPTER TEN

Claire

MY CHEST FLOODS with a painful longing as I watch, and I realize I'm looking at the two people I love most in this world sharing the most beautiful moment I've ever witnessed.

I turn to Ira and the guarded smile he's wearing tells me he knows what I'm feeling. "Is it okay if I take a picture?" I ask, looking back and forth between him and Chris to make sure I don't miss anything.

"Go right ahead."

I hastily pull my phone out of the pocket of my blazer. My hands shake as I open the photo app. Chris looks at me as I point my phone at him and Abigail. The look in his eyes is a mixture of joy and pain. Abigail reaches up and pokes him in the eye and he laughs, which makes her giggle and I seize the opportunity to snap the shot.

Taking one look at the photo on my phone of him in his suit and her with that glowing smile, I can't hold back the tears anymore. Chris turns to me as Abigail continues to claw at his face and giggle; the most musical and precious giggle I've ever heard.

"You ready?" he asks. I nod, wiping away the tears because I don't want to scare her. "I love you, princess," he whispers in Abigail's ear and I bite the inside of my cheek to keep from breaking down.

He hands her to me and I can smell her before I even touch her. She smells so soft and clean, so well taken care of. She looks uncertain about being handed off again so soon, but as soon as her soft, warm body is nestled against mine she scrunches up her nose and lets out a laugh that sounds almost like a cough. Then she smiles and I'm done.

I try to smile through my tears, but she's a child, and children are the most emotionally responsive creatures on this Earth. She reaches up and places her hands on my cheek, her fingers curling clumsily around my flesh as she attempts to wipe my tears.

"I'm sorry, Abby," I whisper. "I'm sorry I wasn't the mom you needed."

Chris rubs my back and it calms me a little. "Are you okay?"

I sniff loudly as I shake my head. "No, I am *so* not okay, but I will be," I say as I turn to look him in the eye. "Thank you. Thank you so much for making this happen."

I turn back to Abby, to really look at her, and I finally see her through the tears. She has Chris's eyes, a rich dark brown that shine with joy. And one look at her fingers and I know she has his hands. Hands that have caressed me, carried me, and played me like a melody. Bringing her hand to my lips, I breathe in her sweet scent as I lay a kiss on the soft palm of her hand.

"You're a part of me that I will never forget. I love you so much," I say as I look her in the eye. "I hope you can feel that and I hope you never forget it."

I hand her to Chris just as the conference-room door opens. I close my eyes and press my fingers into my eyelids so I can't see as Lynette and Brian take her from Chris. As soon as I feel Chris's hand on my back I turn into him and bury my face in his shoulder.

"It hurts so much."

He wraps his arms around me and rubs my back. "I know, but I wouldn't trade this pain for what I was feeling an hour ago. Not any day."

I nod in agreement. I don't know how long we stand there holding each other. It could be ten minutes, an hour, or a day. All I know is that when I finally let go, I can breathe. I can rest. I can live knowing that my baby girl is happy. Knowing that she felt my love.

"You ready to go?" he asks.

I can only imagine how horrible I look. Without even looking in a mirror, I can feel my face is puffy and all my makeup is smeared on his collar. I nod and he kisses my forehead before he lets me go. He begins to pull away from me, but I clutch the front of his coat desperately.

"Chris?"

He looks me straight in the eye as if he knows what I'm about to say. "Yes?"

I take a deep breath and let it out slowly. "I love you."

He closes his eyes and shakes his head as he lets out a breath he must have been holding for the past six weeks. He opens his eyes again and his gaze slides over my face, taking me in.

"I love you so fucking much," he whispers, his voice tender and full of relief. "Let's go home."

By the time we're sitting in the car, my certainty and resolve have solidified. I love Chris. I always have and I always will. All the memories we shared and the plans we made come rushing back to me as he pulls out of the parking lot. I think of the day we lay on the grass in Moore Square two years ago. We promised to love each other forever. Little did we know this was a promise we couldn't break, even if we tried.

I think of the plans we made to grow old together. I was supposed to tour the world with him until we turned thirty. Then we were going to move out to the country and have at least three kids.

I close my eyes and imagine us, lying on the grass the way we did in Moore Square, but with our children lying next to us, the sun warming our skin and love melting our hearts. Maybe it's a stupid dream. Maybe it will never happen. The important thing is that I want it. I never stopped wanting it. I open my eyes and I know I have to speak the words I'm thinking; the words I should have spoken months ago.

"Thank you."

"For what?"

"For not giving up on me or Abigail. I gave up after that visit in the hospital, but you never gave up." I take his hand in mine and squeeze. "I'm sorry I blamed you for not being there after I pushed you away. And, most of all, I'm sorry that I made you feel responsible for the mistakes I've made. I know you've done nothing but love me and forgive me and I repaid you by pushing you away again and again. I even tried to blame you for not knowing I needed you—like you were psychic. I was stupid. I'm so sorry."

He's silent as he focuses on the road ahead of us. Then, he turns quickly into an empty parking lot on our right and parks beneath the umbrage of an overgrown elm tree. He leaves the car on as he turns to me, his expression so serious I'm almost afraid of what he'll say.

"Claire, you only did what you thought you had to do to survive. And I know you, possibly better than I know myself. I knew you'd come around. I knew you'd stop blaming me. But, more importantly, I know you're going to stop blaming yourself. You need to forgive yourself more than you need my forgiveness."

I nod as he brings my hand to his mouth and plants a soft kiss on my knuckles. He pulls my hand away from his lips and the smile on his face makes my heart flutter. Pulling his hand toward me, I lay it on my chest. We lock eyes and I feel the dark night pressing in on us, pushing us, whispering in my ear that everything is going to be okay.

I have Chris. He's the only person strong enough to carry me. Chris is my rock. Always has been and always will be.

His gaze is ravenous as it falls on my lips, his chest heaving. Sliding my hand down, I unbuckle my seatbelt as he grabs the front of my dress in his fist and pulls me across the console. Our mouths crash into each other with cataclysmic force. I clutch his hair as I climb onto his lap. He grabs my face and tilts my head back so he can look at me.

"Do you finally understand how much I love you? That there is nothing I won't do for you?" I nod as I hastily lean in to taste him again, but he holds my face firmly. "Slow down, babe," he murmurs. "I'm not going anywhere."

He gently pulls my face to his and I close my eyes as I wait patiently for his lips to find me. His mouth lands softly over mine and I tilt my head as I breathe in his scent and his presence. His tongue parts my lips and dips into my mouth and every nerve in my body pulses with my need for him.

He traces his tongue along my bottom lip and a soft

whimper sounds in my throat. Then he plunges his tongue into my mouth again and, with every taste of his lips and every stroke of his tongue, I become more and more lost. His hands slide under my dress, caressing my thighs, and I lean my head back as he places his warm lips to my throat. His arms pull me tighter against him as he nips my neck with his teeth.

His fingers slide further up the back of my dress to unhook my bra.

Hastily, I peel off my blazer and dress then toss them, along with my bra, onto the passenger seat. He stares at my breasts for a moment before his fingers whisper over my ribs and he cups my breast in his hand. He bows his head and his eyes are locked on my face as his tongue traces a light circle around my nipple.

I slowly begin to unknot his tie. "You look so good in this suit."

His hand slides into my panties, but his gaze burns into me as he watches my face to see my reaction. He caresses me gently as I slowly pull off his tie.

"Is this mine?" he asks as I grind my hips with the rhythm of his fingers.

"Yes."

I reach for the button on his pants and he shakes his head as he pushes my hands away. "We're not having sex here. I just want to watch you come."

He eases his fingers inside me as his other hand grabs

the back of my neck and pulls my head forward. He kisses me slowly as I rock my hips back and forth. His fingers slide out of me, scooping out my wetness, and I kiss him hungrily as he strokes my clit.

"Oh, Chris," I moan, and I wrap my arms tightly around his neck as my body begins to tremble.

"Who do you belong to?" he growls as he kisses my neck.

"You," I breathe, a searing heat building inside me. "I belong to you."

The orgasm comes suddenly and hard and I bite down on his collar, which still tastes like my tears.

"You'll always belong to me," he insists. "I love you, babe, but don't you ever put me through what you put me through these past three months."

Taking his face in my hands, I kiss him as he slides his hand out of my panties. Without breaking contact with my lips, he grabs my blazer off the passenger seat and drapes it over my shoulders. Wrapping his arms around my waist, he pulls me tightly against his chest. I hold his face firmly as I attempt to show him with this kiss that he will never have to worry about losing me again.

CHAPTER ELEVEN

Adam

THIS IS THE second time I've had to have a difficult conversation with Claire in the past two months. The kind of conversation that could break us, for good, and my stomach is in knots as I stare at my phone. I go over what needs to be said, overthinking my words and rethinking my priorities. I've seen Claire three times in the past two months, and I'd be lying if I said I still feel the same passion for Claire that I felt five weeks ago when I surprised her at Cora's apartment.

I look back on the time I spent with Claire and I'm stunned at how much love we were able to pack into an eight-week relationship. There is no question that I love Claire, but I don't see us surviving all the obstacles we've encountered. I have to go to Australia in March. I'm not giving up surfing again. And I have three competitions between now and March, all of which I'll have to travel overseas for. Claire needs someone who refuses to leave her.

I asked her last week if Chris was going back on tour and she said he'd rescheduled the tour for the summer. It doesn't take a genius to figure out he did it for her. I feel like an idiot for not seeing this coming. I've been so obsessively focused on getting Claire back; I never stopped to think about what was going on in her life. I never stopped to think about her needs.

Just sitting here in my apartment thinking about this makes me sick to my stomach as I realize I'm about to do to Claire what she did to Chris last year.

I dial her number and my heart pounds harder with every ring. She finally answers just as I'm about to hang up.

"Adam."

Hearing her say my name, not as a question but as a statement, makes me nervous. Like she has something she wants to tell me and she's been waiting for me to call.

"Claire, can you talk?"

It's Tuesday, the day after she was supposed to see Abigail, so I know she just got out of class an hour ago. Sometimes, she'll ask me to call her back later because she's studying, but something tells me that she's not going to do that today.

"Yeah, I'm actually just walking down the path toward your apartment. What number are you in? Fourteen?"

Fuck!

"You're here?"

My eyes dart toward the corner of the living room, right next to my drafting table, where Lindsay is crouched on the floor, unbuckling Kaia from her car seat. I promised Lindsay I'd watch Kaia today while she goes on a job interview. I've never actually babysat an infant, but the idea of Lindsay leaving Kaia with a babysitting service or a neighbor filled me with all sorts of conflicted feelings—mainly fear.

"Just stay where you are and I'll meet you outside," I blurt into the phone as I leap over the coffee table and rush toward the front door.

"I'm already here," Claire says as the doorbell rings.

Lindsay looks back at me over her shoulder as she scoops Kaia out of the car seat. "Who's that?"

In the span of about one second, multiple scenarios play out in my mind. I can meet Claire outside the apartment and talk to her there, but it's raining so that would seem very odd. I can ask Lindsay to hide in my bedroom, but that would be even more awkward since she's leaving for her job interview in a few minutes. I guess I'll have to introduce Claire and Lindsay to each other and hope for the best.

"It's Claire," I say as I reach for the doorknob.

Opening the door, the sight of Claire makes my stomach twist. She's dressed in a beautiful blue dress, some tights, and knee-high brown boots. She's shaking out her black umbrella and all I can think of is how I was once Claire's umbrella, her shelter from the storm. But, once again, I'm about to become the rain.

She looks up from her umbrella, but she doesn't smile. "Do you have a minute?"

I want to say, "For you, I have infinite minutes," but that would be weird with Lindsay standing just a few feet behind me.

"Yeah, of course. You didn't tell me you were coming over," I say as I open the door wider for her to come in.

As soon as she steps over the threshold, bringing with her the smell of rain and soft perfume, she and Lindsay see each other. I hold my breath as I wait for one of them to say something.

Lindsay is dressed in a pencil skirt and a blazer— interview clothes—as she cradles six-week-old Kaia. I can only imagine what this must look like to Claire who still knows nothing about the paternity scare in Hawaii.

"Lindsay, this is Claire. Claire this is Lindsay... and Kaia."

I try not to sound nervous, but that's pretty much impossible right now.

Claire smiles at Lindsay then turns to me. "Am I interrupting something?"

"No, Lindsay was just dropping off Kaia. She has a job interview."

I feel like I should clarify that Kaia is not my child, but I can't bring myself to say those words. Even though Kaia isn't my biological daughter, I feel like saying this aloud will give Lindsay the impression that I don't feel a connection to Kaia. And, as much as I didn't want this to happen, I can't deny this girl has burrowed her way into my heart with those tiny fingers.

Lindsay holds out her hand to Claire. "Nice to meet you, Claire." They shake hands and Lindsay turns to me. "Are you sure you're okay to watch her alone?"

I don't know if she's trying to imply that she doesn't want Claire to hang out with me while I'm watching Kaia, but I highly doubt Claire will want to hang out after I say the things I've been planning to say to her.

"I'm fine," I say, reaching for Kaia. "Give her here."

Lindsay smiles as she kisses Kaia's forehead then hands her over. The look on Claire's face is pure confusion and heartbreak as she watches me take Kaia into my arms. *Fuck.* She's probably thinking of Abigail.

"Sorry I can't hang out. I've heard so much about you," Lindsay says to Claire as she squeezes past her then turns to me. "I should be back in an hour or two. She just took a nap; so don't let her fall asleep. I need her to sleep tonight."

"Got it," I reply. "Good luck."

I close the front door as Lindsay takes off. The sound of rain and Kaia's gurgles punctuate the silence as Claire stares at Kaia.

"Is she… yours?"

I shake my head, still not able to verbalize this denial. "She's Lindsay and Nathan's, but Nathan decided to ditch Lindsay a few weeks ago, so I've been helping her out while she tries to find a job."

"Is that why she called you when we were at the game?"

"Yeah, come on in and sit down." I nod toward the living room, which looks very similar to my living room in Wrightsville, except for the glass doors that lead off onto a patio; huge glass doors where the light pours in when it's not raining.

Claire appears conflicted as she takes a seat on the sofa where I once gave her multiple orgasms. Trying not to grin, I think of the time I made her scream so loudly that Cora sent Tina upstairs to my apartment to check on us. I can only imagine how embarrassing that was for Tina.

"Well, I came because you said you had something to talk to me about. I have something I need to talk to you about, too."

She keeps looking at Kaia with hesitation and I feel like, before I say anything, I need to know how her visit with Abigail went.

"First tell me how everything went last night."

She looks down at her hands in her lap and smiles, the kind of smile that makes me think that it went very well.

"She is so beautiful," she says, and her voice is barely louder than a whisper. "I wish I hadn't cried in front of her, but I couldn't help myself. She's perfect. It was the best and worst moment of my life, but I'm still on a high from it."

She looks up from her lap and the smile on her face is unlike any smile I've ever seen.

"You look so happy."

"I am."

Kaia's fingers grab onto the front of my shirt and I look down at her round eyes and dainty nose. She looks so much like Lindsay. Even the way she's drooling reminds me of all the times Lindsay would drool on my chest while we slept. I miss that closeness; that security of going to sleep knowing you'll always wake up with the person you love right next to you.

Then it dawns on me that Claire came here to talk to me unannounced instead of waiting for me to call her, like we had agreed. Suddenly, I have a feeling that I wasn't the only one with some bad news to bear.

"Why did you come here?" I ask. "Not that I don't want you here, but I thought I was supposed to call you."

She turns away from me and glances around the apartment before she answers. Then she reaches into her purse and my heart stops. I was right.

She pulls her hand out of the purse and holds it out to me, palm up, so I can see the promise ring I gave her six weeks ago. I turn back to Kaia because I don't want to look at it. It fills me with shame to think that I lost, even if I was prepared to give up five minutes ago.

"I'm sorry, Adam."

"You don't have to apologize."

"Yes, I do. Please look at me."

I look her in the eye because I don't want to look at the ring. "I don't want the ring. It's yours. It's not like I'm going to give it to someone else."

"I can't take it."

"You mean you don't *want* to take it."

Her fingers curl around the ring as she makes a fist. "Adam, I'm sorry I brought you into this mess, but I'm not sorry about the time we spent together. I'll always cherish that and I'll always be grateful that you were there for me when I needed someone. You will always own a piece of me. But this is a piece of you that I can't keep."

She sets the ring on the coffee table and pulls her purse into her lap. Staring at the ring for a moment, I wonder if things would have been different if that were an engagement ring rather than a promise ring. When Lindsay and I broke up, she claimed that she cheated on me with Nathan because she got tired of waiting for me to propose.

"Why didn't you tell me about her?" she asks, and I know she's referring to Kaia.

I shrug. "I don't know. I guess I thought it would just be something temporary—help her find a job, run a few errands, then we'd part ways again. But things got... well, things changed."

She reaches out and traces her finger along Kaia's

cheek. "She's adorable."

"Are you and Chris back together?"

"Yes. Are you and Lindsay back together?"

"No."

I don't want to say more because I'm afraid I'll say something stupid or hurtful. I can already feel the frustration and anger rising to the surface as I think of Chris touching Claire.

"I guess I should get going."

She looks at Kaia before she stands from the sofa, but in that one-second glance I see the months of anguish and longing for Abigail. Then it hits me. Claire and Chris are back together and Claire has just told me she's happy. I should be happy for her, not angry with him.

I stand up and follow her to the door. "Claire?"

"Yeah?"

"I want you to be happy, but I don't want you to disappear."

She takes a deep breath and turns around to face me. "Look at you."

"What?"

She looks at Kaia then back to me. "You're so generous and I would love to stay friends with you, but I need less confusion in my life. Adam…" She takes a long pause that makes me anxious. "Chris is taking me to meet my father at the end of December. I need to get my head straight before I go there. My therapist says I'm making a lot of progress and he doesn't think he's going to have to get me a psych referral anymore. That's a huge deal to me. I don't want to take medication. I think of my mom and how she self-medicated with heroin and how I was self-medicating with the meditation crap and... I'm so happy that I'm starting to feel *normal* again, the way I felt before Chris left. I think if you and I were to stay friends, I'd be a mess, because I *do* love you, Adam. Seeing you right now, holding that baby... I can't describe what I'm feeling because it would just confuse both of us."

I let out a deep sigh. "I don't want to think of what my life will be like without you. You deserve to be happy. And if this is what you need to be happy, then I'll respect your decision. I won't call you." I reach out to brush a few strands of damp hair off her cheek. "But if you ever need someone to talk to, I'll always be here for you."

I lean over to kiss her forehead and when I pull away Kaia has a chunk of Claire's hair in her hand. We both laugh as we attempt to extract her hair from Kaia's fingers, but our faces are so close that I can't help but look up to see if she's looking at me. She looks up at the same time and her smile disappears. My gaze falls to her lips; lips I've kissed, sucked, licked, and tasted so many times, and it still wasn't enough.

She steps back and opens the door quickly. "Bye, Adam."

As soon as the door closes behind her, my body

instantly feels heavier than it did two seconds ago. I feel weighed down and listless, like I could stand here in this spot, in this moment, for the rest of my life and it wouldn't matter.

This is bullshit. I have to find a way to get Claire back.

Chapter Twelve

CHRIS

SOMETIMES YOU GET lucky and the universe throws you a bone, and you have to sink your teeth in and refuse to let go. That's what happened when Claire showed up at my concert in August. Then there are those other times, when the universe catapults you straight into heaven and you just have to let go and enjoy the ride. This is how I feel after getting to see Abby and getting back together with Claire in the same night last week. My instinct is to keep fighting to make sure I never lose Claire again, but my heart is telling me to let go and enjoy because she's mine.

And I've never been more certain of this as I am when she arrives at Fleming's Steakhouse carrying a silver box tied with a giant white ribbon and wearing that smile that makes me want to give up everything.

"You look beautiful. I missed you," I say as I take the

box from her hands and lean in to kiss the corner of her mouth. "God, it feels good to be able to say those words to you again."

She throws her arms around my neck and I laugh as she plants a loud kiss on my cheek. "I love you."

"This is kind of heavy. What did you get her?"

"It's a surprise. Is she inside?"

"Yeah, we just got here. I got us a private dining room."

She hooks her arm around mine and I lead her toward the entrance. "A private dining room? How fancy."

"Yeah, we've got Grey Poupon and violinists, too."

"Geez, you really know how to impress a girl."

"Only the best for you, babe."

I lead her through the warmly lit dining area toward the private dining room, making an effort not to let her see the discomfort in my leg. When we enter the dining room, my mom is sitting at the far end of a square table that is way too big for the three of us, but it's better than being out in the main dining area where I may be recognized and hassled. I set Claire's gift on the table as she and my mom hug each other.

The day after we saw Abigail last week, I told my mom that Claire and I were back together. I haven't seen her cry so many tears of joy in all my life.

"Happy birthday, Jackie," Claire says as I pull out a chair for her to sit down.

Once we're all seated, a waiter takes our drink order and my mom is grinning as she looks back and forth between Claire and me. I know she's just happy to see us together, but I don't want her enthusiasm to put any pressure on Claire.

"Yeah, we get it, you're happy we're back together."

"Oh, Christopher, don't be such a killjoy and let me enjoy it." She tilts her head as she looks at us. "You two look so adorable together."

Claire reaches across the table and grabs my mom's hand. "How was work?"

My mom smiles before she launches into a long-winded explanation of her day. Claire knows how much my mom loves to talk about the customers at the bakery. I can't help but feel like I'm falling more in love with her by the second as I watch them laughing and gossiping. They love each other just as much as Claire and I love each other.

After a long five-course meal, Claire's eyes light up when it's time to open her gift.

"This better not be anything expensive," my mom says as she unties the white satin ribbon.

"It wasn't. I think all the materials cost like forty dollars." Claire leans forward, her eyes glued to the silver box as my mom lifts the lid.

My mom's hands disappear into the box and when they come out they're holding what looks like a black photo album.

"It's a memory book," Claire announces.

My mom looks up at Claire and I can tell she already wants to cry. She opens the book and instantly smiles.

"The first few pages are just Chris," Claire continues. "Then there are a lot of pages of the three of us. I hope you like it."

"How could I not love it? Look at you, Chris, with your bowl haircut."

Claire jumps out of her chair to peer over my mom's shoulder, as if she didn't just put the album together herself.

"I love that bowl haircut," Claire says, then she looks up and winks at me.

"Oh, my goodness!" my mom squeals. "Look at your prom picture."

Now I jump out of my chair so I can lean over my mom's other shoulder. I took Claire to her senior prom, even though I had dropped out almost two years earlier.

"Look at your Mohawk," Claire teases me as she pokes my ribs.

"I can't believe you wore that to Claire's prom," my mom complains.

I hated high school and Claire gave me permission to wear a Rolling Stones T-shirt and jeans. I wore a blazer over the shirt just so we could get into the dance hall at the hotel, then I took it off as soon as we were inside. When it was our turn to take pictures, I scooped Claire up into my arms at the last second before the camera flashed. The result was a really awkward picture where I'm sticking my tongue out and she's flailing her arms with a terrified look on her face.

My mom gushes over a few more pages of pictures, mostly of Claire and me with a few of her and Claire sprinkled in. When she turns the last page, we all seem to freeze as we look at the final photograph. It's the picture Claire took last week of Abby and me. She showed me the picture that night, but somehow seeing it tonight after all those other pictures just makes it seem bigger, more significant, like Abby doesn't just belong in this memory book—she belongs with us, all three of us.

My mom traces her finger along the edge of the photograph. She's seen pictures of Abby before, but this is the first time she's seen Abby and me together.

After a long silence, Claire stands up straight. "I'm sorry if I upset you."

My mom closes the book and Claire looks at me, her eyes pleading me to interpret this silence for her.

"Mom, are you okay?" I ask.

She nods as she sets the book gently inside the box. "I'm okay. I just wasn't expecting that." She heaves a deep sigh before she stands from her chair and turns to Claire. "Thank you for the most thoughtful birthday gift anyone has ever given me."

Claire looks hesitant for a moment before they embrace, and I can't help but feel an element of tension between them.

"I just wanted you to see what I saw," Claire whispers as my mom lets her go.

"I know, sweetheart. Thank you."

"You girls ready to go?"

Claire nods at me and my mom smiles as she closes the lid on the box.

Once we're outside, my mom holds out her hand for the car keys. "It's freezing out here. I'll wait in the car while you two say your goodbyes." She takes my keys and kisses Claire on the cheek before she sets off across the parking lot.

The first Friday of December has brought a deep chill to Raleigh. Claire instantly begins to shiver as we walk toward her car.

"Are you coming over?" I ask Claire. "I have a surprise for you."

"It's not another engagement ring, is it?"

"Too soon," I say, clutching my chest dramatically.

"Oh, please," she says, her teeth chattering. "What's the surprise?"

I pull her into my arms and rub her back to warm her up. "Do you really want to know now?"

"Yes, I'm not big on surprises anymore."

She slides her arms under my coat and around my waist to keep herself warm. I lean my head back and tilt her face up so I can look her in the eye.

"I've been talking to a real estate agent." Her eyes

widen, but I can't tell if it's with fear or excitement. "Don't freak out."

"I'm not freaking out."

"It's not for now. It's for a few years down the road. I'm looking for an empty lot to build on."

I wait for the recognition to dawn on her face as she realizes what I'm getting at.

She closes her eyes and sighs. "I don't know what to say."

"Claire, baby, look at me."

She opens her eyes and smiles. "I thought we were supposed to wait until we were thirty."

I kiss the tip of her nose and look her in the eye. "That was before I decided to give everything up. I don't want any of that other stuff anymore. I'll produce or I'll write songs—anything that won't take me far away from you... and our family. I want us to have a family. Not now. I want you to finish school and get your dream job first."

She continues to smile as her gaze wanders over my face. "You know how many times I've imagined this conversation? Somehow, I always knew this would happen."

"What did you know would happen?"

"This. I always knew you'd give it all up. But I don't want you to."

"Don't say that, Claire."

"No, I'm not telling you to go. I'm just being honest. I

wish it wasn't this way. I wish you could go and have your career and I could stay here and wait for you."

"I don't want you to wait for me."

This feels like fucking déjà vu.

"Good, 'cause I don't want to wait for you," she says, tightening her arms around my waist.

Gazing into her eyes for a moment, I realize how everything has come full circle from the moment I left to this moment right here. I grab her face and kiss her slowly. Her breathing quickens as I nip her bottom lip and a needy whimper echoes in her throat, feeding the longing I've been burying for the past seven weeks. I want to pull up the skirt of her dress and pin her against the car right here, but I have to be patient.

I pull back, breathing heavily as I speak. "I have something else I want to show you."

"What?" she murmurs as she moves down to kiss my neck.

"I got an apartment... in Chapel Hill."

CHAPTER THIRTEEN

Claire

THE BUTTERFLIES IN my stomach build and build with each mile I drive toward the address Chris texted me. He has to drop his mom off at home before he meets me there, so I'll arrive before him. The address he gave me is very close to Spencer Hall. This makes me nervous, but not because I don't want him nearby. It makes me nervous because I know I'm going to want to be near him all the time.

The building on West Franklin, just half a mile down the road from the dorm, is brand new and very modern. The bottom level is comprised of restaurants and shops that surround a large courtyard bustling with people. Multiple water sculptures sparkle with light from the surrounding shops, which are also decorated with twinkling lights for the holiday season. It's so modern, yet warm, like this is a community on its own.

I park at the Quickee Mart across Franklin because it looks like the underground parking is just for patrons and residents and I don't need a parking ticket right now. Grabbing a hoodie out of the backseat of my car, I pull it on over my dress, not caring at all how bad it looks because it is freezing out here. After I cross the street and make it to the front entrance, I'm not surprised to find a doorman.

He nods and I smile at him as he opens the door for me. Once I'm inside, I'm overcome by a pleasant gust of warm air in the lobby. Pulling my hands out of the front pockets of my hoodie, I look to my left where a man, who looks about my age, stands behind a glossy mahogany desk.

"May I help you, miss?" he asks in a smooth voice.

"I'm waiting for someone, unless he's already arrived. I'm here…" I take a few steps toward the desk so I can whisper, though there's no one but us in the lobby, "…for Chris Knight."

He smiles a knowing smile. "Yes, Mr. Knight just phoned and told me to tell you he will be here very soon."

Mr. Knight?

This is too weird. Just as I begin to wander toward the shiny elevators, Chris's voice grabs my attention.

"What's up, Julian?" he says.

Turning around, I see Chris nod at the guy behind the counter as he walks toward me.

"Just the usual," Julian replies. "Waiting on Pete, who's

late as fuck again."

"Tell Pete I still owe him fifty dollars for that beat-down on Tuesday."

"Lucky you're rich. The Lakers are gonna get raped this season."

I watch as Chris approaches me, my eyebrow cocked as he smiles.

"What?"

"Are you still limping?"

He walks right past me toward the elevator. "I'm fine. Are you ready to see my new place?"

"Don't change the subject. Is your leg still bothering you?"

He presses the call button for the elevator, but he refuses to look at me. "As soon I'm done recording, I'm starting the physical therapy. I already booked the first appointment."

Grabbing the front of his shirt, I force him to look at me as the elevator doors slide open. "You'd better not keep putting this off or I swear to God I will break your other leg."

"You're crazy," he says, shaking his head as he pulls me into the elevator.

"*You're* crazy."

"Crazy for you." He grabs my waist and pins me against the wall of the elevator as it begins to climb. His mouth hovers over mine as his hands hold me firmly in place. His breath is hot against my lips, but he doesn't move.

"What are you waiting for?" I whisper.

"Same thing I've been waiting on for over a year," he says as he lifts my dress and slides his hand down the front of my panties.

A shock of pleasure lights my nerves on fire and my entire body twitches. He watches my face as he strokes me and my eyelids flutter. I reach for the control panel to hit the stop button, but he pushes me into the back corner of the elevator so the panel is out of my reach.

"What are you doing? The doors are going to open. We're gonna get caught."

He smiles and slides his hand out of my panties just as the elevator doors open. "I love seeing that look on your face," he says as he grabs my hand and pulls me out of the elevator. "The way your eyes roll back and you hold your breath whenever I touch you. It's fucking hot."

He lets go of my hand and smacks my butt as we walk down the corridor.

"You're very happy," I say with a laugh.

"Yes, I am."

We reach the front door to his apartment and he opens the door by entering a code on a touchpad.

He looks at me as the lock clicks and he pushes the door open. "The code is eight-nine-nine-two."

"My birthday?"

"I wanted to make sure it was something you'd

remember."

I step inside and I can't believe it's already furnished. "How long have you been here?"

"Four days. The furniture came with it, but I changed a few things."

He places his hand on the small of my back to guide me into the living room. The furnishings are all very modern and clean in shades of soft and dark gray with a few splashes of blue. But I can't help but notice there's no TV.

"Do you like it?" he asks as he strides across the black wood floors to the sliding glass door that leads out onto a small balcony. He opens the door and a gust of cool air blasts me from ten feet away.

"I love it."

Following him out onto the balcony, I step aside so he can slide the door closed behind me. Grabbing the top of the waist-high wall, I lean over a little to glimpse the crowds of people scurrying about the courtyard below. Chris comes behind me and I shudder as his warm lips land on the back of my neck. His lips disturb the hairs on my nape and I shiver. He kisses me lightly as his hands glide over my belly then he slowly gathers up the front of my dress.

"Wanna study?" he whispers in my ear as his hand slides into my panties again, instantly finding my spot.

"Yes," I whisper breathlessly as his fingers caress me slowly and carefully.

His left arm holds me tightly against him so I can feel

the solid heat of his erection against me as he slides two fingers inside me. My eyes close and a soft whimper escapes my throat as I lean my head back. He stretches me with his fingers and gathers my wetness before he slides his hand forward again to caress my clit.

"You want me inside of you?"

"Yes," I reply as the pleasure builds slowly with every stroke of his finger.

He slips his hand out from between my legs and spins me around, crushing his mouth to mine as he pulls my body tightly against him. His fingers crawl over my hips as he gathers my dress up then hooks his thumbs into the waistband of my panties.

He pulls his mouth away and looks me in the eye. "I want all those people down there to hear you scream."

I sigh as he kisses my neck hungrily. He keeps moving down, taking my panties down with him as he kneels before me. Stepping out of my panties, my body trembles with cold and anticipation.

He looks up at me and smiles and the pulsating ache between my legs becomes unbearable. As he lifts my dress, I grab hold of the wall behind me as he lifts my left leg and slowly removes my heel. Gently, he rests my foot on the top of his thigh and I can't help but worry that his leg is in pain, though he doesn't appear to be in any discomfort. He brings his lips to the inside of my knee and I pant as he kisses a trail up the inside of my thigh.

"Chris, are you okay?" I ask as his mouth lands on me and I suck in a sharp breath.

He chuckles and the vibration of his laughter sends chills over every inch of my skin.

"I'm perfect," he murmurs. "Are you okay, babe?"

"Oh, yes."

He uses his fingers to gain access to every piece of me, then he licks me like I'm his favorite flavor ice cream. His lips cover my clit, gently sucking as his tongue massages me.

"Oh... my... God. Chris," I breathe as my legs become too weak to support me.

One of my hands clutches desperately to the wall as my other hand grasps a fistful of his hair. He drapes my leg over his shoulder and firmly grasps my ass to hold me steady as he lovingly sucks, kisses, and teases me with his mouth.

Curling into myself, my body twitches as the orgasm rocks me, rendering my muscles completely useless. He kisses my clit tenderly, a soft goodbye, sending one last chill through me as he pulls his mouth away. I wrap my arms around his neck for support as he stands up.

He smiles as he kisses my forehead. "What grade would you give that?"

I take a few deep breaths before I answer. "An A?"

"Not an A-plus?" he says as he hooks his arm around my waist and pulls my body against his. "Guess I'll have to study *harder*."

Even though he has just given me a mind-blowing orgasm, Chris takes his time making love to me in the bedroom. He moves slowly and methodically, letting the pleasure build then easing off. He kisses me tenderly as he glides in and out of me, and with every stroke I feel us becoming closer and closer.

"You're the love of my life, Claire," he whispers, his hips slowly grinding into me and sending shockwaves through me every time he hits my core.

He kisses me slowly, and each graze of his tongue relaxes me further. Squeezing my legs around his hips, I lift my pelvis, tightening myself around him as a jolt of pain flashes inside me. The moans that come out of my mouth are high-pitched, matching the rhythm of his thrusts.

"Oh, fuck," he whispers as he pulls his head back and his arms begin to tremble. His eyes squeeze shut as he comes.

I grab his face and kiss his damp forehead then lick the salt off my lips. Collapsing on top of me, he nuzzles his face into my neck and I chuckle as he bites my skin. The scent of us mingles and leaves me intoxicated as we both attempt to catch our breath.

We lie in silence for a while before he kisses my neck and pushes himself up so he can look me in the eye. "I don't want you to go."

"Kind of hard for me to leave when you're still inside me."

"No, I'm not talking about tonight. Claire, I want you to live with me."

I shift my hips a little and he winces. "Sorry."

He slides out of me slowly then kisses my temple. "Think about it."

Climbing out of bed, he quickly makes his way toward the bathroom. Even through the dim moonlight shining through his bedroom window, I can just barely see the shadows of the tattoos that decorate his muscular back and arms. He disappears behind the bathroom door and I pull the sheet over me as I turn onto my side. My mind immediately wanders to all the studying I have to do when I get back to the dorm tomorrow. I should text Senia to tell her not to wait up for me. She's probably out with Isabel at the new sushi-karaoke bar that just happens to have go-go dancers.

Not my scene.

Not that I don't like getting a little crazy with Senia every once in a while. Most of the time, I'd much rather be reading ahead for a class or listening to music. Or, now that we're back together, I'd rather be lying in bed with Chris.

Maybe that's my answer to his question.

Letting out a deep sigh, I turn over in bed just as the bathroom door opens. Chris comes out of bathroom and slides in next to me. I lay my head on his shoulder and drape my arm over his chest.

"My therapist raised his eyebrows when I told him we

were back together today."

He chuckles. "He just wants you all to himself."

"Actually, I think it's his way of telling me he approves. He's kind of cryptic like that. He has a really nice voice, but he doesn't talk much. Mostly, he just asks questions and raises one eyebrow when he's skeptical and two when he's pleased."

"Did you just say your therapist has a really nice voice?"

I chuckle as I trace my finger over the tattoo on his chest; the tattoo he got for Abby and me. "Don't worry. You're the only one I think about when he serenades me."

"He'd better watch out or I'm gonna have to challenge him to a sing-off." He grabs my hand and lays a soft kiss on the backs of my fingers then kisses my forehead. "Want me to sing you to sleep?"

"Yes, please."

He clears his throat then launches into a soft rendition of "Kiss Me" by Ed Sheeran. Listening to the words, amazed by the sheer amount of emotion he can pack into each note, I have to keep reminding myself to breathe. When he's done, I kiss him on the cheek and his smile shines through the darkness.

"Goodnight, babe."

I wrap my leg over his hips and he laughs as I squeeze him like an anaconda. "Goodnight, Christopher."

CHAPTER FOURTEEN

Adam

YURI'S REFRIGERATOR IS full of health food. Fruits and vegetables, some I don't even recognize, are bursting out of all the drawers and stacked on every shelf. He and his girlfriend, Lena, are both surfers, though she doesn't surf professionally like Yuri. Lena teaches preschool full-time and surfs with Yuri during the NC season. Yuri will be leaving to Brazil soon to surf for three weeks. If I weren't completely confused about everything going on with Claire, Lindsay, and Kaia, I'd probably be going with him.

Reaching into the far back of the top shelf, I grab an Amstel Light. Getting fucked up to forget the mess you've made of your life is not something I recommend, but it's also the only thing I feel like doing right now.

"You may want to go easy on the beer or you'll get a gut before the qualifier," Lena says as I pop off the bottle cap and toss it into the trash bin.

"I don't even know if I'm going to Australia," I reply then proceed to chug half the bottle in one shot.

The foam lights up my throat and fills my belly. I let out a huge belch as Yuri enters the kitchen.

"Dude, it's only ten o'clock. Am I gonna have to confiscate your car keys?"

"What the fuck are you supposed to do when the person you're in love with is in love with someone else and the person who ripped your heart to shreds needs you more than anyone?"

Yuri and Lena look at each other then slowly turn their heads toward me.

"You have to let her go," Lena says, and for some reason I get the feeling they've already discussed this.

"I know I have to let her go, but I'm fucking miserable. The only thing I've got going for me right now is a child that's not even mine. I know I should cut ties with Lindsay before I get attached to Kaia, but I think it's too fucking late for that." I laugh before I down the rest of the beer. "What the fuck is wrong with me? Don't answer that."

Lena's sister Helen enters the kitchen and I quickly toss the empty beer bottle into the plastic blue recycling bin next to the refrigerator. Lena and Helen get to work arranging some snack trays while Yuri and I grab the last few beers from the fridge and make our way back to the living room where Helen's husband, Jack, is rolling a joint while his friend, Brendan, packs the bowl on the bong.

I've only met Jack once, at Lena's birthday party last year. Brendan is completely new to me, but they both work at the same accounting firm and like to brag about getting stoned on their lunch break. I haven't smoked in two months, but the heady fragrance of the medical-grade stuff they're smoking makes my heart speed up just thinking of inhaling.

Brendan passes me the purple bong and I stare at it for a moment. I'm not with Claire anymore. I don't have to leave Yuri's house at all tonight. They've already offered me the guest bedroom. I'm thinking tonight is a good night to see the world in a different light.

An hour later I'm stoned out of my mind off three bong rips. Two months is a long tolerance-break.

The warm light shining from the floor lamp across the room keeps splitting into pink and yellow, hexagonal shapes. I close my eyes, but the light penetrates my eyelids and the shapes continue invading my vision. The dubstep music playing from the iPod speakers on my left infiltrates my mind and vibrates inside my skull. Every bass drop and every scratching beat or lingering lyric stirs something inside my chest. I'm so fucked up.

I rise carefully from the sofa and make my way to the restroom. I lock the door behind me and grip the edge of the sink as I stare into the mirror. My skin looks a little gray. I turn on the faucet and splash some water in my face, but I can barely feel it. My face is numb from the beer.

I get a strong urge to peel my long-sleeve T-shirt off, but the vibration of my phone in my pocket stops me. Pulling my phone out of my jeans, I stare at it for a moment. Lindsay is calling me on a Saturday night. This is a first. She usually only needs me during the week for appointments and shit.

I answer the phone and she shrieks my name into my ear. *"ADAM!"*

"What the fuck?" I mutter.

"Oh, my God! They found him. The police just called me. They found me. I mean, they found him. Oh, my God."

"What are you talking about? Slow down."

"Nathan… Adam, they found Nathan. He's dead!" She screams the last two words and I feel as if someone has just plunged a knife into my stomach. "He drowned."

She continues to mutter in between her shrieking cries of grief and suddenly I can taste the sharp smoke and the stale sweetness of the beer in my mouth. I can feel the warm air coming from the vent above me. The floor beneath me is solid as gravity seems to shift and suddenly I'm heavy, grounded, resolved.

"I'll be there," I say. "Don't do anything. I'll be there soon."

I rush out of the bathroom and into the living room. Lena is sitting on Yuri's lap and laughing as he blows air onto her stomach.

"Hey, I need a ride."

Yuri looks up. "You leaving already, old man?"

"I need a fucking ride."

"There are nicer ways to ask," Lena says as she slides off Yuri's lap.

I pull my keys out of my pocket and toss them to Yuri. "I'm too fucked up to drive and I need a ride, right *now*, please."

Yuri jumps up from the sofa. "I'm on it, bro."

It feels weird sitting in the passenger seat of my truck, but I don't need a DUI on top of the bomb Lindsay just dropped. It takes Yuri a moment to figure out how to adjust the seat. As he pulls away from the curb in front of his apartment building in Durham, I silently wish that I'm hallucinating this shit.

"Where are we going, Miss Daisy?" he says as the truck slows to a stop at the first intersection.

"Lafayette Street. Lindsay's house."

The movement of the truck combined with the beer sloshing around inside my belly and the THC tickling my brainwaves is making me dizzy. Top it off with the dread I'm feeling about what Nathan's death will do to Lindsay and Kaia and I'm about ready to vomit. I roll down the window and close my eyes as the freezing night air blasts me in the face.

"It's fucking freezing. Are you crazy?" Yuri complains.

"I'm high as fuck," I mutter, attempting to hold down the vomit stinging the back of my throat.

"That's what you get for quitting for a girl. Lena would never make me quit."

"I don't want to fucking talk about it."

I give Yuri the address number and we arrive at Lindsay's duplex five minutes later.

"I'm going to call Lena to pick me up. You okay for now?" Yuri says as he hands me the keys.

"Yeah, I'm cool."

I stumble out of the truck and try not to step on any of the cracks in the concrete driveway leading to the rear unit of the duplex. The porch light is on. It's always on. Lindsay swears it deters burglars from trying to pick her lock. She has what I see as an irrational fear of home invasion robberies brought on by watching too many TV shows about unsolved crimes. When we lived together, she would often interrupt in the middle of having sex to ask if I remembered to lock the front door.

I knock on the door and she opens it immediately. Her cheeks are red and raw and the look of utter shock on her face kills me. I step inside and close the door softly behind me, trying not to let her see that I'm still swaying a little.

"I've been sitting here for weeks thinking he was fucking some other girl; hatching my plans to sue him for child support."

"This isn't your fault. Don't let this fuck with your

head."

She clutches at her hair as she shakes her head. "Why? Is this because I fucked everything up with you? Is this what I deserve?"

"Don't say that. No one deserves this shit."

And in that instant, I don't know if it's the weed, but I have an epiphany I've been waiting on for six years.

"We don't deserve this," I continue. "We can't keep blaming ourselves for the moments that get away from us; those moments where nothing makes sense. This isn't our fault."

She narrows her eyes at me as the tears roll down her cheeks. "Are you stoned?"

Fuck.

"A little."

Her face contorts with excruciating anguish and she falls to her knees. "His dad called me." I kneel down so I can hold her hand as she continues. "They're not having a funeral. They're scattering his ashes in the Pacific because that was his favorite place to surf. But I know the truth because the fucking guy at the county called me first. They had to identify him with dental records because there wasn't enough of him left."

I think of Nathan's gold tooth and how they probably used it to identify his body. I cringe inwardly. He only had that tooth because I beat the shit out of him eight months ago.

"I may be a little stoned, but I know you didn't do anything to deserve this. Because most days I wake up thinking I'm a monster for what happened to Myles. And for a long time I thought you were a complete bitch for cheating on me. But I realized something right now that I wish I would have realized six years ago." I place my index finger under her chin to lift her face and her chin is sticky with tears. "It's not our mistakes that define us. It's the lessons we learn that show our true character."

Her blue eyes are dark with doubt. "What did I learn? To suspect Nathan of cheating on me instead of worrying he might be hurt, or *dead*?"

Her hands grasp the edge of her T-shirt, wringing it, as she awaits my response. I haven't seen Lindsay this desperate since the last time we argued about getting engaged and she conceded defeat after a four-hour argument. She said she'd just wait for me to ask rather than trying to pressure me. That was almost a year ago, last Christmas, approximately one month before she got pregnant with Kaia.

"I think you learned who you can count on."

I think we both learned that.

She whimpers as I take her hand and pull her into my arms. She weeps silently on my shoulder, wiping her face every now and again. Within minutes, we're breathing in unison and she begins to relax.

"Thank you," she whispers.

"For what?"

"Thank you for treating me like the person I'm trying to be instead of the person I was."

I pull my head back and brush her hair away from her damp cheeks. "What do you need me to do? Do you need help paying for the plane ticket?"

She shakes her head. "I just... I don't want to be alone tonight."

"Is Kaia asleep?"

"Yeah, she's in her room. She's been asleep for an hour. Are you leaving?"

Her eyes plead with me to stay and I pause for a moment to take in the curves of her face. I remember the first time I saw her working as a TA in my comparative literature class. I always teased her that her English degree wouldn't be worth shit in the job market.

"You don't have to look at me like that. I'm still stoned. I'm staying whether you want me to or not."

She smiles a little, but the smile quickly disappears. She probably feels she's not allowed to smile right now.

I stand up without wobbling then extend my hand to her. "Come on, you should go to bed. The last thing you need is your mom bitching about your puffy eyes. You should put some hemorrhoid cream under your eyes, Lindsay. Don't look at me like that! The supermodels do it.'"

She takes my hand and lets me help her up. "Wow...

Your impression of my mom is still better than mine."

"It's all in the inflection," I say as I lead her toward the hallway. "And the number of times you mention supermodels."

CHAPTER FIFTEEN

CHRIS

WAKING UP WITH Claire in my bed, in my own apartment, feels like a dream. She's curled up next to me, clutching the corner of the pillow, with her mouth slightly open—looking exactly the way I remember her before we broke up seventeen months ago. Seventeen months and countless mistakes later, we still ended up right where we began, where we were always meant to be.

I watch her for a while before she opens her eyes, squinting one eye against the light pouring in through the window behind her.

"How long have you been awake?" she mutters as she reaches for me.

She lays her head on my shoulder as she wraps her arm around me and I imagine her closing her eyes and going right back to sleep. I tuck her hair behind her ear and kiss the top of her head.

"Just a few minutes. Do you mind going to breakfast with Tristan today? You can invite Senia, if you want."

She laughs at this suggestion then kisses my chest before she looks up at me. "Is this some ploy to get Senia and Tristan together?"

"No, but I know you're not crazy about hanging out with Tristan. I thought Senia might keep him preoccupied while I make you squirm under the table."

"Don't you have something we can eat here?"

"Not unless you want to feast on Capri-Sun for breakfast."

"So predictable."

Grabbing her face, I pull her toward me so I can kiss her. Her breath is hot in my mouth as her hand slides down and finds my erection. I suck in a sharp breath as she curls her fingers around me to get a firm grip.

"Is that a yes?" I whisper into her mouth.

She strokes me slowly, which only gets me hotter and more frustrated. Grabbing her by the sides of her waist, I lift her on top of me so she's straddling my stomach. She sits up and I hold my breath as I take in the beauty of her figure. She's different, softer than when we were together. Having Abigail changed her inside and out; it made her a woman. A woman who makes me want to be a better man.

I lay my hand on her abdomen and she smiles. "You're so fucking beautiful. I want to worship this body day and night."

I trace the tip of my finger over the small scar above her belly button where she used to have a piercing. She got the belly button piercing the same night I got her name tattooed on my right shoulder blade, because she was too afraid to get a tattoo. The piercing ended up coming out accidentally while we were wrestling and she never put it back in.

She grabs my hand and plants a soft kiss on my palm before she pulls my hand against her chest. Her skin is like silk under my fingertips. I grab the back of her neck to pull her lips to mine and kiss her slowly, savoring the taste of her lips and the soft warmth of her breasts against my chest. Her breathing quickens as she grinds against me.

I pull her head back so I can look her in the eye. "I have to tell you something." I wait a moment for her to get her bearings before I continue. "I got your name covered up."

At first, she looks confused, then she sits up and tilts her head. "The tattoo of my name? On your back?"

I nod. "Everyone kept telling me to get it covered up. I was really drunk and convinced you'd moved on with someone else."

She looks heartbroken as she dismounts my stomach and sits cross-legged on the bed next to me. "I know I should have expected this, and you do have that new tattoo on your chest for me and Abigail, but this makes me sad."

I sit up and turn my back to her so she can see the tattoo that covers her name. It's a blonde pinup girl in a red bikini. The girl is winking as she sits backwards on a blue motorcycle.

"I kind of hate myself for this," I say as I turn around to face her. "But I covered your name with one of my favorite memories of you. It was my secret way of not really covering it up at all."

I think back to the last time I took Claire stargazing on the anniversary of her mother's death, just one month before we broke up. We rode out on my motorcycle to Poplar Point in Jordan Lake and camped out for the night. The next day, after a long swim in the lake, we found our backpacks, and all our clothes, had been stolen from the campsite. As soon as we got on the bike, Claire in her red bikini and me in my swim trunks, our skin still wet and our bodies pressed against each other... We had sex right there on top of my bike in the shade of the trees surrounding our campsite.

Claire still looks disappointed. "I don't like to think about what happened while we were apart."

"Neither do I. It was the worst year of my life." I take her hand and kiss her ring finger. "If I could do it over, I never would've left. I would've proposed to you at Jordan Lake. I would've done anything to keep you by my side."

Sometimes the cost of success is more than we can afford. I can't afford to lose Claire again.

She looks me in the eye and shakes her head as she smiles. "It's just a tattoo. Next time, you can get my name tattooed on your forehead."

"I knew you'd understand."

I grab her face and lick her forehead.

"Ew!" she squeals and I laugh as I jump off the bed before she can retaliate. A shooting pain slices through my knee as she shrieks, "You're disgusting!"

"And you love it. Hurry up and get dressed so we can go eat." She hops off the bed and pushes me. I grab her hand before she can make her way to the bathroom. "I'm not finished with you, so don't drag out this breakfast."

She turns around and smiles at me. "I'm going to take my time and you're going to like it."

I laugh as I let go of her hand and slap her ass. "Get out of here."

IT TAKES THIRTY minutes of convincing to get Senia to go to breakfast with us, but we finally get her into the car and make our way to the pancake house. When we pull into the parking lot, I'm not surprised to see Tristan leaning against his motorcycle. Tristan's usually late, but he's acting completely out of character lately with Senia. I asked him if his goal was to fuck her or get her to be his date to Rachel's wedding and he claimed neither.

"He must be really trying to impress you," I say as I pull into an empty parking space and kill the engine.

"Hmph. It's gonna take a lot more than showing up early to a fucking pancake house," Senia replies as she gets out of the car.

Claire turns to me and smiles. "Don't encourage this, Chris. I don't want her to get hurt."

"I'm not encouraging it. I've never seen him act like this. I want to know what he's up to."

"So you're willing to throw Senia under the bus to satisfy your curiosity?"

"I think I have more faith in Senia than you do."

Claire rolls her eyes as she gets out of the car and slams the door shut. I get out of the car as quick as my leg will allow and hurry to her side so I can whisper in her ear.

"Senia's a big girl, but I'll break him in half if he hurts her. Okay?"

She smiles then grabs my hand. Up ahead, Tristan holds the door open for Senia to enter the restaurant.

"Good morning, sunshine," he says with a smile and Senia ignores him.

I nod at him as he holds the door open for Claire and me. "Thank you, kind sir."

"Anything for my Knight in shining armor," Tristan says as he follows us inside.

"Hey, bitch, I didn't see you curtsy."

"You can curtsy on my dick," he mutters, just low

enough for Claire and Senia not to hear.

The hostess seats us in a semi-circular booth and Claire and Senia scoot in first so they're sandwiched between Tristan and me. We grab our menus and Senia and Claire look at their menu together.

"Why are you looking at that menu? You know what you're getting," I say as I slide the plastic menu away from me.

Claire looks up from her menu. "Are you saying I'm predictable?"

"I'm saying I know you and you're getting a damn waffle."

She looks at me as if she's not at all impressed. "Waffles happen to be extremely delicious, Mr. Denver Omelet."

"Hey, I'll bet I can guess what you're ordering," Tristan says to Senia. "The *stuffed* French toast."

She looks up from the menu slowly and turns to Claire. "Do you hear someone talking to me?"

"You heard me loud and clear last night," Tristan remarks.

Claire looks up from the menu again, but this time she turns to Senia. "What is he talking about?"

Senia finally looks at Tristan and her lip curls up in disgust at the devious grin he's wearing. They're keeping secrets from us.

The waitress arrives, providing a nice distraction for Claire's ire. After we order our food, I grab Claire's hand

and pull her a little closer to me so I can kiss her temple.

"Did you think about what I asked you last night?" I whisper in her ear.

She lays her hand on my thigh as she looks at me. "I did."

"And? Do you need more time?"

"Chris, I've already lived with you... for many years," she begins, and I brace myself for the inevitable rejection. "Of course I want to live with you, but are you sure you want to live with *me*?"

"Wait a minute," Senia interjects. "Are you moving out?"

I gaze into Claire's crystal-blue eyes and I swear I feel my soul unravel and settle down inside me. "I've never been more sure of anything."

Claire smiles as she turns to Senia. "I guess I'm moving out, but not until the end of the semester."

"That's eleven days away," Senia replies. "I have *eleven days* to find another roomie?"

"I'll pay your housing for the next semester," I offer immediately. "Not just Claire's half. I'll pay it all."

"You don't have to do that. I'll pay it," Tristan says, his eyes locked on Senia, though she's still refusing to look at him.

Her lips don't move, but I swear her eyes are smiling. "It's not the money; my dad will cover Claire's half."

Claire looks torn and I can already feel the guilt of

leaving her best friend alone working against me. "I don't want to leave you alone."

Senia lets out a deep sigh before she finally drops the bomb. "I'm pregnant."

CHAPTER SIXTEEN

Claire

MY WHOLE BODY feels numb. Senia's brown eyes are locked on me, awaiting my response, as Chris's hand reaches for mine. I push Chris's hand away as I try to collect my thoughts. I'm not angry or sad. I'm confused.

I want to ask her how the hell Tristan knows about this before I do, but I'm afraid to know the answer to that question. I want to slide out of this booth, go to the car, and fall asleep, curled up in the passenger seat. But I can't shut down again. I can't do that to Senia.

Still, I feel so betrayed.

I glance at Tristan before I speak. "How? You and Eddie have been broken up for three months."

She scrunches up her eyebrows, as if she's ashamed with herself. "It's not Eddie's."

She appears to be bracing herself for my wrath, but all I

can do is shake my head because I still don't understand. Finally, she nods toward Tristan and my heart beats painfully in my chest.

"When? What the hell's going on?"

"I'm sorry. I didn't want to tell you because of everything going on with Abigail. It was just a one-night thing a few weeks ago and, we were careful, but I didn't get my period last week."

"Wait a minute. A few weeks ago? Thanksgiving was *two* weeks ago. I thought you were going to tell him to stop texting you."

"We ran into each other at Yogurtland and it just sort of happened. I didn't give him my number. I mean, I'm not stupid."

"Hey!" Tristan says. "How about a little gratitude for the guy whose seed is sprouting inside of you?"

"Ew," Senia remarks before she continues. "That's why I was wondering how he got my number and texted me on Thanksgiving. I'm sorry I didn't tell you about it, but I was ashamed of myself for giving in. I was feeling so shitty because Eddie kept texting and calling. I just wanted to do something to take my mind off of him."

Tristan scoots closer to her and lays his hand on the back of her neck. "There's nothing to be ashamed of, sweetheart."

She quickly shoves his arm away. "Stop it."

He smiles as he leans back, but his smile disappears

when he looks at Chris. Turning to Chris, I'm surprised to find he looks as upset as I feel. His jaw is clenched and I don't know if he's going to explode with anger or cry. Finally, he stands from the table and makes his way toward the exit.

I don't hesitate as I slide out of the booth to go after him. Tristan stands to come with me, but I hold my hand up to stop him. "Not now."

I catch up with Chris outside just as he sits down on a brick planter in front of the restaurant. The dark December clouds above us only punctuate this moment. I almost wish it would rain to cleanse the aching from our souls. He leans forward, resting his elbows on his knees as he buries his face in his hands.

"I don't really want to talk right now."

"You don't have to talk," I say as I take a seat next to him. "But do you mind if I talk?"

He takes a deep breath and shakes his head.

"I think I may need to give you a little space to figure out whether you can forgive me before I move in with you."

His head snaps up to look at me. "What?"

"You're obviously upset about this because of Abigail, and that's my fault."

"Don't do this, Claire. This is not the right way to handle this." He sits up and looks me in the eye. "Yeah, I'm really fucking upset right now, but giving up is not the way to solve our problems. You should know that by now."

"I know. I just hate seeing you like this. I hate knowing that I've hurt you."

"Babe, you're going to hurt me many more times in our lives. Just because I forgive you, doesn't mean the pain goes away instantly. I just need some time... and you. I need you to not leave me again. Okay?"

I nod as I reach for his hand and squeeze. He leans forward, resting his elbows on his knees as he stares at the concrete. I hate seeing Chris in pain, but knowing that I'm the cause is unbearable.

"Are you going to stay out here?"

"Go ahead inside. I'll just be a minute."

As I begin to stand, he pulls me toward him so he can kiss me. It's just a soft peck on the lips, but he lingers for a moment. And in this simple gesture, it's as if he's reminding me that we can get through anything. Even this.

I kiss the tip of his nose before I set off into the restaurant again. Senia and Tristan are deep in conversation as I approach, but the silence returns as soon as I take my seat.

"Is everything okay?" Tristan asks, and he looks genuinely concerned.

"He's fine. He just needs a minute." I turn to Senia and she bites her lip. Reaching out, I beckon her into my arms. "Congratulations, bestie."

"I'm so sorry I didn't tell you right away," she whispers

into my hair as she holds me tightly. "I didn't know what I was going to do. And I knew if I told you how unsure I was, that it would just upset you."

I let her go and try to keep my voice steady as I reply. "So you know what you're going to do?"

"I can't get an abortion. That's just... After everything I've watched you go through this past year, the love I see you struggle with... I can't give that up. I could never do that to myself... or you. I want you to be there for me."

"Oh," I whisper because these might be the most beautiful words I've ever heard. She wants me to be there for her. "Of course I'll be there for you. So, does that mean you want me to stay in the dorm?"

She and Tristan look at each other before he speaks. "She's going to move in with me."

"Wait, so are you guys *together* now?"

"No," Senia replies quickly and Tristan actually looks a little annoyed. "This was not planned and we're just taking it one day at a time. I can't tell my parents yet or they'll freak. I need to figure out what I'm going to do with school and everything."

"You're not quitting, are you?"

"Fuck no!"

The waitress arrives with our plates of food and I feel a pang of guilt as she places Chris's omelet on the table next to my waffle. It kills me to think that Chris is in pain. And it terrifies me to consider the possibility, even for a second, that we may not make it through this. Seeing Tristan and Senia get the very thing that I stole from him, without sharing the love that we shared, must be killing him.

"That's good. I don't want you to fuck up like me."

"You didn't fuck up, Claire."

Chris arrives and slides in next to me. He makes no attempt to eat his food, and I don't blame him. I've completely lost my appetite.

I force Senia to eat her omelet then we leave the restaurant, all four of us in a haze of silence. Tristan reaches for Senia's hand as she attempts to get in the car and I can't help but feel that something has changed in him. She looks over her shoulder at him and he doesn't say anything. He just smiles. She rolls her eyes as she lets go of his hand and climbs into the backseat of the Porsche.

I stare at him for a moment before I get into the car, utterly perplexed by this non-douche-like behavior. "If you hurt her, I'll tell the world you got herpes from a gay cowboy."

"I would never do something like that to her or my child," he says as he turns around and walks toward his bike.

I don't know if it's the way he said it or my own guilt painting his words dark, but I swear that was a dig at me for what I did to Chris.

"Claire, are you coming?"

A chill passes through me as the weight of being judged

returns like a vulture perched on my shoulders. I have yet to atone for my sins. Can I even accept Chris's forgiveness if I haven't paid for my transgressions?

Transgressions.

It seems I have something in common with my father after all.

I slide into the passenger seat and Chris can tell I'm upset. "I want to go get my stuff right now." I turn around to look at Senia. "Is that okay with you?"

She looks a little disappointed at first, then she smiles. "I think it's great. I'll help you pack."

I DON'T HAVE much stuff in the dorm. Moving from the dorm, to Senia's, to Wrightsville, then back to the dorm taught me to pare down my belongings to the bare minimum. There are very few possessions that have any meaning to me. Most of those have been destroyed, lost, or given away. What's left is just two suitcases and two boxes of books and mementos. Four containers like the four chambers of a heart, pushing my blood, my life, from one place to another.

I have to threaten to back out on Chris in order to get him to stay in the car. Not only is his leg too messed up to be carrying boxes, but I don't want any of the girls in the dorm to recognize him and get any funny ideas.

I sigh as Senia and I roll my two suitcases out to the Porsche and Chris throws them in the backseat. When I turn to Senia, she's already crying.

"Pregnancy hormones?" I say, though saying the words aloud makes my stomach turn.

She throws her arms around me and squeezes so hard I can hardly breathe, but I don't attempt to loosen her grip. Instead, I squeeze her just as tightly. I know it's stupid. We'll probably see each other on Monday when we meet for coffee between classes. Still, I can't help but feel like this is a step away from my youth. This is a step toward my future with Chris, as adults.

Senia lets go immediately begins wiping her tear. I pull her hands away from her face and look her in the eye. "I'll see you at the café on Monday. Heck, you'll probably see me tomorrow when I realize I've forgotten my hairbrush or something. You're a block away."

"I know. Go ahead and move in with your sexy rock star. I'll move in with mine next weekend."

I laugh as I kiss her cheek. "We're livin' the dream."

She smacks my ass as I climb into the car. "Don't forget to study!"

Chris grins at this comment as I reach for the door handle. "I won't forget," I say, then I blow her a kiss and shut the door.

When we arrive at Chris's apartment, there are three boxes stacked on top of each other in the entryway.

"Whose are those?" I ask as I set my purse and backpack down on a table near the front door.

"It's some stuff from your room at the house. I asked my mom to pack it up a few days ago. I had it delivered while you were packing."

Julian walks in pushing a rolling cart with my boxes and luggage from the dorm. "Where do you want this?"

"In the living room is fine," Chris says.

Placing his hand on the small of my back, he leads me closer to the boxes. He looks them over for a minute until he finds a heart scrawled in marker on the second box from the top. Lifting the top box off the stack, he sets it down at his feet then pulls a blade out of his back pocket and slices through the tape to open the box.

My heart begins to race as I anticipate what is inside this box that made him mark it with a heart. He lifts the flaps and I see it instantly. And I instantly begin to cry.

He lifts the photograph of my mother and me out of the box; the photograph I thought I had lost when I moved into the dorm my freshman year; the only photograph I have left of the two of us together. He hands it to me, a soft but slightly worried expression on his face.

"My mom found it when she was packing your stuff. I had her frame it for you. Is that okay?"

I nod, unable to speak or tear my gaze away from my mother's smile. "She's…"

"Beautiful."

I clutch the frame against my chest. "Thank you. Do you think... do you think this is what Abby will look like?"

"I don't know." He kisses my forehead and nods toward the hallway. "Go put that on your side of the bed. We can unpack this stuff later. You have some studying to do." My jaw drops and he chuckles. "No, the *real* kind of studying. Why do you think there's no TV in here? I wanted to make sure you don't get distracted?"

He hands Julian some cash and thanks him as he leaves. Taking a deep breath, I look around the room and through the glass door leading onto the patio. Everything about this apartment is new to me, except for Chris. That's when I think of the quote on the little sign hanging from Cora's front door: *Where we love is home.*

I turn around to look him in the eye. "It feels like home."

CHAPTER SEVENTEEN

Lindsay

DECEMBER IN LAGUNA Beach, California, is not as cold as Carolina Beach. It's almost spring-like, with a light mist of rain and barely-gray clouds infused with the glow of the sunlight they're obstructing. Every few minutes, a gentle gust of wind comes along and a skirt flutters or someone's hair is ruined. And all I can do is hope that one of those breezes carried some of Nathan's ashes eastward. Laguna Beach may have been his favorite beach in the country, but it wasn't his home.

I hate thinking of Nathan in the past tense.

I almost wore heels to trudge through the damp sand, until I saw that everyone was removing their shoes for the memorial service. We all stood barefoot in the cold, wet sand at the edge of the water as Nathan's mother, Gianna, walked into the freezing ocean to release the ashes. She walked so tall and proud, showing such strength, while I stood twenty feet away, every muscle in my body clenched tightly so I wouldn't collapse.

Now, as we plod through the sand on the way back to the rental car, I still find it hard to breathe. The beach smells of him.

"It's okay to cry," Adam says as he adjusts the blanket over Kaia's eyes to block the sun.

I don't even want to know what Leo, Nathan's father, thinks of the fact that Adam came to the funeral with me. He called me two nights ago to ask me why I never contacted him or Gianna when Nathan didn't come home.

"It took the county coroner over a week to identify him."

His words have played in my head for two days straight. If I had worried about Nathan's well-being rather than suspect him of cheating on me, there might have been more than just a few bones and teeth left. There would have been more ashes to scatter in the ocean. That was the implication in Leo's words.

"I don't want to cry in front of them," I whisper as I reach for Kaia. She balls up her fists as I pull her against my chest.

Adam is dressed in a black suit that reminds me of the suit he wore to my cousin Luanne's wedding last year. It may even be the same suit. That wedding came just a month before everything started falling apart between us. Before I lost all hope that I would ever see Adam in a suit like that at *our* wedding.

"If you don't cry, they're going to think you don't care."

"They already think that. They haven't even attempted to see Kaia since she was born. They don't give a shit about us, including Nathan."

"Don't say that."

I draw in a deep stuttered breath as I attempt to hold back the tears, but the aching in my chest shoots straight up through my throat and lights my face on fire. The tears come so fast I can hardly catch my breath. This is only the thirtieth time I've broken down in the past seven days. Every time I think of the last time I saw Nathan, I want to bury myself under the covers, or right here in the sand would be great.

Nathan was not the love of my life, but he was there for me when Adam wasn't. When Adam lost himself in the haze of his bong, Nathan would pick me up and take me to the beach. When Adam refused to talk about what was going to happen after graduation, Nathan promised me we would live in a grass hut in Fiji if we had to, as long as we had each other and the ocean—that was all we needed.

The day Nathan left for California, he stood next to his car in the driveway with a big smile on his face, his gold tooth flashing in the morning light, and said, "Fiji is just around the corner." I always told Nathan I didn't want to get married because I didn't want him to feel tied to me by a stupid piece of paper. I wanted us to wake up next to each other every morning by choice, not by law. The truth is that, when I got pregnant with Kaia, I felt I owed it to her to stay with Nathan. When Nathan told me Fiji was just around the corner, his words filled me with sadness for the life we dreamed of that I no longer wanted. The life I never wanted.

Leo and Gianna reach the concrete staircase leading from the sand up to the street where we all parked our rental cars. Gianna looks over her shoulder at me and grabs Leo's arm to stop him. The look she gives me has the power to frighten the ocean away from the shore. I wipe the tears from my face, at first trying not to smear my makeup, then I just say, "Fuck it," and wipe the sleeve of my black dress across my nose.

Adam reaches for Kaia. I don't know if he does it instinctively because he sees me struggling to hold her and keep up with the flow of tears at the same time, but this gesture does not go unnoticed by Gianna as she and Leo approach us. Thankfully, they don't know anything about Adam. Right now, they probably think I've already moved on with some random guy just one week after the news of Nathan's death. Little do they know that Adam and I both moved on months ago.

I give Adam a look to let him know that I'll hold onto Kaia and he should probably take it easy on the dad-like behavior. He doesn't look too pleased, especially since Kaia is beginning to stir.

"Lindsay," Gianna says in her husky voice.

The wind is blowing her unnaturally red curls, but other than that she looks flawless as ever. Leo looks Adam up and down a couple of times before he turns to me just as Kaia lets out a frustrated yelp. I pull the blanket off her face and her face scrunches up. She's going to start wailing.

"Is she hungry?" Adam asks, unable to hide his concern.

Gianna glares at me, but she makes no attempt to offer assistance.

"She's not hungry," I reply, though she automatically begins sucking on my finger when I press my pinky against her lips. I take my finger out of her mouth and she starts crying again. "She needs to be changed."

"Just give her to me. She can feel your anxiety," Adam says as he reaches for her again.

I hand her over just as I start to cry again. How can he already know what she wants?

Gianna watches in disgust as I wipe my face. "Are you going to the wake at the Doubletree?" she asks coldly.

I don't care if she hates me, but the idea that she may hate Kaia for being a part of me makes me want to slap her or collapse into myself like a dying star. How can someone be so cold and still make me feel as if there's something wrong with *me*?

I'm dumbfounded. I don't want to spend another two

or three hours in the presence of these two people. If they feel so repulsed by me, there's no doubt they'll have already told their friends and relatives what a terrible person I am. They've all already made up their minds about me.

"We have to put the baby to sleep," Adam says.

I want to thank him and kick him. He said "we." Now they're really going to think Adam and I are together.

"He means *I* have to put the baby to sleep. We're in separate hotel rooms," I clarify. "This is my friend, Adam. Adam, this is Gianna and Leo Jennings."

Adam holds out his hand to Leo to shake, but the gesture is not returned. Whatever Adam feels about being treated like a dirt-bag by the parents of the person I cheated on him with, he hides it well. In fact, something about the look on his face makes me feel like he's holding his tongue so he doesn't tell a joke at such an inappropriate moment.

"Well, then, thank you for coming," Gianna says awkwardly.

"That's it?" I shriek. "No 'see you in Durham' or 'can I hold my granddaughter, whom I've never even seen?' That's *it?*"

I can't bring myself to say it aloud, but I'm glad Nathan wasn't here to see this.

"Nathan told us about the paternity test," she says, glancing at Adam. "We'll be in touch to arrange visitation with… what's her name again?"

Grabbing hold of Adam's jacket, I yank him toward the

stairs before I say something I truly regret. A gust of wind sweeps over the cliffside and up the stairway. I press my hands against my thighs so my skirt doesn't fly away. A loud scream makes me whip my head around and I catch a glimpse of Gianna a few feet behind Adam. Her beautiful mane of red curls has flown away and Leo is lifting it out of the sand.

"Don't touch that!" she shrieks. "Give me that!"

Adam looks at me and I know there's no way he can hold back now. He leans over and whispers in Kaia's ear, "Your grandmama's so bald, I can see what's on her mind. And right now I think she wants us to leave."

I hold in my laughter as we race up the stairs to the street level and I dive into the backseat with Kaia. By the time I get her strapped into her car seat, the giddiness has passed. Still, I can't help but acknowledge what I'm feeling as Adam pulls out of this tiny side street and onto the main road toward our hotel.

When we arrive at the hotel, Adam carries Kaia up to our room on the fourteenth floor and sets her down gently in the middle of the bed. She never even stirs.

He watches her for a moment before he turns to me. "Want to order room service so she can sleep? I don't know about you, but I'm fucking starved."

"I'm not really hungry," I reply as I take a seat in the desk chair.

"Don't start with that shit. You have to eat."

I shrug my shoulders and grit my teeth as I try to hold back the tears. "Do you think you'll ever forgive me for what I did to you?"

He's about to sit on the edge of the bed when he remembers Kaia is asleep. He leans against the desk instead, so close I can feel the heat of his legs inches from mine.

"I've forgiven you. I just don't know if I can ever forget that feeling... like I can't trust myself to fall in love with the right person anymore."

"I'm so sorry."

I bury my face in my hands because I'm certain I must look as ugly on the outside as the monster I feel like on the inside.

"Hey, you don't have to hide," he says as he kneels before me and pries my fingers away from my face. I turn my head so he can't see me, but he grabs my face roughly and forces me to look him in the eye. "Look at me."

"Stop," I whisper, as I close my eyes.

"It wasn't all your fault. I know that our relationship didn't begin under the best circumstances. I wasn't the easiest person to trust."

I open my eyes and he lets go of my face, but his green eyes are locked on mine. The whole time we were together, Adam never wanted to acknowledge the fact that he left his former girlfriend for me, after cheating on her with me for two weeks. I knew he felt awful about it, but I got so used to him blowing me off every time I tried to talk about it, that I never even brought it up when we broke up. It didn't matter, anyway. I was pregnant. I couldn't fight for Adam anymore.

"And I should have just been honest with you about the fact that I wanted to start competing again after graduation, instead of stringing you along," he continues. "I was stupid to think that you would have held me back. I was the one holding myself back."

"I'm sorry. I didn't even ask you how you felt today, being back at that beach."

The resolve in his expression dissolves as he stands up straight. "Believe it or not, I felt happy being back there."

I've only seen Adam cry once, the day we broke up and he was hauled away in that police car. I don't think he was crying because we broke up. I think he cried because of what he had done to Nathan. As I look at him now, clenching his jaw as the tears well up in his eyes, I realize he's been holding this in since we arrived at the beach this morning.

"It's okay to cry," I say, repeating his words from earlier.

He gives me a faint smile. "I'm happy. I swear these are happy tears. I think being back there today made me realize that, even if there is no heaven, Myles died in a place he loved. In a place and time where he was happy. Like Nathan. I don't think I ever would have realized that if I hadn't come here."

We're silent for a moment, before I finally pull off my sweater and hang it on the back of the chair then pick up the phone on the desk. "What should I order?"

CHAPTER EIGHTEEN

CHRIS

ONE OF MY secrets that I'm most ashamed of is that I have never made a real breakfast. Living with my mom, the best chef on the fucking planet, has made me spoiled as shit. Even when I lived on my own in L.A., I never made breakfast. If I woke up before noon, I'd fix myself a bowl of cereal or grab a coffee on the way to the studio. I've never had the patience for cooking. The only thing I know how to make is steak, but I can't make anything to go with the steak. So the fact that I'm reading a box of waffle mix at eight o'clock in the morning and making a disaster of my kitchen has me questioning my sanity.

My hands tremble a little as I crack the eggs into the bowl. As I whisk the eggs with a fork, I wonder when I should make the coffee. Should I wait until the waffles are done or should I make it now so it's ready when the waffles are finished? How long does it take to make waffles?

"What the hell are you doing?"

"I'm visiting the tenth circle of hell, but you're not allowed in here. I don't need any help. Go away."

"You don't need any help?" she says with a chuckle. "Then why is there flour on the back of your head?"

She comes up behind me and lightly brushes away the flour with her fingers, sending a chill through me. "I'm serious. Go wait somewhere else. I want to do this alone."

She wraps her arms around my waist and presses her body against my back. "I want to help," she says as she slides her hands into my boxers.

She lightly runs her fingertips over the full length of my cock, and it drives me crazy. "Are you fucking kidding me?" I say as I drop the fork in the bowl and turn around. "I gave you like four orgasms last night."

"I know. I just want to even up the score," she says as she slowly kneels before me. "Plus, watching you crack those eggs was really hot."

"Cracking eggs might not be the best topic of conversation while you're down there."

She slides my boxers down and grips the head of my erection firmly in her hand then slides her hand all the way down to the base. I suck in a deep breath, which I hold in as she lightly licks the tip of my cock. Her tongue is warm, but it leaves a cool, wet trail that sends a shiver through me.

I suck in a sharp breath through my teeth as she takes

me into her mouth and I hit the hot, fleshy part at the back of her throat. She moans as she bobs her head and the sound reverberates through my cock. I smile as I thread my fingers through her hair. "Jesus Christ, Claire."

She chuckles and I wince as her bottom teeth scrape me. "Sorry," she says before she lays a soft kiss on the tip of my cock.

"It's okay. Don't stop, babe."

She smiles at me as she takes me into her mouth again, then the doorbell rings.

"Fuck!" I whisper.

"Let me finish," she whispers, grabbing my hips so I can't move. "They'll go away."

I smile as I squat down and kiss her forehead. "Get up."

She stands from the floor. I yank down her panties so they're at her feet and she laughs as she steps out of them. I pick her up to place her on the counter and her ass knocks over the bowl of whipped eggs, sending it tumbling into the steel sink with a loud clunk. Then the doorbell rings again.

"Go away!" I shout as I kiss her stomach.

Her hand grips the bottom of the cabinet behind her head as she leans back. I force her legs apart and smile at her lovely, pink center. Sliding my finger inside her, I'm not surprised to find she's wet as the Portland streets in April. She whimpers as I finger-fuck her and stroke her clit with my thumb, getting her ready for my mouth.

The doorbell rings again.

"Christopher! Open the door!" my mom shouts through the door.

"Fuck!" Claire and I both whisper.

"Oh, my God! Go answer it. I have to get dressed!" Claire whispers as she slides off the counter and reaches for her panties. That's when we both notice the box of waffle mix that must have dropped on the floor.

I grab her around the waist so she can't leave. "You look fine like that. I can't answer the door like this," I say, pointing at my dick.

"I'm not answering the door in panties and a tank top!"

"Fine. Get some pants on. I'll be in the bathroom."

When I come out of the bathroom, grabbing a T-shirt off the bedroom floor on my way out, I find Claire on her knees in the kitchen, sweeping up waffle mix with a wet rag.

"We don't have a broom. Did you know that?" she says, glaring at me.

"Why do I need a broom when I have a cleaning lady?"

"What did you call me?"

"Not you! I have an actual lady who comes to clean the apartment three times a week. Her name is Petra. She's taking a few weeks off for the holidays. Maybe I should buy a broom."

"Or another cleaning lady."

"Yeah, that's a better idea."

"Why are you both home today?" my mom asks from

where she's standing by the glass doors overlooking the balcony.

"It's Sunday," I reply as I squat down and take the rag from Claire's hand. "I'll take care of this."

"That's right. I work every day. I can never keep track of the days of the week," my mom calls to us from the living room.

Claire smiles at me as we squat over a pile of waffle mix. "When are you building that house in the country?"

"Whenever you're ready," I whisper as I kiss her cheekbone.

We clean up the mess together and I toss the rag into the sink before we meet my mom in the living room. She's holding a stack of mail and looks slightly annoyed.

"What were you doing in the kitchen? Wait—I don't want to know," she insists as she holds out the stack of letters.

"Mom, I told you I'd be by to pick up the mail tomorrow. You didn't have to drive all the way down here."

She frowns as I take them from her hand. "There's a certified letter in there."

I flip through the envelopes until I see the green certified sticker and the return address makes my heart race. The letter is from Hirschberg, Leidenbach, & Associates. Tasha and I were finally able to sit down with the Jensens and Ira to discuss the agreement last week. I've been trying not to think about the meeting too much because I left

Hirschberg's office feeling as if the Jensens regretted allowing us to hold Abigail.

"What is it?" Claire asks as she sits cross-legged on the sofa.

I stare at the return address for a moment before I turn the envelope over and rip it open. "I don't know. It's from the Jensens' lawyer."

Claire leaps off the sofa and my heart leaps in my chest as I pull out the folded contents of the envelope. There are at least three pages here and I see a few red signature flags sticking out of the pages.

"What does it say?" Claire demands anxiously.

I unfold the stack of paper and my gaze falls right past the gold logo at the top of the page to the black text in the center.

Mr. Knight:

It was a pleasure speaking with you and Miss Singer this week about the post-adoption contact agreement. As I have previously mentioned, Brian and Lynette Jensen continue to express hesitation about how an open adoption will affect Abigail's well-being in the future. With that in mind, we have drafted what I believe is a reasonable post-adoption contact agreement for your consideration. This decision was not entered into lightly. In the end, I'm sure all any of us wants is what is best for Abigail.

Please read the attached two-page agreement thoroughly and seek counsel from Miss Singer before signing. If the agreement is to your satisfaction, please return to us the fully executed documents and we will file the agreement within five business days of receipt.

Kind regards,
Ira Hirschberg

Claire's nails dig into my bicep as she reads the letter. "Turn the page," she whispers.

The agreement stipulates no visitation rights past Abigail's first birthday. The only contact the Jensens will agree to after that is the exchange of photographs, which Abigail won't have access to until her eighteenth birthday.

"What does it say?" my mom asks, still standing a few feet away as if she's afraid to come any closer.

"To keep dreaming or fuck off. That's what it says."

I toss the agreement and the rest of the mail onto the coffee table and head back to the kitchen. My mom follows me, but Claire just stands there staring at the papers scattered across the surface of the black table. She's probably going through the usual mental self-flagellation. As much as I want to comfort her, I'm too upset. I feel as if I've ripped my own heart out and handed it to the Jensens only to have them stick a fucking red flag on it and ask me to sign it away.

"You can still fight for her. You didn't sign the adoption decree," my mom insists.

I grab the edge of the counter and stare at the dirty rag in the sink. Just moments ago, Claire and I were working together to clean up the mess we made while lost in the throes of passion. It seems that we're always fucking stumbling. We can't seem to find our footing ever since we broke up last year. Like the whole fucking universe is off balance. I'm not strong enough to right the universe.

Turning around to face my mom, I glimpse Claire sitting on the floor next to the coffee table, her eyes closed and hands clasped in her lap.

"I can't talk about this right now. You'll have to come by another time, Mom. And next time, please call before you come."

"Don't shut me out, Christopher. I deserve to know what's going on."

"This is not your battle," I say, placing my hand on her back and gently guiding her toward the door. "Claire and I need to talk right now. Thanks for bringing the mail."

"Thanks for bringing the mail? Listen to yourself."

"Mom, please, we need to work this out without you here."

"But I want what's best for *everyone*," she says, and the painful look in her eyes makes me sick to my stomach.

"I know. I'll call you later."

I kiss her cheek and send her off then make my way

back to the living room. Claire looks up as I enter the room and looks me straight in the eye. She's not crying and she doesn't really look upset.

"What are you thinking?" I ask, pushing the mail aside so I can sit on the table in front of her.

"I'm thinking of the last time we went to Jordan Lake."

"Why are you thinking of that?"

"Because we had sex on your bike and we weren't careful. It was almost exactly a month before we broke up. If I had gotten pregnant then instead of a month later, everything would have been so different."

"Come here," I say, beckoning her into my lap. She stands up and wraps her arms around my shoulders as she sits. "You want to know something crazy?"

"What?"

"I was just standing in the kitchen, silently cursing the universe for everything we've been through this past year, but you just helped me realize something." I pause to brush the hair out of her face and look her in the eye. "The universe hasn't been tossing us around, it's been tipping over on its side trying to push us back together since the day we broke up. It's just taken us a while to stop fighting gravity."

She smiles as she runs her fingers through my hair. "You mean, it was the gravitational pull of your huge head that sucked me back in?"

"That, and my waffle-making skills."

She sighs and rests her head on my shoulder. "If you want to fight for her, I'll understand. I'll do whatever I can to help."

"Just hearing you say that is enough. If I do this, I'll do it on my own. I don't want you to get sidetracked from school. Besides, you already have enough to worry about with the upcoming visit to your dad and the wedding in three weeks."

"Ugh. That's reminds me. Rachel left me a voicemail last night asking whether we prefer steak or chicken for the reception. She said the caterer needs everyone's order now. Which do you want?"

"Steak. Did she happen to mention how many people she's inviting? I told her I didn't want this to be a huge thing."

"I don't think Rachel cares what you want. This is *her* wedding. I think there's going to be, like, fifty or sixty guests."

"That's not bad. I just didn't want it to be a huge crowd. Then I end up spending the whole night signing autographs and filling song requests."

"Again, not *your* wedding, so please don't say anything like that to Rachel. I really don't want to hear the words she will choose to remind you of that."

"Got it." I slide my hand under her tank top and take her breast in my hand. "Can I make you some waffles now?"

She grins as I gently tweak her nipple. I can feel her heart pounding under my fingertips.

"Only if making me waffles is code for making me scream."

"You're going to regret saying that." I scoop her up in my arms as I stand from the table and she lets out a high-pitched squeal. "That scream doesn't count. When I'm done, the cops will be breaking the door down to get to you. But it will be too late."

"Good. I don't want to be saved."

Chapter Nineteen

Claire

DR. GOLDBERG'S OFFICE feels like an oven compared to the nipple-cracking air outside the James A. Taylor Building. I tear off my coat and hang it on the back of the chair before I sit down across from Goldberg for my last session before Winter Break.

"How was your last day of classes?" he asks.

He's leaning back in his chair with his hands folded over his belly. This puts me at ease. I'm so accustomed to him taking notes while I speak. It's nice to have his undivided attention.

"It was okay. It was good to not have to worry about where I'll be spending the holidays. It's also strange."

My stomach clenches inside me as I'm reminded of how I spent last Christmas, balled up on Senia's bed.

"Why is it strange?"

"I'd gotten so used to everything being in flux, the way it was six years ago. It seems everything is settling down again and I feel... restless. Almost uneasy, like I'm just waiting for something terrible to happen."

"That's normal. When we've been through trauma, it's difficult to deal with the feeling that it can happen again at any moment. It's a feeling we all live with, but even more so for those of us who have experienced a deep loss." He finally picks up his notepad and pen and I try not to sigh too loudly. "When we spoke last week, you were upset that you still had not reached an agreement with Abigail's adoptive parents. How are you feeling about that today?"

I should tell him about the agreement we received this past weekend, but instead I blurt out, "Have you ever lost someone close to you?"

He looks up from his notepad and presses his lips together in a hard line before he sets down the pad and pen. "Yes. My first wife died of ovarian cancer eight years ago."

Something about this makes the tears come instantly. I can't imagine what it would be like to listen to people complain about the pressure of exams and botched adoption agreements after experiencing that kind of loss.

"What are you feeling right now?" he asks as I wipe the tears from my eyes.

"I'm feeling scared. I know things can get worse, but I'm not sure I can take any more." I swallow the painful lump in my throat and dig my fingernails into the palm of my hand as I prepare myself for the words I've been thinking for weeks, but haven't had the courage to speak aloud. "I'm also feeling sad because I'm beginning to think that the best thing for everyone, especially Abigail, is for Chris and me to give up on the open adoption."

I ARRIVE AT Tristan's—and Senia's—house at 5:30 p.m., but Tristan and Chris are still at the studio. Senia gives me a very unenthusiastic tour of their 3,500-square-foot house in Cary.

"And this is the room where he plays his bass for about ten hours a day," she says, opening the door to a room the size of a small bedroom where various bass guitars and awards hang from the walls.

"You sound so happy," I remark sarcastically as she leads me back down the hallway toward the great room.

"I hate the commute."

"It's thirty minutes from campus."

"I used to live zero minutes from campus."

"Are you mad that I moved in with Chris?"

"Please. If I were you, I would have jumped on that shit faster than a monkey on a banana. You and Chris need to stop pretending like you're not going to spend the rest of your lives together."

Taking a seat on a fancy stool at the kitchen island, I

gaze around the huge kitchen. If Tristan is making enough money for a house like this, what is Chris pulling in? Senia grabs a bottle of water out of the refrigerator and rolls it across the top of the kitchen island toward me. I catch it and guzzle down the whole bottle in one shot.

"How about you? Are you mad at yourself for moving in with Tristan?"

"Check you out. Picking up cues from Dr. Goldberg, are you?" She jumps up to sit down on the counter and I pull my legs up onto the stool to sit cross-legged. "It's not so much that I'm mad at myself. I think I'm just frustrated with... everything. I'm starting to feel like I may have chosen the wrong major."

"Chemistry?"

"Yeah, I mean, I think I just picked it because it's about as far as I could get from real estate. I don't want to be stuck working in the family business for the rest of my life like my sisters. I want to do something important. Like you, you're going to school to do something important, but what am I doing? I'll probably end up rubbing shampoo in the eyes of lab animals for some cosmetic company."

"You won't end up doing that, and you can do lots of important stuff with a degree in chemistry. Maybe you can help discover a cure for AIDS."

"I think I have pre-partum depression. Tristan came home from the studio last night around six. I was lying on the carpet in the study doing my homework when he walks in and asks me if lying on my stomach is safe for the baby. I started bawling my eyes out. I mean, how fucked up is it that Tristan cares more about the baby than I do?"

I laugh so hard at this that I nearly piss out the water I just guzzled down. "That's hilarious!"

"It's not funny! I don't know what the fuck I'm doing!"

"Oh, my God. That's classic. Thank you for making me laugh." I wipe the tears of laughter from the corners of my eyes and catch my breath. "Of course, you don't know what you're doing. You're experiencing this all for the first time. Your next pregnancy will probably be a breeze."

"Next pregnancy? I am *never* doing this again. You know I've thrown up five times this week and I've only taken a dump twice. I think my body doesn't know which end the food is supposed to come out of anymore."

"That's disgusting."

"Yeah, well, at least Tristan has been good about it. He went to the store to get me some Gatorade a few days ago. When he came back, I was passed out in my bedroom, so he left the Gatorade in a cooler next to my bed."

"You've got to be kidding me? Are we still talking about Tristan Pollock?"

She leans back to lie across the granite breakfast bar and I quickly push a bowl of red apples out of the way. "He's really not as bad as I thought he was. I mean, don't get me wrong, he's still an asshole sometimes, but he has his moments. I know we're not together, so technically I can't tell him not to fuck other girls since *we're* not fucking, but I do wish he wouldn't fuck other girls."

"How do you know he's fucking other girls?"

"I don't know. It's just a feeling. Like, he normally gets home at six, but he got home at nine on Tuesday and he went straight to take a shower."

"That's your evidence that he's sleeping with other girls?"

"Whatever. I just know that this arrangement is going to drive me nuts. It's not as if I can start a new relationship while I'm pregnant *and* living with the guy who knocked me up."

I grab an apple out of the bowl and take a large bite. The juice runs down my hand and I lick it up quickly then munch on my apple for a bit before I answer.

"I don't know. Maybe this is going to be good for both of you. If you can't get involved with any new creeps and he can't bring home a new girl every night, maybe you'll both grow up a little and learn to trust each other."

"That sounded kind of harsh."

"Sorry."

She stares at the ceiling for a while before the sound of the front door opening makes her sit up and slide off the counter. "If he sees me lying on the counter, he'll probably ask me if it's safe. Granite countertops emit radiation, you know."

I shake my head and watch as Chris, Tristan, Jake, and

Rachel come walking into the kitchen. Chris smiles when he sees me and my stomach flutters.

"Hey, babe," he says as he leans in and plants a soft kiss on my lips. "How'd it go today?"

He asked me this same question last week, which was my first session with Dr. Goldberg after moving in with him. I assumed he wanted to know if I spoke to my therapist about moving in and what he thought about it. Goldberg actually gave me some important academic advice during last week's session, which I couldn't share with Chris. So I just told Chris that it went well and that Goldberg was pleased to see that we were reconnecting.

"It was okay," I say as Chris stands behind the barstool I'm sitting in and begins massaging my shoulders. "I'll talk to you about it later. Did you guys finish up today?"

"Hell fucking yes, we finished," Tristan answers for Chris as he sits on the huge white sofa in the family room, which is open to the dining area and kitchen.

He swipes the remote off the coffee table and turns on the TV. Looking over his shoulder at Senia, he nods toward the living room, beckoning her to join him. Senia stares at the back of his head for a moment before she walks into the family room and sits next to him on the sofa. He flips to the Science Channel and grins, proud of himself for knowing her favorite channel. If I didn't know better, I'd think Tristan and Senia are entering the stage in their relationship where words are no longer needed to communicate.

Chris continues to knead the knots in my neck and shoulders and it's both relaxing me and turning me on, so I turn my head and bite his fingers to get him to stop. "Sit down and rest your leg," I order him.

"Yes, dear," he says as he takes a seat on the barstool next to me.

Rachel immediately opens the pantry and takes out a box of cheese crackers. "How did the fitting go?" she asks me as she grabs a large handful and passes me the box.

"It was fine. I was in and out of there in, like, twenty minutes. But damn, that woman was wearing a lot of perfume."

"Oh, yeah, Sheri loves her Victoria's Secret body spray. Do you know what song you want to dance to with Chris?"

I chuckle as I pop a cracker in my mouth. "What? Is this one of those weddings where the entire wedding party has to dance?"

Rachel looks uncomfortable and now I feel bad for laughing. "It's not like that," she says as she turns to Chris. "I just figured you guys would want a song to dance to since you've been together so long. You don't have to, but I think it would be kind of romantic."

"I'll give you a song," Chris says as he reaches for my half-eaten apple. "Is this yours?"

"Yeah, it's mine. How about one of your songs?" I suggest. He smiles as he chews the apple slowly. "What are you smiling at?"

"Nothing. I just have something I want to give you, but I have to wait until Wednesday. It's killing me to wait." I open my mouth to speak and he cuts me off. "It's *not* another engagement ring. I'm still waiting for you to give me an answer on the first one."

Jake grabs a few beers out of the fridge and passes one to Tristan and one to Rachel. Chris refuses the beer and Jake doesn't even bother offering me. He knows I don't drink. Rachel and Jake lock eyes as they drink their beers, initiating a drinking contest, but Rachel gives up first when she chokes on her beer. She slams the half-full bottle of beer on the counter and bends over in a coughing fit. Jake finishes his beer and rubs her back.

"I can't believe I'm marrying such a lightweight," Jake teases her and she slaps his hand away.

That's when it hits me. I know what I'm giving Chris for Christmas.

CHAPTER TWENTY

Claire

WHEN CHRIS AND I arrive at Jackie's house, I can't help but feel a little nostalgic as the smell of home-cooked food embraces us and pulls us into the kitchen. Chris looks as confused as I feel when we find Jackie bent over and pulling something out of the oven.

"I thought we were going out for dinner," he says as Jackie places a glass dish covered in foil on the counter.

"I decided to cook instead. I haven't cooked for you two in a while. I'm making your favorite," she says to me. "Rotisserie chicken and bacon mac 'n' cheese."

Macaroni and cheese.

I try not to let anyone see how this simple phrase affects me. Instead, I smile and keep myself busy by setting the table. I set the placemats and silverware out while Chris brings the dishes and napkins.

"Are you okay?" he asks as he sets down a plate at the head of the table for Jackie.

He can sense that my mind is elsewhere. I look at him across the table wearing a black, long-sleeved shirt that's just snug enough to show off his muscular arms and chest. In so many ways, Chris has grown from the person he was before he left to L.A. last year. But even after a year apart, he still knows me better than anyone.

"I'm fine. Just a little nervous," I reply, which is true.

Chris and I set up this Sunday dinner with Jackie to talk to her about Abigail. Thinking back on the conversation we had last night only makes me more nervous.

Last night, as I massaged Chris's knee in bed, I told him everything Dr. Goldberg and I spoke about on Friday, even the part where I expressed my hesitance about moving forward with the open adoption. I expected him to get pissed or refuse to speak to me after that. But, once again, he surprised me with how much he's grown.

"I've been feeling the same way," he said as he adjusted the pillows behind his back to get more comfortable. "I didn't want to say anything. I don't want you to think that I'm giving up on the agreement because I don't love her. It's the opposite. I keep thinking of what will happen to her if she grows up with two sets of parents who would both do anything for her."

"She'll always wonder why I gave her up. She might even resent me for it. Or worse... she may think I gave her up because I didn't want her. And any time something gets rough at home, she'll wish she were with us instead of them."

"I feel like a terrible person for even thinking of giving up. But I'll feel even worse for not putting Abigail first." We look each other in the eye and I can tell he's trying to hold it together. "I never told you this, but the day we met, when you were complaining about not having slept and I convinced you to come downstairs to listen to us play... I've always regretted that."

"Why?"

"After I found out what you had been through with your mom and all the other foster homes, I felt like I should have let you sleep that day instead of asking you to come downstairs so I could put on a show for you."

"It's not like I didn't have a choice. I could have gone to sleep. I *wanted* to go downstairs."

"I know, but you also probably didn't want to say no because you were in yet *another* new home. Anyway, I've thought about that day a lot and how I should have let you sleep. I should have, from the day you moved in, showed you that you would always come first. That's what you needed. And I know that's what Abigail needs, too."

We held each other for what must have been four or five hours, until the tears that soaked through my pillowcase had dried. It was at that moment that I realized the most important lesson Abigail has taught me.

Though she won't grow up knowing us, Abigail will still be happy. She will never know the sacrifice we made for her, but she will be happy. We feel the love of strangers every day in the beautiful things they do that affect our lives without our knowledge. That is how we will love Abigail. And that is how she will feel our love.

Jackie's voice jolts me out of this memory and my nerves are once again zinging beneath my skin. I smile at her as she walks in carrying a serving platter with a beautiful roast chicken. She sets the platter down and sits at the head of the table. I sit in the chair next to her and Chris kisses the top of my head before he sits on my other side.

Jackie smiles at me as she begins carving the chicken. She cuts off a leg and motions for me to pass her my plate. She still remembers my favorite part of the chicken. She lays the meat gently on my plate and looks to Chris.

"Pass me your plate, honey."

When everyone's food is served, Chris glances at me and I try not to make it obvious that we're silently communicating, but Jackie quickly catches on.

"All right, what kind of secret are you two keeping from me now? Is it some kind of Christmas surprise? "Cause you know I hate surprises."

Chris sighs as he sets down his fork. "We want to talk to you about Abigail. We've decided not to pursue the open adoption."

Jackie's face falls, and just when I think she's going to

say something, she throws her napkin on the table and gets up to leave.

"Mom, come on. Please sit down so we can talk."

"I forgot the wine," she says as she heads for the wine chiller. She pulls out a bottle of white wine and begins loudly rummaging through the drawer. "Where's the corkscrew?"

I can feel Chris looking at me, but I can't bear to look at him right now. Covering my face with my hands, I manage to keep the tears from flowing by the time Jackie joins us at the table again. She only brought herself a glass, but neither Chris nor I drink wine, so it doesn't bother me. It's the way her lips are pressed together and trembling, as if she's trying to keep from crying, that makes me want to hide under the table.

"Jackie, we're only trying to do what's best for Abby," I begin. "Please look at me. I need you to understand."

Jackie tears her gaze away from the glass of wine she hasn't touched yet and glares at me. She appears more hurt than angry, which only makes this more difficult.

"I don't know if I can listen to any more of this. I go to bed every night thinking of that little girl."

"So do we," Chris says, his voice thick with emotion. "I want to be selfish. I want to have her all to myself, but she's not ours anymore. And trying to change that now would take months or years of suffering and a miracle."

"And she's so happy." I whisper these words that are

dirty and true and precious all at the same time; a paradox too painful to carry inside me. "I want her to be happy, and I want her to be happy with me. But if she can't be happy with me, then I just want her to be happy."

Chris takes my hand in both of his and I close my eyes as I try to imagine what the next few months or years will be like, trying to forget the joy I felt for that brief moment when I held her in my arms. I'll have to just keep reminding myself of all the joy and love both Abby and I feel every day.

"This was not an easy decision, but it's the right decision," Chris says as he squeezes my hand, and when I look up he's looking straight at me. "If there's one thing I've learned recently, it's that sometimes letting someone go is the ultimate act of love."

I throw my arms around his neck and squeeze him as tight as I can. He returns my embrace with just as much vigor.

"I won't ever let you go again," I whisper in his ear.

"What about me?" Jackie says, and I reluctantly release my grip on Chris so I can look at her.

"What about you?" Chris asks.

"Do I get a hug?" she replies, and I bolt up from my chair. She stands up and wrap my arms tightly around her middle. "Oh, Claire. I can see the fear in your eyes. I don't want you to be afraid of me."

"I'm just so afraid that you'll always resent me for what

I did, but I really just did what I thought was best for Chris and Abby. I'm sorry." She strokes my hair as I hold her tightly. "I'm so sorry."

She lets go of me and grabs both my hands as she looks me in the eye. "I know the pain will become less sharp as the years go by. I also know that whatever pain I'm feeling, you two are feeling it tenfold, so I'm just happy to see you haven't given up on each other. I know a little about losing a child and I know you two will need each other more than anyone else in the coming months and years. Just promise me you'll never leave us again."

"You'll have to change your name and move out of the country to get rid of me."

She smiles and kisses my forehead. "I love you. Don't you ever doubt that."

CHAPTER TWENTY-ONE

CHRIS

CHRISTMAS DAY: I'VE been waiting for this day for over four months, since the day I ran into Claire at the Home Sweet Home concert in Raleigh. Today, I'm giving her a gift I've been working on for years.

I already gave the gift to my mom for her to wrap it. She cried like a baby when she realized what it was. I hope Claire loves it and finally understands how I never stopped loving her.

Claire and I take our time showering together, both of us wearing mischievous grins that hide the secrets of the gifts we have planned for each other.

I sweep her hair over her shoulder and rub body wash over her back. "I'll tell you what I'm giving you if you tell me what you're giving me?"

She shakes her head adamantly. "Nope. If I tell you, it

will completely ruin the gift. I want to see a genuine reaction when I hand it to you."

I kiss the back of her neck, which tastes clean and a little sweet. My hands glide over the wet skin on her belly and under her breasts. She tilts her head to the side, opening her neck to me as I cup her breasts in my hands.

"You can't give me a little hint?" I trace my tongue down the length of her neck and she gasps as I bite her shoulder. "I promise I'll act surprised."

I slide my hand down between her legs and she moans as I stroke her gently.

"No, I'm not telling you," she says breathlessly.

I caress her steadily and she lets out a soft whine as she bends over, priming herself to receive me. I slide into her from behind and she whimpers as she presses her hands against the wall for support. No matter how many times I make love to Claire, it never feels the same. Wrapped up inside of her, I feel as if I'm the man I always wanted to be; the man who was lucky enough to get and keep a girl as beautiful as Claire.

"Harder," she begs. I grasp her hips to thrust deeper and she gasps. "Don't. Stop."

She whimpers every time I hit her core, but this position always gets me and soon I have to slow down so I don't explode. Moving firmly in and out of her, I roll my hips slowly as I stretch her, savoring the way I fit so tightly inside of her. I reach around to stroke her clit as I dip in and out, diving into the depths of her. With every movement of my finger, her cries come sharper and the muscles in her stomach contract under my hand. She releases a piercing cry of pleasure, but I continue stroking her lightly as I move inside of her. Finally, she screams my name, begging me to stop.

"Tell me what you got me for Christmas."

She laughs as she squirms in my arms. "No! Oh, my God. Please stop!"

I keep my arm locked tightly around her waist as I come. It takes a moment for both our bodies to stop convulsing, then we sit back on the shower floor together to catch our breath.

"Merry Christmas, babe," I whisper in her ear.

"That better not be your Christmas gift."

"Oh, my God. Please stop," I tease her and she elbows me in the ribs. "Ow! Of course that's not my Christmas gift. My gift won't be quite so wet."

WHEN WE PULL into the driveway at my mom's house, the house that we all once shared together as a family, I grab Claire's knee to stop her from getting out of the car.

"What's wrong?" she asks, her teeth chattering from the freezing temperatures.

It's supposed to snow tonight. I'm not looking forward

to driving home through that, but it will be our first snow since we've been back together. I miss watching the snowfall outside my window with Claire.

"Nothing's wrong. I just need to say something before we go in there."

She squints her eyes as she looks at me. "What?"

I take a deep breath before I begin. "I've been waiting a long time for today, to give you what I'm about to give you. And it's not an engagement ring, but it means a lot to me. I just want you to know how much love and pain went into this gift. This is me baring my soul to you."

She smiles and reaches across to lay her hand on my cheek. "You didn't have to tell me that. I would never scoff at a gift from you. You could give me a piece of thread and I'd put it in a frame and treasure it for the rest of my life."

"You're full of shit, but I promise I'll never give you a piece of thread."

"Good, because I'd just set it on fire and change the locks."

I shake my head as I climb out of the Porsche and wait for Claire to round the front of the car. I grab her hand and we walk to the front door together. She opens the door and the warm aromas of roast turkey and homemade pumpkin pie are thick in the air.

"God, I swear your mom is trying to fatten me up for the kill."

I pinch her side and she giggles as she slaps my arm

away. "You'll make a tender stew."

"Are you calling me fat?"

"What? First I'm calling you the cleaning lady and now I'm calling you fat?" She tries to punch my arm, but I swerve out of the way. "Your aim sucks as much as your cleaning skills."

She rolls her eyes as we enter the kitchen and find my mom hovering over the stove as usual, but there's someone standing next to her. I'm both surprised and a little pissed. My mom never said she would be inviting someone else to celebrate Christmas with us.

"Mom?"

She turns around and smiles broadly as she sets down the wooden spoon on the stove and greets me with a bone-crushing hug.

"Merry Christmas, honey," she says as she lets me go and takes Claire in her arms. "Merry Christmas. I'm so happy you guys came early. You can help me with the sweet potatoes."

She releases Claire and heads straight back to the stove.

Claire looks just as confused as I feel. "What do you need help with?" she asks as she follows my mom.

"Honey, this is Joel," my mom says, motioning to the guy with the grayish beard and thick brown hair as if he's just an oversight. "He's a friend of the bakery. I invited him to share some turkey with us."

He's wearing a burgundy sweater that screams

Christmas. With the gray beard and the brown hair, he looks like a young Santa Claus. I guess I should be civil to my mom's guest.

I hold out my hand to him. "Nice to meet you, Joel."

He nods as he shakes my hand. "Merry Christmas. Your mom has told me so much about you." He turns to Claire and she smiles. "And you, too. You must be Claire?"

"That's me. Nice to meet you."

I don't like the idea of my mom forcing us to share our Christmas with a stranger, but I don't want to be *that guy*—the son who keeps his mom from dating and ends up looking like a creepy mama's boy. If this is how she wants to spend Christmas, then so be it. Anyway, all I need tonight is Claire.

Joel and I sit in the living room, having been banished from the kitchen. I flip on the news because I have no idea what Joel wants to watch and I really don't feel like asking.

"Your mom talks about you a lot. She's very proud of you," Joel says from where he sits in the armchair I normally sit in while I practice.

I nod as I change the channel. "Yeah, she tells everyone she meets. I told her she needs to stop doing that or she's going to get some crazy stalker following her home one of these days."

Joel is silent. I don't know if he thinks I'm calling him a stalker, and I really don't care. I've warned my mom about being so free with that kind of information, but she doesn't seem to care. She thinks that if nothing bad has happened yet that nothing bad ever will happen.

I sit through another twenty minutes of painful silence before Claire comes in to call us.

She smiles at the scowl I'm wearing as she grabs the front of my shirt. "No pouting on Christmas," she says, and I can't help but smile as she pulls me up from the sofa.

"If you say so. I know better than to argue with the cleaning lady."

"If you didn't already have a bad leg, I'd kick you in the shin," she replies as she grabs my hand and pulls me toward the dining area. "By the way, I'm going with you to your physical therapy appointment tomorrow."

"I don't need you to go. In fact, I don't want you to go. I don't want you to see me getting groped by my physical therapist."

"Why not? I might learn a thing or two." She growls and I smack her ass as she takes a seat at the table.

"Not at the table, please," my mom says as she sets a dish of mashed potatoes next to the turkey.

Joel smiles uncomfortably as he moves around my mom to the opposite side of the table. Claire takes her seat and I quickly grab her hand under the table. She looks at me and I smile as I bring her hand to my lips. The back of her hand is soft and smells like the coconut hand lotion my mom keeps in the kitchen. She tilts her head as she smiles at me and I know this will be the best Christmas, no matter how many strangers my mom invites.

Mom clears her throat from the head of the table and we all turn to her. She folds her hands on the table, but she keeps her eyes focused on the food.

"I know that we have all had a rough year. And we've never been the kind of family to say grace before a meal. But I want to take the time to give thanks right now." She looks at Joel and he smiles. "Thank you, Joel, for joining us today. I know this must feel awkward to you, but I want you to know that your presence is both appreciated and welcomed." She turns to me and her smile fades. "Christopher, thank you for being the most supportive son a mother could ask for and the kind of man I am proud to have raised." She turns to Claire and her eyes instantly well up. "My dearest Claire. My girl. Thank you for making me a proud mother and for making my son stronger and more focused."

Claire bites her lip for a moment before she takes a deep breath and turns to Joel. "Thank you for being here with us today, Joel." He nods at her as she turns to my mom and the long pause worries me since I can't see her face from this angle. "Mom, thank you for being the mother I always wished for." My mom grabs her hand and I rub Claire's back as she wipes her face with her napkin then turns to me. "Chris... There's really nothing I could say to fully express the gratitude I feel for having met you six years ago. To call you my soul mate would be like calling Romeo and Juliet soul mates. It means nothing in the context of real life and it's easily dismissible. You are more than my soul mate. You are me."

I reach up and wipe the tears from her eyes and she closes her eyes in an expression of relief. Taking her hand in mine, I grip it tightly as I turn to Joel. "Thank you, Joel, for having dinner with us today. I hope you join us again... some other time." My mom eyes me warily at this awkward delivery, but I shrug off her glare. "Mom, thank you for knowing and being exactly what Claire and I have always needed." I turn to Claire and she casts her gaze downward, as if she's almost afraid to hear what I'm about to say. I reach across and lift up her chin so she can look me in the eye. "Claire, the love of my life and mother of my child. The owner of my heart and soul and the inspiration for every song I write. If you ever doubt how much I love you, I'll always be there to remind you. And if I should leave this Earth before you, I'll haunt the fuck out of you."

"Christopher!" my mom cries.

Claire smiles as I kiss her temple and let go of her hand. Everyone looks to Joel and he smiles sheepishly.

"Thank you all for this wonderful Christmas dinner and for welcoming me into your home." He turns to my mom and she smiles as he grabs her hand. "Jackie and I are moving in together."

My vision goes a little blurry. "What the fuck?"

My mom shrugs as if this information is a small

oversight. "It's not a big deal. You moved out and Joel and I have been seeing each other for a few months."

"A few months! Are you fucking kidding me?"

"Chris, your mom is allowed to have her own life," Claire says as she takes my hand in both of her hands. "Calm down."

I take a deep breath as I try to figure out what's going on here. My mom must have thought introducing Joel at Christmas, when all the warm emotions were flowing freely, would make everything go smoothly. I know my mom has put off getting remarried for a long time. Part of me always suspected she did it because she didn't want anyone to try to be my father. I guess I just got so used to her being alone, I never stopped to think that she might not *want* to be alone.

I let out a deep sigh. "Congratulations," I mutter.

One of my mom's eyebrows shoots up skeptically. "Fine. I guess I'll accept that for now."

We finish the rest of our dinner without any more surprises. After Claire and I finish washing the dishes, we join my mom and Joel in the living room to open gifts. My mom sits on her knees on the rug in front of the Christmas tree as she hands out gifts from Joel and her to all of us. Claire and I apologize for not getting Joel a gift, though we had no idea he existed before today. My mom loves the new laptop I got her and the sign Claire made for her office that reads: *Moms make the sun and stars shine brighter.* When my mom hands Claire my gift, I freeze.

She looks at me as she holds the red box in her hands. "It's kind of heavy. Is it a photo album?"

I shake my head. "Open it and you'll find out."

CHAPTER TWENTY-TWO

Claire

I UNTIE THE white ribbon first then lift the lid on the shiny, red box. My stomach flips when I see the red, leather-bound book the size of a photo album. Lifting the book out of the box, I lay it on my lap and set the box on the coffee table. I'm almost afraid to open the book for fear that there are pictures of Abigail in here, but I gather my courage and slowly lift the front cover.

My chest fills with a warm sensation as I read the dedication written in Chris's handwriting:

FOR CLAIRE, THE LOVE OF MY LIFE AND THE MELODY OF MY SOUL.

I turn the page and find a sheet of lined paper tucked safely beneath a thin plastic film. Scrawled in Chris's handwriting, the way he used to write when we were in high school, is the song "Sleepyhead" —the first song he ever wrote for me.

"It's a songbook, with every song I've ever written for you," he explains. "I tried to put the original sheet of paper I wrote the song on whenever I had it available. Some of them I had to type up—well, Farrah typed them."

I can barely breathe as I turn the pages and see the names of songs he used to sing to me before we broke up. Each song is bursting with the emotions and memories of the love we shared and lost. After about forty pages, I come to a song I don't recognize.

"What's this?"

"It's the first song I wrote after we broke up."

"Telescope"

The darkest night
The brightest light
Is still in you
You see through me
You see me through
The colors too

But you're so far away

Distance is not my friend
So close but so far away
No light at the end
Of this telescope
The deepest truth
The hardest proof
Is still with you
You set me up
You point me out
And then you're through

But I'm so far away
Distance is not your friend
So close, maybe I should stay
No light at the end
Of this telescope
No eye at the end
Of this telescope

"I don't know what to say," I whisper as I flip through the pages. "Part of me wants to read every single word and another part of me doesn't want to know what I did to you."

"What we did to each other. You said it before: No one knows how to love me like you and no one knows how to hurt me like you."

"You remember that?"

"Of course I remember, and I hope I never forget it. I hope you don't either because the sentiment goes both ways. You shattered my heart, but only because I knew you were the only one who could fix it, and you were gone. I lost hope, but those days are over. And you remind me of that every day just in the way you look at me."

I continue flipping through the pages and the lyrics become darker with each page I turn.

"There are over fifty songs I wrote while we were broken up, and a new song I wrote last week, but I don't want you to read that one yet. You have to promise you won't look at the last page in the book."

"Are you seriously asking me not to look?"

"Chris, that's cruel," Jackie says, giving him a severe look of disapproval. "At least take the song out of the book if she can't look at it."

"No, don't take it out. I want to see it."

Chris laughs as he attempts to take the book out of my hands, but I tighten my grip. "Let go. I don't want you to peek. You're not ready to see it yet."

"I hate you," I mutter as I let go of the book and he sets it down gently inside the red box.

"I hate you harder."

I look at Jackie and we exchange a look because we both know it's time for me to give Chris his gift. Suddenly, my stomach cramps up with nerves and Chris can sense the shift.

"What's going on? Are you two keeping a secret from me?"

Jackie raises an eyebrow, trying to look unimpressed with Chris's deductive reasoning skills. She takes a seat on the arm of the chair where Joel is seated and it warms my heart to see him instinctively lean in toward her. But I'm still nervous as hell.

"I'll be right back," I say as I stand from the sofa and retrieve Chris's car keys from the table by the front door.

"Where are you going? The mall is closed," Chris teases me, but I'm too nervous to acknowledge his joke as I walk outside and close the front door behind me.

As soon as I look out, I'm mesmerized by the fine layer of snow that covers everything from the front lawn and down to the end of the street. I quickly open the door to call Chris and he's just inside the door putting his coat on.

"It's snowing," I say excitedly.

"I can see that."

He follows me outside with my coat in his hands and I slip my arms into the sleeves as he holds it up for me.

"Come with me," I say, taking his hand and yanking him toward the driveway where his Porsche is parked.

I deactivate the alarm and he laughs. "Are we going somewhere?"

"This is where I hid your gift."

"You hid my Christmas gift in my car?"

"It was the one place I knew you wouldn't look."

I pop the hood open for the trunk and quickly make my way to the front of the car. I feel under the top-left part of the trunk and quickly find the small box I taped there. As soon as I rip off the tape, my heart begins to pound wildly against my chest.

Chris sees the box and his face changes. The excitement he was feeling just a moment ago is gone.

"Why are you giving that back to me?"

"No, I'm not giving it back."

"Then what are you doing?"

The snow falls all around us and I close my eyes as I silently wish with all my might that it's the ghosts of our past falling away. My hand trembles as I open my eyes and hold the box out to him. He eyes it warily, but he doesn't take it.

"I've been secretly spending a lot of time with this ring," I say, my voice shaky with nerves and the cold that penetrates my coat and seeps into my bones.

He chuckles softly. "What have you been doing with it?"

"Oh, you know, just wearing it around the house every second you're gone, while I play dress-up and have tea with my dolls."

"That's so fucking creepy."

I smile as my entire body trembles. "I can't help it. This ring is a symbol of everything I've always wanted with you." I draw in and let out a deep breath that comes out in a big cloud of steam. "Ever since you proposed to me two months ago, I've thought about what our lives would be like if I had said yes. And I've regretted saying no from the moment I said it. Then Senia said something to me last week that made me realize what an idiot I've been by holding onto this ring. She said, 'You and Chris need to stop pretending like you're not going to be spend the rest of your lives together.'" Chris laughs and I nod. "Yeah, typical Senia, but she hit the nail on the head. I need to stop pretending this isn't forever... I want you to put this ring on my finger. I want to spend the rest of my life with you. I want all those dreams we have for ourselves and for each other to come true. And I want—"

Before I can finish my next sentence, he grabs my face and kisses me hard. I drop the ring box as my limbs turn to jelly at my sides. His lips are warm and taste like pumpkin pie. I reach up to wrap my arms around his neck just as the sound of applause reaches us. Chris and I both turn toward the sound. Joel is clapping while Jackie covers her mouth and sobs.

Chris looks at me and smiles as he kneels down to retrieve the box from the snow. "I can't believe you just proposed to me."

He takes the ring out of the box and tosses the box over his shoulder. I hold out my left hand and he smiles as he slowly slides the ring onto my finger. He lays a soft kiss on my hand and the crooked smile on his face could melt snow.

Standing up, he brushes some snow off my hair then kisses my cold nose. "Is this the part of the marriage proposal where I start screaming and jumping up and down?"

"Only if you truly love me."

CHAPTER TWENTY-THREE

Adam

THE PHONE CALL from Tina leaves my stomach in knots as I attempt to finish out the workday so I can call Claire. I pack up my laptop and, just as I'm closing my office door, Maddie calls my name from further down the corridor. She's walking toward me with a fruit basket.

"Hey, Maddie," I say as I begin making my way toward the front office so I can leave.

"I'll walk you out," she says, her feathery brown curls bouncing as she lugs that big basket.

"Give me the basket and you can carry my bag," I say, handing her my laptop bag as I take the basket off her hands.

"How was your Christmas?" she asks as she holds the door open for me and I step outside into the snow-covered parking lot.

"It was pretty quiet. I spent Christmas Eve with a friend in Carolina Beach then went to my parents' house in Wilmington on Christmas Day."

"Ooh, how was everything with your dad?"

"Well, we didn't talk at all on Thanksgiving, but it's hard to be a complete dick in front of company, so he was civil on Christmas. How was your Christmas? Buy yourself something nice online?"

"You bet I did. Bought myself a nice pair of Chanel boots and John got a new snowmobile," she says as we arrive at the parking space where her silver SUV is parked crooked.

"Wow. That's a nice gift," I say as I wait for her to unlock her door. "I hope you didn't spend your entire bonus on it."

"I didn't," she says as we exchange the basket for the laptop bag. "I've been saving up to get him a snowmobile for four years, ever since Janelle went off to college. He loves the snow." She places the fruit basket in the trunk of her car then climbs into the front seat. "Have a good weekend, kid."

I stand still as I watch her pull out of her parking space and drive out of the parking lot. It's funny how a simple phrase can put things into perspective. "He loves the snow." Sometimes you have to give someone something they love in order to show how much you love them. It seems simple, but sometimes the thing they love has nothing to do with you. And that's okay.

As I walk to my car, I think of the things I love most: the ocean, surfing, and my family. Claire used to be one of those things, and I still love her, but it's been a month since she moved on; since we both moved on. Spending Christmas with Lindsay and Kaia only solidified this feeling of closure. I love Kaia. Sometimes I wish I didn't love her because she's not mine, but most of the time I don't know what I'd do if Lindsay were to suddenly stop needing me. All I know is that I'm glad neither of us is ready for a relationship right now. It means we have time to regain each other's trust before we do anything stupid to lose it again.

And there's one other thing I know: Lindsay and Kaia are coming with me to Australia in January and March. I hope that, by then, Lindsay and I have figured things out.

Climbing into my truck, I stare at my phone for a few minutes as I try to think of what I'm going to say to Claire—if she answers. Finally, I send the call and wait as it begins to ring… one ring… two rings… three rings…

"Adam?"

I didn't even think of it until now, but she probably deleted my number from her phone. She probably didn't recognize my number right away. I don't know why this feels like a punch in the chest, but it does.

"Yeah, it's me. Do you have a minute?"

"Is everything okay?"

"Yeah, well, sort of. I'm calling for Cora—actually, I'm

calling for Tina. She called me this morning to say that Cora wants to see us—and Senia. Her daughter is putting her in a full-time care facility in Idaho and Cora wants to see us before she leaves."

She's silent and I don't know if this is because she's upset about the news or upset that I contacted her.

"When is she leaving?" she asks softly.

"Friday, January second."

"In one week? I'm leaving the twenty-ninth and I won't be back until the following Sunday, the fourth."

"So... what does that mean?" I know she's probably going with Chris to California to see her father, like she said she was, but I need to at least try to get her to visit Cora before she leaves.

"It means that the only time I'll be able to go is tomorrow, and this is really short notice. I'll see what I can do. I really want to see her. Thank you for calling."

"Yeah, no problem. You can text me your answer if you're more comfortable with that."

"Yeah, I'll text you." She's silent for a moment, then, "I hope you're doing well."

I let out a deep sigh to ease the anger building inside me. "Yeah, you too. Take care."

I hang up before she can say anything else that I may interpret as a patronizing remark, when I know she only means well.

Chapter Twenty-Four

Claire

"WHAT WAS THAT about?" Chris asks as I end the call and set the phone back on the coffee table where it was before Adam called.

"Cora. She's moving into a care facility in Idaho, where her family lives. She wants to see me and Senia before she leaves."

Chris looks even more worried now than when I was on the phone. "And he's going to be there?"

"I don't know. I can ask him to go another time. I can call Tina myself."

"But you told him you were going to text him. And now he knows the only day you can make it out there is tomorrow."

I let out a frustrated sigh. "Right. Well, I'm going with Senia, and you could come, if you want."

He smiles weakly as he shakes his head. "I don't think that's a good idea."

My nerves are buzzing as I try to think of how to handle this situation gracefully. I want to see Cora, but I don't want to have to do it under the pressure of what Adam and I will say and do when we see each other. And I especially don't want Chris to worry about that. But I know that I need to settle things with Adam as much as I need to see Cora.

I climb onto Chris's lap and grab his face. "I know you trust me."

He leans his cheek into my hand as I brush my thumb over the two days of hair growth on his face, then he grabs my hand and holds it against his chest. "This means something, doesn't it?" he asks, indicating the ring on my finger.

"It means everything."

He smiles again, a little wider than the last time, but it still doesn't reach his eyes. "Then you should go. I trust you. I know I said that the last time you went to Cora's, but I meant it then and I mean it now. I know you were sort of asleep at the wheel before, just trying to get from one day to the next. But you're awake now."

I wrap my arms around his neck and squeeze him tight. We sit like this for so long, feeling totally at peace, that I actually start to fall asleep in his arms.

He rubs my back and whispers in my ear. "Wake up,

sleepyhead. You have a text to send."

I tighten my arms around his neck and smile as I breathe in the scent of his skin. "I don't want to."

"Come on, babe," he says, grabbing my sides and pushing me back. "Just get it over with so you can call Senia."

I reach behind me and grab my phone off the coffee table then I hold it in front of me where Chris can see as I type.

Me: *Okay. I'll be there tomorrow at noon.*

"Happy now?" I say as I send the message then dial Senia's number.

"Not really. I actually think that made me a little sick to my stomach, but I'll survive."

I lay a soft kiss on the corner of his lips as Senia answers the phone.

"Hello?"

"Hey, we're taking a little road trip tomorrow. Cora's leaving to Idaho next week and she wants to see us before she leaves."

"Tomorrow? I can't go tomorrow," she replies.

"Why not? It's a Saturday. You don't have class."

"I can't go. I'm introducing Tristan to my parents tomorrow."

"You're telling them about the baby?"

My heart starts racing as I remember the inner turmoil I experienced last night after realizing my period is late. I can't tell Chris. I can't bear to get his hopes up; especially since we've used protection every single time we've had sex except the time we had sex in the shower two days ago, and there's no way I could get pregnant the day my period was supposed to begin. This is probably just a false alarm. But I need to find a way to sneak away from him soon to take a test. That's the problem when you live with your fiancé and both of you are on a break from school and work. We spend every waking minute together.

"No, I'm not telling my parents yet!" Senia squeals, and I can hear Tristan in the background asking Senia who she's talking to. "I'm just introducing them to Tristan so I can go to Vegas with you guys next week without them bitching."

"Oh. But what about Cora?"

"Well, when is she leaving?" she asks.

"Next Friday."

"I'll go see her on Thursday."

"But I won't be back from Vegas on Thursday. Chris and I are staying a few more days."

"I'll go with Tristan and you can go tomorrow with Chris."

"Chris isn't going."

"Why not? It's not as if Adam's going to be there." I'm silent as I wait for her to catch on. "Wait... is Adam going to be there?"

"Yes."

"Oh…" Her voice trails off and I wait for what seems like an eternity before she finally continues. "I'm sorry, Claire. I still can't go. I already made the reservation for the restaurant and my dad rescheduled his appointments. Do you hate me?"

"Yes, but not anymore than I did yesterday when you told me about your craving for pig's feet."

"You don't know what you're missing."

"Okay, well, good luck tomorrow. I will pray for your soul."

"And Tristan's, too," Senia adds excitedly.

"I don't need to pray for Tristan with you there to protect him."

"Damn right. See you in Vegas, baby."

"See you Tuesday."

After I end the call with Senia, I see the notification on my screen of a new text from Adam. I touch the notification and his text is short, but it still puts me on edge.

Adam: *See you then.*

I set my phone on the coffee table again and I don't give Chris a chance to say anything before I kiss him. I trace my tongue along his top lip and I smile as I taste the berry-flavored Capri-Sun he was drinking earlier.

"Why are you smiling?" he says as he leans his head back.

"Because you taste good."

"You're making me hungry."

"You want me to make you something?" I ask as I sit up.

"I'm not hungry for food," he replies, his hand sliding underneath my shirt as he pulls me toward him.

Once again, I remember the pregnancy test I'm dying to take to ease my mind and I grab his hand to stop it from moving further up.

"What's wrong?" he murmurs as he kisses my neck.

"Nothing. I just thought we were going to watch a movie."

He looks up at me and smiles. "Okay, I can take a hint."

"No, it's not like that."

If I say no to sex right now, he may think it's because I just spoke to Adam. Not that I don't want to have sex with Chris, I would just rather not do it while worrying whether I'm knocked up.

"Then what is it?"

"Nothing. I'm just worried about something right now and it has nothing to do with Adam or Cora. I can't really talk about it, but I promise I'll talk to you about it tomorrow. Is that okay?"

"Of course it's okay."

I run my fingers through his dark hair and he closes his eyes as he begins to relax. "Tell me again what the plan is for Sunday."

"We're flying out to San Francisco and we're going to rent a car to go see your dad. Then we're staying the night in the hotel and we're flying out to Vegas Monday morning."

"Rachel wants me to be there by noon on Monday. She said she arranged a lunch for me, her, and Jackie."

"A bachelorette party?"

"That's what I said, but Rachel didn't think it was funny."

"Good, because you're not a bachelorette. You're mine."

"Well, we're not married yet, so technically I am still a bachelorette."

He opens his eyes and his expression is serious. "You just said that ring on your finger means everything. Or does it only mean something when it comes with a marriage license?"

I swallow hard. "It does mean everything. I was only kidding about being a bachelorette."

"I'm not trying to scare you. I just want to be clear about this before you leave tomorrow."

"Shit."

"What?"

"Are you having doubts about me going to Cora's tomorrow?"

"I don't know. I trust you. I just don't know if I trust

him."

"I think you should come with me."

"I don't think that's a good idea." I grab his ears and he smiles. "Don't do that."

His ears are the only place on his body where he's ticklish. "Come with me and I'll let go."

"Claire, let go of my ears."

I lean forward and blow in his left ear and he squirms under me. "Come with me."

"I'm not coming with you. This is something you have to do without me. I swear I trust you." He slides his hands up my shirt and chuckles as he grabs both my breasts. "But if he tries to touch you, you have to promise you'll tell me. And then you'll have to promise to visit me in jail after I murder him."

He smiles as he squeezes my breasts as if they're car horns. "Ow! That hurts," I protest as I push his hands down.

"Why does it hurt? Are you okay?"

Oh, no.

My mind draws back to the memory of the first time I felt the tenderness in my breasts when I was pregnant with Abigail. I was putting on my bra while getting ready to go to a party with Senia. I didn't know what it meant at the time. I thought it was just a symptom of PMS.

"It always happens before my period."

"I don't remember that happening when we were

together before. Is that because… because of Abigail?"

Two days. Two days late is not a big deal. Don't worry him.

"I don't know, but it's nothing to worry about," I say as I stand from the sofa and hold my hand out to him. "Let's go to bed."

"It's only six thirty."

"Then don't forget your Capri-Sun so you can rehydrate. We've got lots of studying to do."

CHAPTER TWENTY-FIVE

Claire

CHRIS SENDS ME off on my road trip with a long, deep kiss that he knows will not be soon forgotten. As I pull onto the highway, I'm reminded of the few times Adam drove from Wrightsville Beach to Chapel Hill to see me in the dorm. I wonder if he's driving on this same road right now. If we were friends, we could have carpooled.

The thought of Adam and me not being friends makes me sad.

Turning on the stereo, I smile when I hear the end of "I Will Follow You Into the Dark" by Death Cab for Cutie. Chris taught me to play this song on the guitar when I was seventeen. It took him almost eight weeks to teach me a song he learned to play by ear in a couple of days. Sometimes, I forget how talented and driven he is and how lucky I am that his heart belongs to me.

I make a stop at a grocery store in Wilmington to get Cora some flowers and a card, and to get myself a pregnancy test. I consider going into the grocery-store bathroom to get the test over with, but the thought of pissing on a stick in a public restroom just seems wrong. Besides, now that I have the test, I can wait until I get home where I can break the news to Chris in person should the test come up positive.

The light patches of snow along the edge of the highway clear up the further I get from Chapel Hill and the closer I get to the coastline. Shrugging off my coat, I turn up the heater so I can feel more comfortable. I turn on my phone and plug it into the car stereo to listen to some music. My phone screen displays a new text from Chris.

Chris: *I made you a playlist to listen to while you're driving. No texting and driving. I love you.*

I smile as I keep my eyes half-focused on the road and open up my music app to see the playlist. None of the songs on the list are his, but they're all songs that mean something to us.

The first song on the list is "I Want You" by The Beatles, which was the song he was playing on the guitar when I walked into his living room nearly six years ago. The second song is "In Your Eyes" by Peter Gabriel; the first song he played for me that same day. The third song on the list makes me laugh: "Crank That (Soulja Boy)." Chris and Tristan had a contest to see who could do the Soulja Boy dance better. Jake and I both agreed that Chris won and Tristan ended up destroying all the video evidence because he thought he was robbed.

The next song on the list makes my heart leap into my throat. It's a cover of "Falling Slowly" by Kris Allen. He used to make fun of me for watching American Idol, and he pretended to be jealous whenever I rooted for Kris Allen. Then he asked the DJ at my senior prom to play this song for us to dance to.

The rest of the playlist has me laughing and weeping. Ultimately, I think the playlist does what I'm sure Chris intended for it to do: to help me remember how much he loves me and how far we've come. And how I'll never do anything to risk breaking us again.

My stomach begins to ache the moment I pull into the parking lot of Cora's apartment complex and I see Adam's truck. It's funny how inanimate objects can prompt such emotional reactions. After I broke up with Chris, I never knew when I was going to get punched in the gut by a memory. One minute I'd be sailing smoothly through life and the next, I'd see a restaurant we once frequented or I'd get a whiff of something that smelled like him, and the whole world was turned upside down.

Pulling into the parking space next to Adam's truck, I pause to take a few deep breaths. This is nothing like the last time I visited Cora, when Adam surprised me by coming back from Hawaii early. Everything has changed in the two months since that day. I got to hold Abigail in my arms. Chris finished recording his album. I got engaged three days ago.

I hold up my left hand to look at the ring. I told Chris that this ring means everything, but the truth is that it's just a ring. Without this ring, I still belong to Chris. I always have.

I slide out of the driver's seat and the asphalt is wet from the rain. Luckily, the carport above me provides some protection, but I have to get my umbrella out of the backseat so I can make it across the parking lot without getting drenched. I step out of the car and see Adam coming out of Cora's front door with an umbrella. He sees the umbrella in my hand and stops.

Reaching back into the front seat, I grab the bouquet of flowers and the greeting card. I slam the door shut and pop open my umbrella. Staring at the ground, I cross the parking lot toward the apartment. As soon as I reach the shelter of the eves, I let down my umbrella and shake off the rainwater.

"I didn't know if you brought an umbrella," Adam says, and his voice sounds different, deeper.

"Thanks," I say as I close my umbrella and walk toward Cora's open front door.

I stop at the threshold, shocked to see Lindsay sitting

on the side of the sofa closest to Cora's armchair. Her baby is asleep in a car seat at her feet. She looks at me and smiles; a faint, uncomfortable smile.

"Are you okay?" Adam asks from behind me.

I nod as I step inside and try not to think about why Adam would bring Lindsay here today. The room is really warm, but I don't remove my coat. I have a feeling I won't be here very long.

I lean down and kiss Cora's fuzzy cheek and she giggles. "Claire, did they tell you I'm flying the coop?"

"Yes, they did," I reply, setting the flowers and the card on her TV tray table as I squat down next to Cora's armchair. "Are you happy to be leaving?"

"Oh, well, a girl my age can't ask for too much. You'll see when you get older. You learn to accept the simple pleasures people offer, like a warm bed and a different flavor of Cream o' Wheat every day. I'm going to get to see my great-grandkids for the first time ever."

Grabbing her hand, I try to not think of the possibility of Cora living in a place where she's not treated like the angel she is. It eases my mind a little to know that Chris will take me to visit her in Idaho whenever I want.

"I think I know what you mean," I say as I kiss her hand then reach across to pet Bigfoot, who's sleeping in her lap.

When I scratch behind his ears, he wakes up and lazily stretches his limbs. I glance at Lindsay and Adam and they're both looking at the ring on my finger. I remove my hand from Bigfoot's head and hide it away.

"Where's Senia?" Cora asks.

"She couldn't make it. She's coming to see you on Thursday. She has some big news to share with you."

"What kind of news? You can't keep secrets from a lady my age. I may not wake up tomorrow."

"Don't say that," Adam and I both say at the same time.

"Oh, don't you worry about me. I'm not afraid to die. I'm more afraid to live till I'm so old I can't remember my kids' names."

"Senia's having a baby," I say, and the way Cora's eyes crinkle up even more when she smiles just makes me want to cry.

"Senia and Eddie are having a baby!" she says, her voice a bit more energetic now.

"No, not Senia and Eddie. Senia and Tristan."

I grit my teeth and force myself not to look at Adam. I can sense his tension from six feet away.

"I don't know Tristan. Who's he?" Cora asks, her white, wispy eyebrows scrunching together in confusion.

"Tristan is her new boyfriend," I say.

This is a tiny white lie. Tristan and Senia may not be together now, but they have a romantic trip to Vegas in a couple of days, which may change everything before Senia visits Cora. I have to give Tristan and her the benefit of the doubt that they will make this work. I still can't believe she's pregnant.

I nearly reach down to touch my abdomen before I realize where I am. "Cora, I want you to know that you've been the closest thing I've ever had to a grandmother," I say, and as much as I don't want to cry in front of Lindsay, the tears come immediately.

"Honey, don't say stuff like that or you'll make me cry."

"It's true. I don't think you understand how much your friendship meant to me when I moved here." I try not to think of the nights I spent sitting on the bathroom floor when I first moved to Wrightsville. "Your kindness… Taking care of you gave me something to look forward to. Thank you for being my friend."

I feel so uncomfortable saying these things in front of everyone, but my need to say this far surpasses my embarrassment.

"Claire, dear, can you put those flowers in some water for me." I quickly stand up and grab the flowers off the tray table. "And while you're in there, I have something for you on the counter next to the phone."

I wipe away the tears as I make my way to the kitchen. The first thing I see on the counter is the wooden sign that usually hangs on Cora's front door.

Where we love is home.

I take a deep breath in a vain attempt to stifle the tears. Reaching into her cupboard, I pull down a tall glass and fill it with water. I remove the plastic film from the flowers and stick the bouquet in the water, grabbing the wooden sign off the counter as I make my way back to the living room.

I set the flowers on the tray table and Cora smiles. "I love mums. Did you pick those?"

"I sure did. I got you a card, too, but you can read that when I'm gone." I don't want her to read what I wrote inside the card in front of everybody. "I should probably get going. They say it's supposed to snow later this afternoon and I'm driving home alone."

"So soon?" Cora protests gently.

"I'm sorry. I don't have snow chains. I haven't been driving very much lately now that I'm on break."

And Chris drives me everywhere I need to go.

"Okay, honey, you have a safe trip," Cora says with a grin that lights up the room.

"But I'll visit you in Idaho soon. You can count on that."

"I would love that. Get those straight 'A's and tell Senia I miss her."

I don't bother reminding her that Senia is coming on Thursday. It will be a nice surprise for her.

I give her a long hug and, as much as I try to fight it, the tears come again along with a painful lump in my throat. Cora is the last thing tying me to Wrightsville. Once she's gone, I won't have any reason to come back here.

"I'm going to miss you so much, Cora," I whisper. "I'll

make sure to call Tina to get all your addresses and phone numbers."

I smooth her hair back and her eyes are brimming with tears. I kiss her forehead then kiss the top of Bigfoot's head. I try not to think horrible things like the fact that this may be the last time I'll see her alive. Instead, I think of how happy she'll be to finally see all her family after all these years. I have to be happy for her. Cora's going home.

I stand up, letting the wooden sign dangle from my arm as I make my way toward the door.

Adam quickly follows. "I'll walk you out."

I turn to Lindsay and she appears even more uncomfortable than when I first walked in. "It was nice seeing you again," I say to her and she smiles without saying a word as I reach for the doorknob.

I open the door and a stiff winter breeze sweeps over me. I grab the umbrella I left outside as Adam closes the front door behind him. I don't move. I just stare at the rain pounding the pavement in the parking lot and wondering how much change and heartache one person can endure in a lifetime.

"Are you okay to drive back?" he asks, and I turn around to face him.

It's strange the things we notice about someone when we're no longer in love with them. He's wearing a Duke hoodie and some jeans. I didn't realize it until now, but he never wore any Duke sweatshirts or T-shirts when we were together. I don't know if he did it out of respect for me, but I never noticed this until now.

"I'm fine," I reply. "I didn't know you were going to bring Lindsay. I thought that maybe you and I could talk, but…"

"But, what? We can still talk. I only brought Lindsay because I'm taking her to her parents in Carolina Beach and Cora's house is on the way. I didn't bring her here because I don't want to talk to you."

"I just feel like everything has gotten so awkward between us. I hate it."

I wipe the last remnants of tears from my cheeks and Adam cringes a little when he sees my finger. I quickly tuck my hand inside my coat pocket, but it's too late.

"You're getting married?"

I nod my head and try to think of an appropriate response to this. I don't want to say something about how happy I am or anything that will seem like I'm rubbing the engagement in his face. But I *am* happy; so happy it scares me.

"How have you been?" I ask and he smiles.

"I'm putting in my notice on January first. I got sponsored."

"That's awesome. I'm so happy for you." I want to hug him because that's what you do when a friend tells you something like that. Instead, I dig my hand further into my coat pocket and tighten my grip on the umbrella in my other hand. "So… does that mean you're going on tour?"

He nods and the way he looks at me makes me think we've run out of safe things to talk about. That must be it because all I can think right now is that he had to let me go to get everything he ever wanted.

"Claire, I want you to know that I meant it when I said you'll always own a piece of me."

I bite my lip to keep from crying, but it doesn't work. "I'm sorry."

"For what?"

"For not being the person we both thought I was. I'm sorry you met me when you did."

"You don't have to apologize. We were both running away without knowing where the hell we were running to. And I swear I'm okay. I'm *better* than okay." He smiles and this time the smile reaches every part of his face. "I think I needed you to show me that I do have it in me to forgive, not just others, but myself. You didn't do anything wrong. I'm the one who fucked up when I went to Hawaii, but I don't regret it. I only have one regret."

"What's that?"

"The last time you came here to Cora's, when you got out of your car and walked toward the apartment, I was watching you from the window. I saw how happy you were—like, *really* happy—and in those few seconds, I knew that you had probably already moved on with Chris. I should have left you alone instead of confusing you even more. I apologize for that."

I take a deep breath and I realize that the rain has stopped falling. "Thank you for calling me to come here. I know that must have been difficult for you. I hope… Good luck in Australia. I mean it when I say I'm happy for you."

"I know. Congratulations on the engagement."

I glance toward my car and smile. "I guess I should get going before it starts coming down again."

"Yeah, you don't want to get caught in the snow with that nerd-mobile."

I roll my eyes as I tuck my umbrella under my arm and look up at him nervously. "Goodbye, Adam."

"Goodbye, Claire."

As I walk to my car, I feel that final thread of uncertainty unraveling and falling away behind me. I lay the wooden sign and the umbrella on the backseat then I sit in the driver's seat and smile. Adam is happy and so am I. What more could I ask for out of this trip?

Then I see the grocery bag on the passenger seat and I remember the pregnancy test. It's time to go home.

CHAPTER TWENTY-SIX

Adam

I WALK BACK into Cora's apartment and Lindsay is gently placing Kaia in Cora's arms while Bigfoot purrs and rubs himself against Lindsay's legs, having been banished to the floor.

Cora's eyebrows shoot up as she holds Kaia. "Look at you, pretty girl."

I can see Lindsay struggling with whether or not she should adjust Kaia's head, which is lolling to the side over Cora's arm. Kaia's eyes are unfocused until I come closer to kneel down next to the chair and she sees me. Her arms go stiff as she flails them around, the way she does when she's excited. I let her latch onto my finger to calm her down.

"Want to play some poker, Cora?" I ask.

Cora lightly taps Kaia's chin and Kaia reaches for Cora's finger. "I think I'm going to take a nap soon. I've seen too much excitement for a girl my age."

Lindsay shoots up from the sofa to take Kaia from Cora, and I get a whiff of her perfume. It's the same beachy scent she's worn since I met her more than two years ago. I've smelled that perfume for weeks now, but it seems warmer today. She grabs Kaia to pick her up, but I put my hand on her hand to stop her.

"I'll take her."

She looks at my hand on hers, but she doesn't move. "Are you sure?"

Cora answers for me. "Of course, look at her reaching for her daddy."

My eyes shoot up at this remark, but Cora's eyes are fixed on Kaia's face—and Kaia *is* reaching for me. I scoop Kaia up in my arms and she mashes her face into my chest looking for something to suck on.

I laugh as I watch her growing more frustrated with my lack of milk. "Can I borrow one of yours?" I ask Lindsay.

Her eyes widen with shock. "Is there somewhere I can feed her? I have to save the bottle I pumped for when we're at the restaurant."

"I'm sure Cora won't mind if you feed her in the bedroom. Is that all right with you, Cora?" I ask and Cora seems a little confused for a moment.

"Oh, you want to breastfeed her? Of course, you can lie down in my bed. That's how I used to do it with my kids. Be a good boy and show her where it is."

I nod toward the hallway and Lindsay follows me as I lead her into Cora's bedroom, which is just as bare as the living room. Everything is packed away except for her furniture, the bed linens, and one lamp.

Lindsay sits down on the edge of the bed and immediately begins unbuttoning her blouse. I can't tear my eyes away as she unsnaps the clasp over her breastbone and peels away the fabric covering her left breast. I glance down at Kaia before I hand her over, and she's asleep in my arms.

"She's asleep," I say, trying not to stare at Lindsay's chest, but my eyes keep falling.

"Really? I don't know if I should let her sleep or wake her up. I want her to sleep through dinner."

Gently, I set Kaia down in the center of the mattress then I can't help but watch as Lindsay gets dressed. She stands from the bed and glances at Kaia before she looks me in the eye.

"Why do you look at me like that?"

"Like what?"

"Like you want to touch me."

I take a step closer to her so our noses are inches apart. "Because I do want to touch you," I say, my hand slowly inching forward until it finds her face. She closes her eyes as I sweep her hair back over her shoulder, exposing her neck. I lay a soft kiss on her jaw then whisper in her ear, "But not here."

DINNER WITH LINDSAY'S mom and stepdad goes well, as I knew it would. Lillian loved me until the very end when she became convinced I was never going to propose to Lindsay. She must think that me inviting Lindsay and Kaia to come with me to Australia in January and March means that Lindsay and I are back together. I told Lindsay that she could tell her mom whatever she needs to about our relationship to get her blessing. If that means telling her that we're back together, I'm fine with that. At this point, I'm willing to do pretty much anything not to miss out on the important moments in Kaia's life.

"I'm sorry I didn't say anything to her," Lindsay says.

The snow is coming down again now that we're only twenty minutes from Durham. The rumbling sound of the snow chains tearing over the highway is so loud, I'm not sure whether I misheard her or I don't understand what she means.

"What are you talking about?"

"Claire. I'm sorry I didn't say anything when she spoke to me at Cora's house. I just froze."

"It's fine. I didn't expect you two to have a long conversation while painting each other's toenails."

"I know, but I could have said something. I just couldn't get my mouth to work. She's stunning and she wears her heart on her sleeve. I can see why you fell for her." She waits for me to respond, but I don't know what I'm supposed to say. "Adam?"

"Yeah."

"Do you still love her?"

"Yeah, I do, but not the way I used to. I just want the best for her, the same way I want the best for you and Kaia."

She sighs and I take my eyes off the road for a moment to look at her. She's leaning her head back against the headrest with her eyes closed. A tear rolls down her temple and down the side of her face. I reach across and brush my thumb across her temple.

"I'm sorry," she says as she pushes my hand away from her face. "I'm sitting here thinking of how horrible it is that Nathan has been gone for less than two months and I'm already trying to figure out how to tell you that I'm in love with you."

I stare at the road in front of me, focusing on keeping my tires aligned with the tracks of the car in front of me. I rub my right thumb and index finger together, as if the moisture from her tears will give me some clue as to what to say.

I love Kaia and I will always love Lindsay for being my friend and for allowing me to be a part of Kaia's life. I don't know if that longing I've been feeling to touch her and to kiss her is because I love her or because it's been more than two months since I've felt that closeness with anyone. With so much uncertainty, I don't want to lead Lindsay on. But I also don't want to unnecessarily reject her if what I'm feeling is real.

"I don't know how to feel about that," I say, as I reach for her hand and lace my fingers through hers. "I do love you, but I don't know if I can trust that feeling or if it's the same kind of love that we shared before. All I know is that I don't want you to go and the thought of you being with someone else makes me physically sick. I just think we should take this slow... for Kaia's sake."

She squeezes my hand and nods. "You're right. I just had to say it aloud because it's been driving me crazy, watching you with Kaia and making plans to go to your competitions. Letting you pay my *rent*. I just... I know you do it mostly for Kaia—"

"I do it for you, too. I wouldn't pay your rent or invite you to travel the world, and I would never have dinner with your parents just for Kaia. I need someone to laugh at my jokes and, no matter how many times I try to teach her, Kaia still can't say "Who's there?"."

We're both silent for a while until we almost reach her house and she speaks again. "Remember the time we took my niece Shayla to the beach last year and you saved her from drowning?"

She runs her fingertips over the back of my hand and forearm as she talks and it sends chills through me. She probably doesn't even realize she's doing it. She did it all the time while we were together, whenever we watched a movie or went on long car rides. It's one of the things I missed the most after we broke up.

"Yeah, I remember."

"She asked me about you the other day. She said her mom made her take swimming lessons and now she's going to start swimming competitively. She wanted me to tell you that."

I pull into her driveway and she sets off to unlock the front door while I get Kaia and her car seat out of the car. When we walk into the house, it's almost colder inside than it is outside.

"Is your heater not working?" I ask.

I set the car seat on the dining table and begin unbuckling the straps over Kaia's torso. I gently scoop her up and quickly grab the blanket she was lying on top of so I can cover her up.

"The thermostat stopped working yesterday."

"Why didn't you tell me? We could have fixed it today. Kaia can't sleep in this."

"She slept with me last night so we could keep each other warm. It was kind of nice."

"Fuck that. Get your stuff and I'll take you guys to my apartment. I'll fix the thermostat tomorrow."

After we get to my apartment and Kaia is settled into my bed, Lindsay disappears into the bathroom to change into her pajamas and get ready for bed. When she comes out of the bathroom, I can't help but smile when I see what she's wearing.

"You still have that shirt?" I say, referring to the Duke T-shirt she stole from me when we first started dating, before we moved in together, because she wanted to feel close to me while she slept.

"Yes. I hope you don't think it's weird, but I've been wearing it ever since we broke up. Nathan didn't know it was yours."

"Have you at least washed it?" I ask and she rolls her eyes. "It doesn't matter. You look hot in that shirt no matter how filthy it is."

Grabbing her hand, I pull her toward me. She clutches the front of my shirt as she looks up into my eyes. My heart thumps against my chest as I hold her face and slowly lean in to kiss her.

CHAPTER TWENTY-SEVEN

Claire

I CALL CHRIS when I'm a few minutes from the apartment to see if he's home. When I pull into the underground parking space, he's leaning against a concrete column waiting for me. I park the car and he opens my door, as if he can't wait for me to do it myself. I look up at him and he looks a little scared, like he expects me to blurt out that I'm leaving him for Adam.

I smile at him and sigh as he smiles back. "I'm so happy to be home," I say as I grab my purse, where the pregnancy test is tucked safely inside.

Stepping out of the car, I wrap my arms around his waist and nuzzle my face into the crook of his neck. He feels so solid and warm.

"You said what you needed to say?" he asks as he takes my car keys and activates the car alarm.

I grab his hand as we walk toward the elevator. "Yeah. And I promised Cora I would visit her in Idaho. Is that okay?"

"Of course. Anything you want is okay."

"Anything?"

He presses the call button for the elevator and grins. "What are you thinking?"

My stomach clenches inside me as I think of the pregnancy test in my purse. "Chris, I wasn't going to tell you this, but I want to be one hundred percent honest with you. I don't want us to have any more secrets."

The elevator doors slide open and he looks worried as I pull him into the cabin. "What is it you want to tell me?"

"I'm late."

His brow furrows as he attempts to work out what this means. "Do you mean... your period is late?"

I nod and take a deep breath. "It's probably nothing because we've been pretty careful, but I got a test just to be sure. I'm going to take it right now."

"Wow..."

I look down at the floor. "I didn't want to tell you because of everything that happened with Abigail. But on the way here I realized that I can't keep stuff like that from you any more. Even if we're disappointed or surprised by the results, we should face this stuff together, right?"

He stares into my eyes for a moment, not saying anything, and I begin to worry that maybe I shouldn't have told him. Finally, his lips curl into a faint, guarded smile, as if he's trying not to smile.

"I don't want to get my hopes up, but I'd be lying if I said that the idea of you carrying my baby doesn't make me want to jump in the air and click my heels together."

I laugh as I imagine this. "I don't want you to get your hopes up either. Hell, I don't want to get *my* hopes up."

"Is that what you want? Do you want to have a baby?"

"No. I mean, I don't think I'm ready right now. But I will admit I've been thinking about it for the past few days and... I keep thinking of how having you with me this time would make everything so different than the last time. And I want that. I want to share that with you."

The elevator doors open and we're silent as we make our way down the corridor to our apartment. He opens the door and I breathe in the scent of home. I love that smell. I set my purse down on the kitchen counter and Chris joins me in the kitchen after he locks the front door.

He helps me out of my coat then looks me in the eye. "Go ahead and take the test and we'll talk about it after that. Whatever the result, we're in it together this time, so you have nothing to worry about."

I kiss him before I disappear into the bathroom and attempt not to freak out as I read the instructions for the test. I follow the instructions then set the test on the counter. I consider waiting in the bathroom, but I don't think I could sit alone in here for five minutes. I wash my hands and go out to join Chris in the bedroom.

"You're done?" he asks as he pulls off his shirt.

"No. I have a few minutes to wait, but I didn't want to wait in there."

I sit on the edge of the bed and he sits next to me. "Are you nervous?"

"Yes."

"This is probably something we should discuss, even if you're not pregnant."

"What do you want to discuss?"

"What would happen? With school and with us."

"What do you mean? What do you think would happen to us?"

"I don't mean we'd break up, but we can't raise a baby in an apartment."

"I guess we'd have to move."

"But what about school?"

I pause as I recall the conversation I had with Dr. Goldberg a couple of weeks ago that ended with me scheduling an appointment with an academic advisor. I've been holding off on telling Chris because I wanted to save the news for a special moment. New Year's Eve seemed like the perfect time to tell him, but I wonder if right now would be better.

"What are you thinking about?" he asks with a smile.

I try not to grin too broadly. "I'll tell you later. I have to go check the results now."

"Can I go in there with you?"

"Of course."

My hand trembles as I grab the test off the vanity in the bathroom and hold it up for both of us to see: One pink line. Not two.

"I'm not pregnant."

I toss the test into the small trashcan next to the toilet and head for the door, but Chris grabs my hand to stop me from leaving.

"Are you disappointed?" he asks.

I turn to face him and the confused look on his face makes my stomach cramp. "I know it's stupid because we're totally not ready for a baby, but yeah. I'm disappointed. I've been fantasizing about what it would be like, and I know it won't be perfect. I know it will remind us of Abigail, but I also know it would be beautiful. I just really wanted to see that joy that I saw on your face when you held Abigail."

"I love that you said that."

"Why?"

"Because you're thinking of my happiness. You're always thinking of me."

For some reason, him saying this aloud makes me blush with embarrassment, as if he's just undressed my soul. He's right, I'm always thinking of his happiness. I don't think I even notice when I'm doing it.

"That's because you're my real-life hero," I say as I drape my arms over his shoulders and rest my forehead against his. "How do you feel? Are you disappointed?"

"Yes, but I know as long as I keep studying and drinking my Capri-Sun, I'll grow up big and strong and we'll make lots of babies."

He kisses the tip of my nose and I lick his chin. "Yum," I murmur. He chuckles as he locks his arms around my waist, then I wrap my legs around his hips as he lifts me off the floor. "Ooh, you don't need Capri-Sun. You're already strong."

I rest my head on his shoulder as he carries me out of the bathroom and walks straight through the bedroom toward the kitchen.

"It would have been nice to be surprised with a baby," he says as he sits me on top of the kitchen counter then goes to the refrigerator. "But I have a surprise I think you'll like just as much."

He opens the refrigerator and pulls out a box of Capri-Sun. He sets it next to me on the countertop and starts taking out every pouch of juice in the box.

"I'm not really into that stuff like you are," I say and he smiles as he removes the last pouch.

He reaches into the box again and pulls out a small black box. "My mom wanted me to give you this for Christmas, but you hadn't proposed to me yet so I thought the songbook would be better." He lifts the lid on the box revealing a gold necklace with a teardrop pearl pendant suspended in the center of a diamond-encrusted gold ring.

This is the necklace I've seen Jackie wear on special occasions. "You know both my grandparents are gone, but this was my grandmother's wedding ring. My mom had it made into a necklace after my grandma died so she could keep it close to her heart. She wants you to use it as your wedding ring."

I rub my finger over the smooth pearl and smile. "It's beautiful, but we haven't even set a date."

"It's okay. She still needs to take it to the jeweler so he can take out the pendant and turn it back into a ring. Do you want it?"

I nod and he replaces the lid on the box then sets it aside. "Well, that takes care of the 'something old' part. Now we just need something new, borrowed, and blue."

"When do you want to get married?"

He shrugs as he puts the drinks back into the box. "Your birthday's in seven months, but it will be too hot to get married in August. Maybe we could do it in April then my birthday gift will come early when I take you on our honeymoon during Spring Break."

Chris's birthday is in May, but he doesn't know that I've been planning a much better gift than a honeymoon during Spring Break.

"April sounds good," I reply. "It's not going to be a huge wedding. We can totally put it together in three months."

He puts the box of Capri-Sun back in the fridge then he

grabs my knees and spreads my legs apart. He grins as he wraps his arms around me and slides me forward until my butt is on the edge of the counter. "I honestly don't care where, when, or how we get married as long as it's just you and me and the people we love. No reporters or photographers or hundreds of people we don't know."

I run my fingers through his hair and he closes his eyes. "I'll ask Senia and Rachel to help me with the planning when we get back from Vegas. I'm sure I can get a lot done before next semester starts."

"Let's talk about the wedding later."

"What do you want to do right now?"

"I'm not going to lie. I was stressed as fuck today at the PT appointment. I kept thinking of you and hoping you were okay. I just want to take a long, hot shower and lie in bed for the rest of the day. We can pack for Vegas tomorrow morning."

"I can handle that." I slide off the counter, feeling a little guilty for allowing him to carry me here with his knee the way it is. Sometimes, I forget about it because he never complains. But he insists it's getting a lot better since he started therapy.

As soon as we've showered, we lie down in bed and I pull the red songbook he gave me out of the top drawer of my nightstand.

"I promise I haven't peeked at the last page. I just want to read while we lie here. Is that okay?"

He grabs the book from me and lays it on his nightstand. "Just tell me what you want to hear and I'll sing it to you."

He hops out of bed and grabs his acoustic guitar off the wall. He sits on the edge of the bed and I slide off the bed so I can sit cross-legged on the carpet in front of him.

His eyes are locked on mine as he sings each word to me, his voice soft as a lullaby and I'm mesmerized. Bombs could be going off outside our window and I'd never know.

I may be the melody of Chris's soul, but Chris is my harmony. He is the one who fills my heart and soul with peace. I'm so glad he will be standing next to me when I see my father on Monday.

Chapter Twenty-Eight

CHRIS

TRYING TO KEEP a secret from someone you live with, someone who knows everything about you, is like hiding under a box with pinpricks for windows. If you put your eye next to one of those holes, you can see everything on the outside, but no one can see what you're hiding inside.

Every time Claire says something about Rachel's wedding, I want to shake her and say, "Can't you see what's going on right under your nose?"

"She said she'll have my dress waiting for me in our hotel room. I can't believe I don't even get to try it on again before the wedding," Claire says as she packs some face soap and creams into her makeup bag. "I mean, the dress looked okay at the fitting, but it was so rough. What if it looks hideous or the seamstress messed up? I just think it was a bad idea to rush this wedding. She and Jake have been together more than seven years. Why do they *have* to get married on New Year's Eve?"

I grab her hairbrush out of the top drawer and hand it to her so she doesn't forget it. "Maybe they didn't want to wait anymore. Don't you ever feel like going to the courthouse and getting married without anyone knowing?"

"Not really. I want your mom there at the very least."

"I think they're doing the right thing. They've put it off for too long as it is. They've been living together for more than three years," I reply as I follow her into the bedroom.

She stuffs her makeup bag into her suitcase and zips the suitcase closed. "*We've* lived together for more than three years. That doesn't mean I want to rush to set a date for the wedding. Anyway, the point is, if I hate this dress, Rachel is going to owe me big time."

I grab her suitcase off the bed and set it on the floor. "Are you ready to go?"

Her eyes widen as she realizes this is it. "No, I'm not ready, but I've got no choice. I have to see my sister."

"And you're sure you don't want to at least try to call before you show up?"

"I don't want to give him any opportunity to put on a mask. That whole letter reeked of someone with something to hide."

I can see that she's trying to be strong despite her growing anxiety. I smooth her hair back and kiss her forehead and she lets out a deep sigh.

"Everything is going to be fine."

WE ARRIVE AT my mom's house to pick up a pair of heels Claire ordered for the wedding. She had them delivered to the house in case they arrived after Claire and I left to California. When we pull into the driveway, Joel is rolling my mom's red suitcase down the walkway toward us.

"What the fuck?" I mutter.

"Be nice," Claire insists as I get out of the car.

"What's going on?" I ask as Joel approaches me with the suitcase.

"Your mom is almost ready."

"We're just here for the shoes. My mom's flight isn't until tomorrow."

Joel raises his eyebrows as if this is out of his control. "She said she was going with you two. She wants to be there for Claire."

My mom comes strutting down the walkway with her coat on and her purse over her shoulder.

"Mom, what are you doing? Claire and I are going to California alone."

"She's my daughter. I'm going with her whether you like it or not." She kisses Joel on the cheek and he shrugs apologetically as my mom climbs into the backseat.

Claire hops out of the car and insists that my mom take

the front seat, but my mom doesn't budge. I place her suitcase on the backseat next to her and she doesn't look at me. She's pissed. I didn't tell her about the letter from Claire's father until last night. I didn't want to give her anything more to worry about, after everything we went through with Abigail. But she did not appreciate being kept out of the loop.

The silence inside the car is making me uncomfortable. I reach for the stereo and Claire reaches for my hand to stop me. She shakes her head imperceptibly and I sigh as I pull my hand back.

"I'm happy that you're coming," Claire says.

I crane my neck a little to get a better view of my mom's face in the rearview mirror. She looks more worried than angry.

"I just can't believe you two have been keeping so many secrets from me."

After a brief, but still agonizing nonetheless, silence, I ask the question that needs to be asked. "Did you book yourself a room at the hotel?"

Claire smacks my arm. "God, Chris."

"What?"

I don't want to share a hotel room with my mom. I had plans for Claire tonight.

"Don't worry about me. I'll get my own room."

Claire throws me a look that could make my nuts shrivel up. "Jackie, I'm sorry we waited so long to tell you. I just didn't want to bring it up in case I changed my mind. I'm still not sure I'm making the right choice, but I'm happy you'll be with me."

My mom spares a tight smile. "Is there anything else you two are keeping from me? Do you have a sixth toe or an evil twin I should know about, Chris?"

"Well, Mom, I didn't want to tell you this, but… I'm pregnant."

Once again, Claire smacks my arm.

"Shit! Take it easy on the arm. I need that to perform."

"Are you pregnant, Claire?"

"No!" Claire shrieks. "You see what you started?"

Claire ignores me all the way to the airport. After we park the car and check our baggage, we get in line for the security check and I can't help but smile when she takes off her shoes and puts them in a plastic tray to be scanned.

"Why are you smiling?" she asks as we push our trays down the steel table toward the conveyor belt.

"No reason."

"You're such a jerk."

I laugh as she slides her tray onto the conveyor and gets in line to be scanned. "You're so fucking adorable when you're pissed."

My mom slides her tray after mine and gets in line behind me. "Stop antagonizing her," she warns me. "She doesn't need you to be cute; she needs you to be supportive."

Once we get on the plane, I try to switch seats with my mom so she can sit next to Claire, but she insists on sitting alone so she can read. After takeoff, Claire orders a bottle of water and I consider asking for a Capri-Sun, just to see if I can get a smile out of her, but I have a feeling it would just annoy her right now, so I settle for water.

"I'm sorry for the comment about being pregnant. I think I'm just nervous about this trip and I'm deflecting."

She glances at me then stares at the water bottle on her tray table. "I know you didn't mean anything by it, and it was kind of funny, but I'm still upset. And I know it's stupid to be upset about not being pregnant, but I think I'm just stressed about the trip and I'm probably PMS-ing. I'm sorry if I'm being a bitch. I just feel so... *angry* today. I'm afraid of what I'm going to say when I see my father."

"You don't have to be afraid. Anything you say to him will only be a reflection of how you feel. You deserve to speak those words. He wasn't there for you."

Suddenly, I feel angry, too. I'm angry for Claire and for myself. I never talk about my dad because, as far as I'm concerned, he's dead. I don't want to know what kind of man abandons his own child. I think of the lengths I would have gone to for Abigail, if I knew it were in her best interest, and it makes me want to kill anyone who would willingly make their child feel unwanted. And Claire and I have always felt that way.

Everyone thinks about how lucky Claire was to find us

when she did. No one ever thinks about how lucky we were to find her. Claire filled a gaping hole in our hearts. I'm not surprised my mom wanted to be with us today.

CHAPTER TWENTY-NINE

Jackie

NO MATTER HOW hard you try, you can't shelter your children from suffering. And the suffering is what allows them to experience true bliss, so maybe I shouldn't be so upset that Claire and Chris were going to visit Claire's father without me. But I feel as if they're slipping from my grasp, and so quickly. I don't know what to do other than be there for them.

Chris's plan to have a surprise wedding for Claire is beautiful. When Claire came to me and told me she wanted to propose to Chris, I couldn't believe how alike they are and yet they're still able to surprise each other. As happy as I am to see them preparing to spend the rest of their lives together, I really wanted to have the experience of helping them plan their wedding. I should be happy for them, but it's hard to be happy when you realize your children no longer depend on you.

After we take our luggage to our hotel rooms, we meet in the hotel lobby and the color is drained from Claire's cheeks. She clutches Chris's hand as she stares at the hotel entrance with a faraway look in her eyes and it breaks my heart.

"I'm going to pick up the car," Chris says. "You two can stay here. It's cold outside."

He kisses her cheek before he sets off across the lobby toward the hotel entrance. Claire squeezes her hand into a fist then wiggles her fingers, like she's grasping for a phantom limb.

I grab her hand and look her in the eye. "Honey, you let me do the worrying. You're going to go in there and tell him everything that's on your mind and demand the answers you deserve. And don't you worry about how it will all turn out. Because no matter what happens, you are loved. You are cherished."

She throws her arms around my waist and I hold her tightly as I think of the day that her caseworker, Carol, called me to ask if I could take in a fifteen-year-old girl. Carol gave me a complete rundown on Claire's past.

Her mother had died of a heroin overdose when she was seven. She was kicked out of her first four foster homes for locking herself in the bathroom for hours at a time. They didn't know why she was doing this, but it doesn't take a degree in psychology to know she was afraid. After that, she got thrown out of a few more homes for physical altercations with the males in each of those foster homes. She ran away from the foster home she was in before she came to us. She lived behind a grocery store for eight days before she was discovered and taken to the police station, which was when they called me.

Every fiber of my being told me to say no to Carol, but a tiny shred of guilt wouldn't allow me to turn her away. I feared what this teenage runaway would do to Chris. Would she introduce him to drugs or sex? Would she assault me or my son? I had the normal prejudiced thoughts that most people recognize as survival instincts. But looking back now, I realize I was prejudging her. Claire didn't bring the turmoil I thought she would bring. And I wasn't the one who got through to her; it was Chris. Through his music, he opened her heart and calmed her spirit.

I honestly believe that Chris and Claire may have known each other in a former life. I couldn't imagine two people more perfectly suited for one another. So I will hug her and comfort her and I will assist him in keeping his surprise wedding a secret. I will do anything for these two to find the happiness they are destined for.

I give her one last squeeze before I let her go and this puts a smile on her face. "Chris and I will be right there waiting to knock some sense into this man if he so much as looks at you wrong." I lock my arm in hers and we head outside to meet Chris. "Don't forget that I was a cheerleader in high school. I won't hesitate to give him a swift cartwheel-kick in the face."

Chris asks me to drive the rental car so he can sit in the back with Claire, and I'm happy to do it, but I'm not happy with Chris sitting in the backseat and barking directions at me. And the way these people drive in California makes me want to never get behind the wheel again.

"Get off on Washington and make a right," Chris says.

"My hands are going numb," Claire whispers.

"Take deep breaths, babe," Chris replies.

The sound of her panicked breathing makes me nervous. I take the turn onto Washington Street too fast and the tires skid a little.

"I don't feel good," Claire says. "Please pull over."

Before I can even pull into the Bank of America parking lot, the sounds of her retches make me cringe. I pull into a parking space and she throws the door open to vomit onto the asphalt. I jump out of the car and hold her hair back as she finishes spitting out the last remnants of the cookie she ate on the plane.

"Chris, go into that nail salon and get something to clean up the backseat and some water for her to drink."

I help her sit back down in the driver's seat where it's clean and she leans forward as she wipes the tears from her face. "I'm sorry. I'm just so nervous about meeting him. I felt like my heart was about to pop out of my chest."

"Are you feeling better now?"

"A little."

"It's not too late to change your mind, Claire."

I don't tell her that I think seeing her father is a mistake. I don't tell her this because I could be wrong. But my experience with Michael leaving Chris and me has taught me that you can't *make* someone love you.

"I'm not here for myself," she says as she looks up at me.

Something about her face seems different and I don't think it's the flush in her skin from vomiting.

"Are you sure you're feeling okay? We can go back to the hotel so you can rest and we'll all come back here after the wedding."

She shakes her head. "No, I don't want to go back. I want to get this over with."

I take a deep breath as I prepare to reveal a secret I've been keeping from Claire for many years. "Claire, do you remember the day you came to me and asked if your caseworker had told me anything about your mother or father?"

She looks confused for a moment, then, "Yeah. That was a couple of days after you found out about me and Chris."

"Yes. You asked me that question and I told you I didn't know anything more than you knew, but that wasn't the truth."

She frowns as she anticipates what I'm about to tell her.

"What do you mean?"

"When you came to us in April, your caseworker, Carol, told me that you didn't know your father and your mother had died of a drug overdose when you were seven. Months later, when I found out you and Chris were dating—almost two years before you two confessed to me—I called Carol to dig a little further into your history."

"Why?"

"You have to understand that you had lived with us for just over six months at that point. I wanted to protect both you and Chris."

"Protect us from what?"

"I was afraid that you may have been sexually assaulted in a previous foster home and I wanted Chris to take things slow with you. I knew you'd had problems with some of the men and boys in your other homes. I wasn't sure about the details. I didn't want you or Chris to get hurt."

"And what did you find?"

"I found that you had done an excellent job of keeping yourself safe in the foster care system." For some reason, these words make her cry. I can only imagine it's the years of loneliness that she's recalling. "Claire, Carol also told me something about your mother. She'd spoken to your neighbor, who said that your father and mother carried on a brief, but consensual, relationship when she was sixteen and he was twenty."

She shakes her head in disbelief. "That doesn't make

sense. Why would the neighbor know all this? And why would Henry Wilkins tell me she was raped?"

"Claire, honey, you remember your neighbor, the one you used to call Grandma?"

"I remember, but why would my mother tell Henry Wilkins that she was raped?" As soon as she asks the question, her face falls as she realizes she already knows the answer to this question. "Henry was in love with my mother?"

"Henry helped your mother set up the trust fund for you. Your mother was sick, but she did everything she could to ensure you would be taken care of after she passed."

"You mean, after she killed herself."

"What's going on?" Chris asks when he arrives with a bottle of water and sees Claire crying.

The concern in his voice both worries me and comforts me. I know Chris would take on all of Claire's pain if he could.

"Do you still want to go? Or do you need some more time to think?" I ask Claire and Chris looks confused.

"I don't know," she says, wiping her face as she stands from the driver's seat. "I think I need a minute." Chris hands her the bottle of water and she takes a few small sips. "Can you walk with me?" she asks him and they set off through the parking lot toward Washington Street.

I watch them leave and my heart aches for them.

They're not kids anymore, but they still have so much to learn about the world. I hope this visit brings Claire the closure she so desperately needs.

CHAPTER THIRTY

Claire

CHRIS AND I walk in silence for a few minutes until we reach a gas station. We walk through the parking lot, holding my breath as we pass the dumpsters, and find ourselves at a café behind the gas station. I'm not at all hungry or in the mood for coffee, so I take a seat in one of the chairs outside the café and Chris sits across the small table from me.

"You want to tell me what happened back there?"

"Your mom shared some information about my dad with me. I guess he didn't rape my mom. At least, that's what my old neighbor told my caseworker."

He reaches across the table and grabs my hand and I hold on tightly. "Do you believe what your neighbor said?"

"I don't think she would have any reason to lie. She was the one who found me... and my mom. I don't remember her that well, but I remember I was over the moon the few times I went to her house because she had a real granddaughter who I played with a couple of times. I think her name was Misty."

"Yeah, I remember you telling me about her. I hope you know that I won't be upset if you decide to back out. I came here for you. If you want to go back to the hotel, that's what we'll do."

I pull my coat tighter as a large system of dark clouds settles above us and the purplish dusk quickly transforms into a gray night. I can smell the rain that has just finished drying on the concrete below us. We should get back to the car before we get soaked.

I stand up and Chris does the same. "I want to go back to the hotel and sleep on it. The wedding isn't until midnight on Tuesday. That's over two days away. We can catch a flight tomorrow night instead of tomorrow morning, if I do decide to see him in the morning. Is that okay?"

I can't decide if he looks disappointed or worried. "Like I said, we'll do whatever you want. As long as we're back in Vegas by Tuesday morning, Rachel will just have to deal with it."

"Oh, that's right. She wants to have brunch with your mom and me tomorrow," I say as I sneak closer to him. "Well, Senia's not getting there until Tuesday morning, so it's not like I'm going to be the last one there."

"She'll get over it."

"You look worried. Are you that afraid of Rachel?"

He grabs my face and his hands are warm despite how cold it is out here. "I always worry about you. I just want you to be happy."

He kisses my cheekbone so softly that it tickles and I grin stupidly. He smiles and my breath catches in my chest.

"You're so beautiful," I whisper and he chuckles. "Really, you are. Sometimes, I watch you sleep."

"I know."

"No, you don't."

"Yes, I do. And I caught you feeling me up the other night."

"Shut up."

"Oh, right. That was me who was feeling you up. Sorry."

I wrap my arms tightly around his neck and squeeze him as hard as I can. "Take me home."

"To the hotel?"

"I don't care, just take me with you."

He lifts me off the ground and tilts his head back so he can look me in the eye. "What are you going to do when I'm gone?"

"Wherever you go, I go."

WE WALK JACKIE to her hotel room even though she insists she doesn't need us to escort her. It's weird that I've known Joel less than a week, but I already find myself wishing he were here to keep her company. It may be too soon to say this, but Joel may be the missing piece our family has been waiting for.

After we shower and Chris texts his assistant to change the time of our flight, we settle down in bed. The hotel room is too cold for me, but Chris always complains about how hot he gets when I'm snuggled up next to him. It doesn't bother me one bit. I spent more than a year craving his body next to mine. I'm never letting go again.

"Do you ever wonder what life would have been like if you had come on tour with me?" he asks.

I trace my finger lightly over his chest in a figure-eight pattern as I contemplate this question. "I thought about it almost every day."

"Do you think you'll go on tour with me this summer?"

The uncertainty in his voice kills me and I can't keep this secret any longer. "Chris, I'll go on tour with you tomorrow, if that's what you want. I changed my classes for next semester. I'm taking all my classes online."

He sits up suddenly and, even through the darkness, I can see the incredulous look on his face. "You can't do that."

"Yes, I can. And don't tell me I can't." I sit up so I can look him in the eye. "Do you have any idea what it feels like knowing that one of the reasons I gave up Abigail was so that you wouldn't have to give up your career and here we are without Abigail and you on the verge of giving everything up? Have you any clue how that makes me feel? I feel like a failure. I failed her *and* you."

"Don't say that. Don't even think that."

"I can't help thinking it. This is the only way to stop feeling like it was all in vain. *Please* let me do this."

"Fuck," he whispers as he shakes his head. "I don't feel good about this."

"But I do."

I reach for his face and he kisses the palm of my hand. "How did I get so fucking lucky? I don't feel like I deserve this."

"When I told Dr. Goldberg that I wanted to do this, he laughed. I don't think I've ever heard that man laugh."

"Why did he laugh?"

"I couldn't figure out why he kept cheering us on. Every time I told him I was moving forward with you, I kept expecting him to tell me to slow down, that I'm not ready." I sigh as I think of Goldberg's words. "He told me his first wife, the one who died eight years ago, was his first love. And she got sick before they had children. He said that if he could go back and change one thing in his life, he would have given up his practice before she got sick so they could have enjoyed the time they had together while she was healthy." I grab his face so he knows how serious I am.

"I don't want to let time get away from us. I can study from anywhere in the world. I don't need to stay here. The only reason I went to UNC was because of the scholarship. But I talked to my advisor and I can still use the scholarship for the online classes."

"You don't even need the scholarship. You should donate it to someone else who needs it."

"Is that a yes?"

He pulls my hands off his face and smiles. "How could I ever say no to you?"

I throw my arms around his neck as I climb into his lap. "I'm so happy."

He nuzzles his face in my neck and the softness of his lips against my skin comforts me. His hands slide under my T-shirt and glide over my skin. His erection grows beneath me, feeding my hunger for him.

"Did you start?" he whispers as he kisses his way up my neck to the back of my ear.

"Start what?"

"Your period."

"Oh, shit."

He pulls away and he's smiling even though he looks confused. "How late are you?"

I think for a moment. "Five days."

He lifts me up off his lap and sets me on the bed. "I have to make a phone call."

"Who are you calling?"

"Concierge."

An hour later, a very embarrassed bellhop brings up an unmarked brown paper bag containing three different brands of pregnancy tests and two large bottles of water. Chris tips him well before we race to the bathroom.

"You can't be in here," I insist as I twist open the cap on the first bottle of water then guzzle it down.

"Let me read the instructions, to make sure you do it right."

"You are *not* going to watch me piss on a stick!"

"Just let me read the instructions."

He reads all the instructions for each test and quizzes me until he's satisfied I know what I'm doing.

"You're such a pain in the ass," I say as I push him out of the restroom.

"I want to have sex tonight. I'd love to do it without a condom."

"Get out. I have to pee."

I can hear him laughing as I close the door behind him. Luckily, I drank enough water to supply all three tests with the right amount of fluid. After I wash up, I unlock the door and let Chris inside.

"All three tests in one shot? That's talent."

"I'm nervous."

I sit on the toilet and Chris kneels before me. "Why? Are you afraid of being pregnant?"

"I'm nervous that it's going to say I'm not pregnant and

then what? Maybe I haven't gotten my period because something is wrong with me? What if I have a tumor or something?"

"There's nothing wrong with you," he insists.

"You don't know that."

"Yes, I do." The look in his eyes is almost daring me to challenge him on this.

"How long has it been?" I ask.

"Let me check." He stands up and grabs the first test off the counter while I watch his face anxiously for a sign. He's serious as he picks up the second and third tests. Then he closes his eyes and takes a deep breath. The silence kills me. Then a tear rolls down his cheek and I feel as if I might be sick.

"We're having a baby," he whispers.

I shoot to my feet so I can get a better look at the results. "Really?"

He opens his eyes to look at me and I haven't seen Chris cry since his grandfather died three years ago. Just the sight of it takes my breath away. I grab his face and lean my forehead against his as I attempt to catch my breath.

"I didn't think it would feel like this," he whispers.

"Like what?"

"Like the happiest day of my life."

I kiss his cheek and lick the moisture from my lips before I crush my mouth to his. "I love you so much."

He lifts me off the floor and I wrap my legs around his

hips. "I love your heart," he whispers as he kisses my neck and carries me to the bed. He lies me down and the ravenous look in his eyes makes my entire body pulse with desire. "But your body is a close second to your heart."

He lies on the bed next to me and his hand slides into my panties. His fingers glide into me as his mouth covers mine, swallowing my whimpers. He pulls his hand out of my panties, and I'm about to protest when he grabs my panties and yanks them down roughly, leaving a burning trail on my skin. I bite my lip as he tosses them on the floor. I reach for his boxers, but he pushes my hand away.

"Just because we can have sex without protection, doesn't mean we don't have to take our time."

I smile uncontrollably as he sits up on his knees between my legs. He rubs my clit gently with his thumb then lifts his thumb to his mouth and sucks it clean.

"I'm addicted to that flavor."

He grabs my hips and I squeal as he flips me over onto my stomach. He lifts my hips so my ass is in the air then he spreads my knees apart so he can lie on his back between my legs. His hands are firm on my ass as he eases me down onto his mouth. I gasp as he sucks gently on my clit.

"Oh, God," I breathe as I press the side of my face into the pillow.

His tongue and his lips work in unison, stirring a fever inside me. Then his fingers plunge into me, gathering my wetness before he slowly eases his finger between my cheeks. He massages my opening and I hold my breath, unsure if I want this, but it feels too good to stop. His finger slides into me and I let out the breath I've been holding.

I want to cry out in both pain and pleasure, but I don't want him to think he should stop. It's a sensation unlike anything I've ever felt as he licks me at the same time as he's massaging me from the inside. I don't want it to end. A soft whimper escapes my throat and he slides his finger out of me.

"Are you okay?"

"Oh, my God, Chris. Don't stop."

He laughs as he kisses the inside of my thigh then dips his finger inside me again. My thighs tremble as his tongue circles my clit and his hand works wonders until I'm so swollen with pleasure I think my entire body might explode. I turn my face into the pillow and let go a scream so loud that my ears pop. He slides his finger out of me, but he keeps the warm pressure of his mouth on me, lapping up my juices as I climax.

My body trembles as he scoots out from beneath me and I collapse onto my belly. "Holy shit," I whisper as he lies next to me and lightly runs his fingertips over the backs of my legs.

"That's only the beginning, babe." He turns me onto my back and takes off his boxers. He begins to lie on top of me, but I push him off. "What's wrong?"

I quickly sit up and peel my shirt off as I climb into his lap. "I don't want to lie down."

I hook one arm around his neck and reach down to grab his cock as I ease him inside me.

His eyelids flutter as they close. I ride him gently, slowly moving up and down, savoring the delicious friction as he hits that spot deep inside me.

"Do you think that's safe?" he says, grabbing my hips to stop me.

"I don't know. Google it." He grabs my hips to try to lift me off his lap, but I hold on tight. "I'm kidding. Of course it's safe."

"Don't fuck with me like that. You have no idea how scared I am."

I cradle his face in my hands and kiss his forehead. "That's why I love you."

I kiss him slowly as we rock our hips back and forth together.

"I want to live inside you," he whispers. I suck on his tongue as his hand slides down to find my clit. "I want you to come with me."

Grabbing fistfuls of his hair, I plunge my tongue into his mouth as I attempt to not scream the way I did a few minutes ago. "Faster," I urge him.

He groans, his fingers still caressing me as his cock twitches inside me. He continues stroking me long after he's finished, making no move to pull out of me. I curl into him and bite his shoulder to suppress my cries as the second orgasm rolls through me.

"Claire…"

"Yes."

"I want to have three kids… at least." I can't help but laugh and he pinches my side. "I'm serious. And after this album, I'm not going to tour anymore until you graduate." I open my mouth to speak, but he continues. "And I want to make little T-shirts that say, "My Dad Rocks." And I want to teach them all to play an instrument. And we'll have some animals, like horses and chickens, and I'll teach them to take care of the animals. And—"

"Slow down, cowboy. I know your sperm is quite potent, but let's not count our chickens before they hatch."

He lifts me off his lap and sets me on the bed, then pushes me back so he can lie on top of me. He slides his hand behind my knee and lifts my leg onto his shoulder. He eases himself into me and I gasp.

"Don't tell me not to get my hopes up," he growls as he pierces me at an agonizingly slow pace. "Hope is the only thing that has kept me going for the past year and a half."

"You don't have to hope anymore. I'm yours… forever."

CHAPTER THIRTY-ONE

CHRIS

I WAKE CLAIRE up slowly.

I open the curtains in our room just a smidge to let in a crack of gray morning light. Then I lie next to her and wait until she can feel me watching her. I could write a song about her face; the way her top lip is fuller than her bottom lip; the tiny, barely noticeable dip on the tip of her nose; the graceful arc of her eyebrows; the crystal-blue color of her eyes. She slowly opens her eyelids and smiles when she sees my face inches away from hers.

"Are you stalking me in my sleep again?" she says as her arms reach for me and she nuzzles her head against my neck.

I lightly stroke her arm as she squeezes me tightly. "How do you feel?"

"A little hungry."

"Do you want to order room service or do you want to go out?"

"Call your mom and ask her what she wants to do."

I tilt her chin up and stare at her face for a minute. "Are we going to tell her right now?"

"No! I think we should wait until we get back home from Vegas."

"Why?"

"I don't know. I'm scared. What if she thinks we're not ready or she gets really emotional?"

"Well, I can guarantee you she's going to get really emotional and who cares if she thinks we're not ready. You and I know we're ready. We're being responsible. We're not giving up anything to do this."

"I know, but I'm still scared to let anyone know before the wedding. Let's let Rachel have her day, then we'll tell everyone when we get back."

I can't tell Claire that Rachel has been planning our wedding in Vegas since we got back together a month ago. Or that Rachel is probably more excited about our wedding than I am. She's been coaching me on what to say and what not to say to Claire to make sure our secret stays hidden. I probably would have told Claire by now if it weren't for the fact that I think Rachel would slowly disembowel me.

"Yeah, let's let Rachel have her day," I say, trying my hardest not to grin.

"Why are you smiling?"

"I'm just happy we're having a baby," I say as I slide my arm out from underneath her neck and head for the desk phone.

I call my mom to join us in our room, but she insists she'll wait for us to get showered and dressed first. After Claire and I eat a light breakfast of toast and eggs, we both shower and she allows me one last taste of her before we invite my mom up. I laugh as Claire makes the bed and she laughs as I spray the room with her perfume to cover up the smell of sex.

My mom comes in and she glances into the trashcan before she sits on the edge of the bed. "You're not going to shave?" she asks me pointedly.

I scratch the scruff on my jaw and shake my head. "Claire likes it. Don't you, babe?"

She rolls her eyes at me as she leans against the dresser. "Rachel will probably make him shave."

"Rachel's in for a surprise. Jake's getting his first tattoo tomorrow."

Claire's mouth drops. Jake isn't a sissy, but he's the most whipped motherfucker I know. He pretty much does whatever Rachel wants. And Rachel doesn't like tattoos. She thinks our bodies are like sacred temples, or some shit. I'm assuming this is why Jake is so whipped. She must worship his temple often.

"She's going to kill him," my mom says as she digs in her purse for something. "You should try to talk him out of it."

"I can't. It was a bet between him and Tristan."

"What kind of tattoo is he getting?" Claire asks.

I can't tell her because I agreed to get the same tattoo he's getting.

"You'll see."

"Enough talk about tattoos," my mom says, turning to Claire. "Have you made up your mind, honey?"

"I'm going," Claire replies. "I want to meet my sister."

"What if she's not there? What if no one's there?"

"We'll wait," I answer for Claire and she smiles.

I get an anxious feeling inside me as I realize we're about to meet the aunt and grandfather of my child—my *children*.

I have to stop thinking of Abby like that.

"Chris?"

Claire is looking at me as if she knows what I'm thinking, but of course she doesn't.

"Yeah, let's get going," I say, clapping my hands together. "We have a flight to catch at five o'clock."

Rachel was counting on us checking into our hotel suite in Vegas by this afternoon so she could sneak into our room while we're having dinner. The plan was for her to leave the wedding rings and Claire's dress under the bed. Then tomorrow, my mom is supposed to come in and get them while we're gone and take them to the wedding venue. Rachel is going to be pissed that I'm fucking with her schedule.

CHAPTER THIRTY-TWO

Claire

CHRIS DRIVES SLOWLY on the ride to my father's house so I don't get sick. As usual, Jackie notices everything.

"Why are you driving like a grandma?" she asks Chris. "Claire, are you feeling better today?"

"I feel great. I had a good breakfast," I reply, knowing how much Jackie prizes a healthy breakfast.

"Good girl. You need to eat well and drink lots of water."

My heart races as my mind tries to conjure reasons why she would say this. She doesn't think I'm pregnant. One vomiting fit does not a pregnancy make. She must be giving me advice to heed *in general*.

Now I feel like throwing up again. The egg-flavored vomit stings the back of my throat and I swallow it down multiple times, all the while staring out the passenger window so no one can see me struggling. Suddenly, I break out in a cold sweat and my chest heaves involuntarily. Oh, God. It's coming.

"Pull over!"

Chris quickly pulls into a gas station, but I can't get the door open fast enough. Some of the vomit hits the inside of the car door. The car rental company is going to hate me. The rest of my breakfast comes up, painfully. When I'm done vomiting, my eyes are bloodshot and tearing and the back of my neck is dripping sweat.

Jackie goes inside the gas station to get me some water this time and Chris squats down in front of me as I sit on the passenger seat.

"Are you okay to go? We can do this another time. We don't even have to go to Vegas. You can just lie down in the hotel room until you feel better. Or maybe I should take you to the hospital. Do you think you need to see a doctor?"

"Chris, I'm fine. Well, not fine, but this isn't any worse than… than it was with Abigail. It will get better… eventually."

I bite my lip so hard as I think of her that I draw blood. The metallic-tang makes me gag and I quickly wipe my lips on the inside of my shirt.

Jackie arrives with a plastic bag of goodies. She hands it to me then gets into the backseat without another word. I look inside the bag and find two bottle of water and a bottle of multi-vitamins.

She knows. She has to know.

"What's this?" Chris asks, holding up the vitamins.

"Well, if she can't hold anything down, she should at least be taking a multi-vitamin."

The way she says this as if I'm not in the car worries me. "Jackie, I'm fine. I just can't stand the smell in this car. And I'm beyond nervous."

"I know, honey, but you have to take care of yourself."

Chris kisses my forehead as he stands and I swing my legs into the car so he can close the door. I take one of the vitamins with a small sip of water. Chris sets off down Washington Street again and my stomach begins to hurt the second he turns into the residential housing tract where my father lives. The houses all have red clay tile roofs and rich, green lawns. The overcast sky dulls the shine on the cars, which are all mostly brand new.

My breaths come shorter and quicker the closer we get to his house. As soon as we pull up in front of the two-story house with the cream-colored stucco and the brand-new SUV in the driveway, I feel as if I might pass out. I clutch the handgrip on the inside of the car door and stare at the rust-colored door of the house.

Chris grabs my hand and I jump a little in my seat. "Take your time."

I nod and take a few deep breaths before I open the car door. Chris and Jackie follow and my heartbeat pounds in my ears as I shut the door. He places his hand on my back to guide me forward and I wiggle my fingers and arms, like a fighter about to enter the ring.

"Claire, you're very pale," Jackie remarks. "Are you sure you're feeling all right?"

I nod again as I continue up the concrete driveway, past the box hedges that stand like pillars on each side of the garage door. Walking up the brick-paved path to the front door, I try to imagine that each step is literally making me stronger. It's much harder to fool our brains into thinking we're strong than it is to believe we are weak. But if we are taught to see the good in others, we should also try to see the good in ourselves.

I am strong.

I've endured the stench and agony of my mother's death. I've battled the loneliness of not having a home. I've survived willingly handing over a piece of my soul to two complete strangers after losing the love of my life.

I will survive this.

Chris looks at me as he reaches for the doorbell. "You ready?"

"Yes."

He presses the doorbell and Jackie links her arm with mine. She winks at me and I *finally* realize that no matter what happens today, I already have a family.

A woman answers the door, her light-brown penciled eyebrows raised in a question beneath her blonde-streaked hair.

"May I help you?" she asks in a pleasant voice that's definitely tinged with annoyance at being disturbed at ten in the morning.

Her black yoga pants and baby-pink T-shirt hug a youthful body, which betrays her late-forties face.

"We're here to see Phillip Lungren," Chris replies, making no attempt to offer our identities because the woman suddenly recognizes him.

"Phil is at work. Are you... you're not...?"

"I'm his daughter," I respond for Chris. "Claire... Nixon."

The woman looks at me and back at Chris then she shakes her head. "Phil didn't tell me he was related to Chris Knight."

"He's not," I reply, trying not to sound too annoyed. "I'm his daughter. Will he be home soon?"

Her lip curls up then she sighs as she seems to remember her manners. "You're the one from North Carolina?" she asks, as if my father has left a trail of illegitimate children traversing the nation.

"Yes, I'm the one from North Carolina. Raleigh."

Jackie squeezes my arm tighter. I'm sure it's a gesture of support, until I look at her face and she appears on the verge of breaking this woman in half. She's trying to draw on *me* for support.

"Well, then come on in," she says, taking a step back to

make way for us. "I'm Elsie, Phil's wife. I'll call him right now to let him know you're here. He works less than ten minutes from here."

She leads us into a living room with black leather sofas and more high-end electronics than I've ever seen in a home before. Not even Tristan and his flashy house have this kind of setup.

"Have a seat," she says, waving at the couches. "Would you like something to drink? I've got iced tea, water, juice…" She glances at Chris. "Beer, bourbon, vodka, pretty much any kind of liquor you want."

Chris grabs my hand as we take a seat and the smell of leather surrounds us as a puff of air explodes from the sofa cushions. "We're fine, thank you," he replies.

Elsie disappears into the kitchen—to grab her phone, I assume—and Chris whispers in my ear. "Didn't mean to answer for you about the drink, but I don't trust this woman not to poison us."

I laugh softly and Jackie smiles at us. The wistful expression on her face makes me wonder if she's happy that Chris can make me laugh at a time like this or if she's nervous. I want to tell her that she has nothing to be nervous about. I'm going to get through this and nothing my father says or does will ever affect my love for her.

Elsie enters the living room and sets her iPhone on the coffee table as she takes a seat on the other sofa. "Phil will be here in about twenty minutes." Her eyes take everything in, from Chris and I holding hands to the stubborn look on Jackie's face. "So, you two are a couple?"

"Claire is my heart," Chris responds and I smile as I get a swooping sensation in my belly.

I never think of Chris as the rock star everyone else sees him as. To me, he's just Chris: the guy who patiently glued the broken pieces of my shattered heart back together. The same guy who cried last night when he discovered I'm carrying his child. It's always weird when I see others regard him as a celebrity.

Still, as wonderful as that simple statement, *Claire is my heart*, makes me feel, I know that this is partially a threat from Chris to Elsie: Fuck with Claire and you're fucking with my heart.

"Is Nichelle here?" I ask to ease the growing tension in the room.

"No, Nichelle is on Winter Break. She's out with some friends right now. You know kids that age. If they're not at the mall or at home, they're off getting into trouble." She snatches her phone off the coffee table and begins typing something. "I'll text her to see if she can come home to meet you."

The tone in Elsie's voice sounds annoyed, as if she knows Nichelle will not come home, but she'll send the text anyway just to satisfy my curiosity.

"That's not necessary," I say. "I don't want to interrupt her plans."

"Oh, please. She does the same thing every day. You're not interrupting anything." Elsie rolls her eyes as Nichelle responds quickly. "She says she can't come. She's sitting inside the movie theater right now."

I guess she's not as anxious to meet me as I am to meet her. I try not to let this hurt me—she's just a teenager, after all—but it stings.

Jackie squeezes my knee when she sees the disappointment in my face. "It's just bad timing."

I'm not sure why I put myself in a position to be rejected. I guess we never really know if the path we've chosen was the wrong one until we reach the end. The important thing is whether you enjoyed the journey. And telling Chris about the letter from my father only brought us closer. If nothing else comes out of this visit, I've already won because I have Chris.

After twenty minutes of awkward conversation punctuated by long silences, the sound of the front door opening makes us all perk up. Elsie grabs her phone off the table again and we all stand as my father walks into the living room.

He's thin and tall with ropy muscles snaking underneath his tanned skin. His grayish-brown mustache matches the hair on his head. The yellow T-shirt he wears tucked into his jeans has the words "*Kelly Co.*" splashed across the left side of his chest in green letters.

Kelly Company.

How ironic. The father who abandoned me and my mother works at a company with the same name as my mother, and he has to wear her name over his heart every day when he goes to work.

He smiles at me, but it's such a phony smile that I can't even bring myself to smile back. "You're Claire?" he asks with even more phony enthusiasm.

I don't know what I expected from the person who never attempted to contact me until I refused the trust fund he contributed to. What was I thinking coming here?

Chris reaches out his hand to Phil. "Nice to meet you. I'm Chris."

They shake and Phil raises one of his eyebrows, as if he's sizing Chris up, then he laughs. "Great to meet you, Chris."

He turns to Jackie and she holds out her hand. "I'm Jackie. Claire's foster mother. It's a pleasure to finally meet you."

Phil looks a little taken aback by Jackie's presence. He probably didn't expect to meet the person who took care of me when he refused to. He turns to me and I take a deep breath as he holds out his hand.

I don't want to shake his hand. I don't want to feel the callous built over the years of working a blue-collar job to support his family. I don't want to feel the warmth that belies the truth of how coldly he abandoned my mother and me.

"Claire has been through a lot," Jackie says. "I think she deserves to know why you weren't there for her."

As soon as she says this, my father's eyes widen and I realize I don't need to know why he wasn't there. I don't need anything from this man.

"We were young," he says, glancing back and forth between Chris and me as if we should understand.

Chris shakes his head. He's just as appalled as I am.

"I should have been there, but I was dumb. Then I got offered a job in Kentucky, and I took it. Then I got offered another job in California… And by the time your mom contacted me, I had already married Elsie and Nichelle was on the way."

"You moved on," I say, summarizing the sorry excuse he just gave me. "Well, while you were busy moving on, my mom was busy dying from a heroine overdose. And I was busy being kicked around from one place to another like a piece of trash. Nobody wants a piece of trash and that's what I felt like. Because you didn't want me."

Jackie watches me with tears in her eyes, but she still smiles as she mouths, *I'm proud of you.*

Phil looks very uncomfortable and a little defensive, like a dog backed into a corner. "Well, I did deposit all that money into your account all these years. I wasn't a deadbeat or nothing like that."

"That money is nothing but a reminder of a childhood I want to forget. I don't want your money. I want my childhood back. I want my *mother* back."

My entire body trembles as the adrenaline courses through me. These are the words I've dreamed of speaking, but always wished I would never have to. In my happiest dreams, this meeting included a heartfelt apology from my father followed by the kind of hug that heals from the inside out.

Jackie wipes the tears from my face and I wait another couple of minutes for an apology that was never coming to me. "You ready to go, honey?" she whispers and I nod as I let out a deep breath that I think I've been holding for twenty-one years.

"Are you sure you don't want to stick around to meet your sister?" Jackie asks.

"We have a flight to catch," I reply. "And she didn't seem so *eager* to meet me after all."

Chris nods toward the door. "Mom, take Claire to the car. I'm going to have a talk with Phil." I look at Chris questioningly and he shakes his head. "I'll be right there. You two go ahead."

"It was nice meeting you," Elsie says and I nod as Jackie and I walk out of the house arm-in-arm.

It's raining when we get outside and we quickly deactivate the car alarm so we can both get into the backseat. As soon as the car door closes, Jackie takes me into her arms and I cry on her shoulder for a few minutes as she strokes my hair.

"You said what you needed to say, Claire. If he can't see what he did wrong then he's not your father. A father loves his child and would never allow his child to feel unwanted. That is what you deserved and I hope with every bone in my body that I have given you that."

"You have. You've given me so much more than that," I reply as I think of Chris.

I'm worried about what he's doing inside that house. But my worrying ends when he walks down the brick path toward us. He slides into the driver's seat and quickly turns the key in the ignition.

"What happened?" I ask anxiously.

He shakes his head and I can feel the anger pulsing off of him with every breath he takes. "Exactly what I thought was going to happen." He pulls away from the curb and makes a U-turn to go back the way we came. "I offered him a check in the amount of the trust fund and he took it."

Chapter Thirty-Three

CHRIS

WE ALREADY PACKED our luggage into the trunk of the rental car, in anticipation of having to make a swift getaway for the airport. The visit with Claire's father was such a flop that we arrive at our gate in the airport three hours early. Claire sits in my lap and closes her eyes as she rests her head on my shoulder. Within minutes, she's asleep and I can only imagine how tired she must be with everything her body and mind have been put through these past two days.

"I'm going to get you two something to eat," my mom whispers before she sets off down the concourse.

Claire's chest rises and falls slowly and I think of the life growing inside of her at this very moment. I can't believe I just handed over a check for two hundred and seventeen thousand dollars to a man who didn't understand the beauty of the life he created. But I guess it's a small price to pay for

Claire's peace of mind. Now she can do whatever she wants with the money in that trust fund.

Claire wakes before my mom returns, but her eyes are still rolling around with grogginess. "Where's your mom?"

"I think she went to get you something to eat. Are you hungry?"

She blinks a few times until her eyes are focused then she looks around at the people sitting around us with their carry-on bags at their feet and their electronic devices in their hands.

"I'm starving."

We find my mom sitting inside a pub, talking on the phone and looking very upset. When she sees us approach, she quickly says goodbye and ends the call.

"Are you okay?" I ask as she tucks her phone into her purse.

"I'm fine. I was just talking to Joel. He wanted to know how it went. How are you two doing?"

I look to Claire and she shrugs. "Can you get me a sandwich? I'll be right back. I have to call Senia."

"Yeah, I'll take care of it."

She pulls her phone out of her pocket as she sets off toward the exit. I take a seat across from my mom and she lets out an exasperated sigh.

"We shouldn't have brought her here."

"She'll be fine. She needed this. Have you talked to Rachel?"

"Yes, I spoke to her right before Joel. She said that she'll send Jake's assistant, I can never remember her name, to drop off the dress tomorrow morning. So no room service for you two. You need to get Claire out of the room by nine a.m."

"Her name is Irlina. You didn't tell Rachel about the tattoo, did you?"

"Of course not. Do you want to tell me about this tattoo or do I have to be surprised again the way I am with everything you two have been keeping from me?"

I'm almost certain she knows that Claire is pregnant, but I can't confirm her suspicions. She'll find out about the baby the moment everyone else finds out. Since we found out about the baby last night, I've been planning how I'm going to tell my mom and I'm pretty sure she'll be glad I waited.

"I can't tell you about the tattoo, but you'll see it soon enough."

She shakes her head then flags down a waitress. She orders Claire a sandwich and a plain club soda. The food arrives a couple of minutes before Claire returns. Her eyes are rimmed pink and I wish I could reach inside her and pluck out the pain like a weed from a lush garden.

"Senia said she picked up the bridesmaid dress from Rachel last night and it was very classy and fit her perfectly, so I shouldn't worry about my dress."

"I told you you had nothing to worry about," I reply as

I think of the day Rachel brought me a selection of pictures of wedding dresses she thought would look perfect on Claire.

I don't know much about fashion or wedding dresses, but I almost kissed Rachel when she showed me this one particular picture. Claire is going to look so beautiful in her wedding dress. But I know that even if she doesn't love it, she'll pretend to because she loves me.

OUR FLIGHT LANDS in Vegas at 7 p.m. When we arrive at the hotel, Joel is waiting for us in the lobby.

I like Joel, and my mom deserves to be happy, but I don't like the idea that she may get hurt if it doesn't work out with him. He doesn't seem like the kind of guy who would hurt her, but you never really know someone until you've seen them react under pressure.

I pull out my wallet to tip the bellhop before he takes my mom's luggage, but Joel puts his hand up to stop me. "I've got it."

Suddenly, a loud scream gets our attention and we all turn toward the sound coming from my right. About twenty feet away, a dark-haired girl is staring at me with her mouth agape.

"Oh, my God!" she squeals.

I force a smile because everyone in the lobby is looking in our direction now. Instinctively, I pull my hood up over my head so that no one else can recognize me. The girl jumps up and down a few times as she converses with her friend, then they both walk toward us.

Claire smiles and I kiss the corner of her mouth, letting my lips linger against her skin for a moment so there's no confusion about whether I'm available. Claire pokes me in the ribs and I laugh as I finally pull away. The two girls in their scarves and Ugg boots are staring at Claire and me with wide-eyed excitement.

"Chris Knight?"

"That would be me."

"Oh, my God! Can we get a picture with you? *Please*?"

After a brief photo shoot with Nova and Mandy, Claire and I make it up to the suite. Claire immediately goes to the window to gaze out onto the dazzling lights of the Las Vegas Strip. When I come up behind her, she turns around so our noses are touching.

"Let's get married in Vegas?" she says with a gleam in her eyes.

"Don't you want to have a wedding at home where you can invite all your friends and pick out your dress and all that stuff?"

I'm *so* going to hell for this.

"We have all our friends here. All we have to do is call them and tell them to meet us at the drive-in chapel and— *boom!*—we're married."

"You want to get married with a boom? How about

Rachel? Don't you think she'll be a little pissed if you steal her thunder?"

She pouts as she realizes I'm right. "Fine. We'll wait. I just really wanted to wake up tomorrow as Claire Knight."

"Claire Knight. Like a clear night sky," I whisper then plant a soft kiss on her lips. "The stars will wait for us."

CHAPTER THIRTY-FOUR

Claire

CHRIS WAKES ME up early to get showered and downstairs for breakfast with Tristan and Senia. As usual, Tristan and Senia are forty fashionable minutes late. Senia looks a little pale as they approach our table in the café.

I stand up to give her a hug and she gives me a weak hug. "Worst flight ever," she complains as she sits down in the chair next to me. "We flew through a snow storm over Oklahoma. I haven't been knocked around like that since my dad found out I'm pregnant."

"Your dad knows!" I cry. "How? Oh, my God, what happened?"

"He happened," she says, pointing her thumb at Tristan. "I threw up a couple of times yesterday and he goes out to get me crackers. He gets back from the store a few minutes after Claudia gets there and blurts out, 'I've got your crackers. How's my incubator?'"

"Incubator?" I reply incredulously.

"Yeah, can he be any more of an asshole?"

"Hey, save the name-calling for the later," Tristan says with a wink. "And your family was going to find out anyway. Your mom gave me the stinkeye on Saturday when I suggested you should cut back on your workout routine."

"She gave you the stinkeye because you poured ketchup on your fish."

"Ketchup is delicious with fried fish. And I ate every last morsel. She should take that as a compliment."

She shakes her head in disgust. "Claudia told my mom and she told my dad and I thought he was literally going to have a heart attack. My mom had to give him a muscle relaxer to calm him down." Senia's face perks up a bit and a smile forms on her full lips. "But that was last night. He called me this morning when we got off the plane to tell me he's proud of me for not quitting school."

I want to blurt out, "I'm pregnant, too!" But I promised Chris we would wait until we get home. There will be no thunder-stealing on this trip.

After breakfast, Chris and Tristan set off to pick up Jake so they can all get their tattoos. Tristan leaves Senia at the elevator with a kiss on her temple. The bashful smile on her face tells me there is more going on with them than she is letting on. As soon as the elevator door closes and I punch the number for the thirty-second floor, I round on

Senia.

"So are you and Tristan finally…?"

She shrugs as she stares at the numbers flashing on the LED screen above the elevator doors. "I may have let him give me multiple orgasms last night."

"I knew it."

She turns to me with a quiet desperation in her eyes. "He's so sweet when we're alone, but he was a total douche with my cousins yesterday while they were watching football. I asked him if he could get my sweater out of the car and he reached into his pocket and handed me the keys. And it was snowing!"

I don't know what to tell her. Chris would never do something like that to me, but Chris has known me for years so he knows better.

"You have to cut the guy a little slack. I don't think I've seen him in a relationship since Ashley dumped him when we were seventeen. And I know this sounds like a total cliché, but I think you've changed him. He's not the same brooding asshole he was a few months ago. In fact, I don't think I've seen him brood once since you all had your little tryst last month. I think you make him feel like he's conquered something."

"Conquered something? Conquered what? My womb?"

"Maybe. Who knows and who cares? The point is that you or this baby may have cracked the unbreakable code that is Tristan Pollock."

"Oh, please. Any guy will crack if you apply the right amount of pressure. It's all in the grip."

I have to tell her I'm pregnant. If I don't tell her, I'm never going to get rid of this bubbly feeling inside of me and I may throw up during the ceremony. As soon as we get to the suite, I wait for her to set out her makeup and plug in her curlers as she prepares to get us both ready for the wedding.

"I'm going to get you ready first, then I'll do myself and Jackie. Where is she?"

"I think she said she was going to pick up some name cards for the reception. I don't know why Rachel asked her to do it. I'm her maid of honor. She should be asking me to do this stuff instead of making Jackie run all over town. Jackie should be enjoying her trip with Joel."

Senia's eyebrows shoot up as she begins applying primer to my face. "She probably figured you have too much going on with saying goodbye to Cora and Adam and meeting your dad."

Just the mention of Cora and Adam makes my throat thicken. "I feel like everyone is babying me. I'm not as fragile as you all believe I am."

"I know you're not fragile. You're one of the baddest bitches I know. I'd be in a mental institution if I were you."

She picks up my makeup bag and digs around until she finds my foundation. Then she grabs her foundation brush and proceeds with erasing all my imperfections. Life would be so much easier if we could just paint broad strokes of color over the ugly parts to make them beautiful.

"Then again, you do have Chris's healing love to get you through. Did he *heal* you last night?"

I grab her hand to pull it away from my face, then I look her in the eye. "I have something to tell you but you have to promise not to tell anyone until we get back home."

"You know I won't say a word. What is it?"

"You can't even tell Tristan. I know he'll just blab about it to Jake and then Jake will tell Rachel and then I'm going to be accused of ruining her big day."

"Okay, that is definitely not going to happen, but I'll play along. I promise not to tell Tristan. Now spill."

"I'm pregnant."

She screams so loud, my ears tingle. "I'm sorry, but—" She screams again and this time I cover my ears. She jumps up and down as she throws her arms around me. "I knew it! I knew it!"

"You did not."

She lets go of me and looks me in the eye with a serious expression. "Yes, I did. I had a dream that we were both pregnant, but I didn't want to tell you about it because I didn't want to upset you. But I knew it! I knew you wouldn't leave me hanging."

"Leave you hanging?" I reply with a laugh.

"I can't do this alone. If you didn't get pregnant, I was about to get one of those lactation consultants just so I could bitch about all the stuff I've been dealing with."

"You can always bitch to me."

"Now I can. Gah! I'm so happy for you!"

She hugs me again and when she finally lets go there are fat tears rolling down her cheeks. "Why are you crying?"

"I'm just so happy for you. I was just telling Tristan the other night how you and Chris deserve to have a baby more than we do."

"Don't say that."

"It's true. I've never known anyone who would do the kind of thing you did for Chris. That's the kind of love we all wish for."

"Stop crying or we're both going to look like shit for this wedding," I say as I wipe the tears, and the makeup, from my cheeks.

She fans her face and sniffs loudly as she picks up her makeup tools again. She begins reapplying the makeup in the spots where I wiped it off. Then she stops and looks at me.

"Our kids are going to grow up together."

I grin stupidly at the thought of this. "After the tour."

"What tour?"

"I'm going on tour with Chris. I changed my schedule. I'm taking all online classes next semester."

"You're leaving me."

"Not for long; just a few months. I don't even know what's going to happen. It's probably too late to change the tour dates now and I can't go on tour in the summer when I'm seven or eight months' pregnant."

"Chris will not go on tour if you can't go with him."

"I know."

She shrugs. "You two will work it out."

"What about Tristan? He'll be going on tour with Chris."

"He said he's not going." She grabs some concealer out of my makeup bag and begins dotting it under my eyes. "He said anyone can play bass for Chris. He can skip this tour."

I can't help but pout as I think of how this will make Chris feel and how complicated it has all suddenly become.

"Don't be sad. I'm sure Chris will figure something out. Worst-case scenario, they cancel the tour and he loses millions of dollars."

"Then he'll resent me."

"He will not resent you. Trust me, you two are going to live happily ever after with a brood of mini rock stars running around your house."

I sigh as I close my eyes so she can dab more concealer on my eyelids. "You don't know that."

"I do know that because I know something you don't."

"What is that?"

"I can't tell you, but you'll find out very soon."

"You're such a bitch. First Chris tells me he's getting a secret tattoo and now you have a secret. I swear to God, you think we'd all have learned the destructive nature of secrets by now."

"It's not a secret. It's a surprise. And you're going to love it."

A knock comes at the door and Senia runs to answer it. Jackie walks in with Joel trailing close behind her. Joel is carrying a long, black nylon bag that looks like it could be for golf clubs. Senia and Jackie hug and Senia fills Jackie in on everything that is going on with her and Tristan and the pregnancy. Jackie casts me a few sideways glances as she listens to Senia.

"What's that?" I ask Joel as he sets the black bag on the bed.

"Chris asked me to bring it for you."

"What is it?"

"He asked me not to let you open it until he gets here. He said he should be here in less than an hour."

I stand up from the chair and walk toward the bed. "What happens if I open it?"

"If you get any closer, I'll tackle you," Jackie says. Senia and I laugh, but Jackie looks dead serious. "I am not kidding. You are not allowed to open that bag, young lady. Now step away." I smile as I step back and take my seat in the chair. "Good girl. Chris will be here soon and he'll explain everything. Right now, let's get your hair and makeup done so Senia can come up to my room and make me pretty."

"You're not going to get ready in here?" I ask as Senia

picks up her tools to continue applying my makeup.

"I have all my stuff in my room. I don't want to haul it all down here then haul it back," Jackie replies. "I'll see you later, honey."

She kisses the top of my head then she and Joel leave the suite. My knee starts bouncing with anxiety as I wonder what the hell is inside that bag.

Senia smiles as she hands me the eyelash curler. "Happily ever after. Just you wait and see."

CHAPTER THIRTY-FIVE

CHRIS

WHEN TRISTAN AND I walk into the hotel suite, Claire is sitting on the edge of the bed next to the black bag I asked Joel to bring up here. Senia is busy packing away her makeup in a large purple makeup case.

Claire narrows her eyes at me. "Can I open it?"

I smile as I lean down to kiss the tip of her nose. "Not yet."

"We're leaving," Senia proclaims as she and Tristan head for the door. "I'll see you later, my love."

She blows a kiss to Claire and I wait until the door closes behind them to peel off my shirt. The tattoo is covered with gauze right now, so she can't see it, but that doesn't stop her from staring at the gauze taped over the inside of my left wrist.

"When do I get to see that?"

"Very soon." I pull on a clean T-shirt and a hoodie and Claire watches me with a slightly amused expression.

"You're the best man. Aren't you supposed to wear a tux?"

"I'm wearing a suit, but not until later. It's five o'clock. We don't have to be there until eleven. Right now we're going somewhere else, so get your coat on."

"We can't show up there at eleven. She has my dress there—I have to get there early enough to get dressed and freshen up."

"You'll get there on time." She grabs her coat out of the closet and puts it on over her jeans and T-shirt. "On second thought, put a sweater on underneath your coat. It's really cold out there tonight."

"We're going outside?"

She pulls off her coat and searches through the drawers for the white cardigan I told her to bring.

I turn the black nylon bag over until I find the zipper. I unzip the bag and lift the flap so Claire can see what's inside. She looks confused at first, then she sees the long optical tube of the telescope and her mouth drops.

"Are we going stargazing?"

I nod as I zip up the case. "Ever since you told me that you didn't get to go stargazing last June, I've been planning this in my mind. The wedding just presented the perfect location and the perfect conditions: the desert on a clear night."

Clear night.

I'll never think of that phrase the same way again.

She presses her lips together and fans her face, probably trying not to cry so she doesn't mess up the makeup Senia just applied.

"I can't believe you're doing this tonight. If we're late, Rachel and Jake will never let us live it down."

"Don't worry about that. We're not going to be late."

She shakes her head as she grabs her purse in one hand and her heels in the other hand.

"You can leave the heels. We'll be back in time for you to get your shoes later."

I can't tell her that these shoes were meant to match the dress we supposedly had made for her to walk down the aisle as Rachel's maid of honor. These heels don't match her wedding dress.

She looks at me skeptically, but she sets the heels down on the bed before we leave the suite. "You're making me nervous."

We make it down to the front of the hotel and the black SUV pulls up in front of us. "I don't feel like driving today," I say as I pull open the back door for her to get in.

I throw the telescope into the trunk then climb into the backseat. Her knee is bouncing as the driver takes us onto the 15 freeway. I grab her knee and she turns to me.

My nerves are buzzing. I'm so afraid that she's not going to be happy with what we planned for tonight. Seeing her so nervous is only making it worse.

"Why are you so nervous?" I ask.

"I don't know. I just have this weird feeling, like something is about to happen. Why are *you* nervous?"

I can't hide anything from her—well, except for a wedding.

"I'm just excited about tonight."

"Excited for Jake?" she asks as she hugs my arm and lays her head on my shoulder.

"Aren't you excited for them? They've been together since they were fifteen."

She lets out a deep sigh. "Don't say stuff like that or you're going to make me cry. God, I can't wait to hear their vows."

I smile as I kiss the top of her head. Though Senia gave her a natural-looking wavy hairstyle for the wedding, I can still feel and smell a lot of hair products were used to achieve it. I would have married Claire in her pajamas at a drive-in chapel, but I want her to look back on the pictures from today's wedding and feel proud of herself, and me.

After twenty-five minutes, Claire sits up and looks around at the desert on each side of the highway. "Where are we going? This is too far. We're not going to make it back in time for the wedding."

"Yes, we will. Trust me."

The driver exits near Sloan and the SUV slows as we go off-road, over the rough desert terrain. It's nearly six o'clock in the middle of winter, so the sun set almost an hour ago over the horizon of mountains in the west. Claire clutches my hand tightly as the SUV bounces over the rocky soil. The tires spit up sand and dirt, which surrounds the back half of the vehicle in a cloud of dust.

Claire shakes her head as she leans her head back and closes her eyes. "I'm going to be sick."

"Stop the car," I tell the driver and he eases to a stop. "This is fine."

I kiss her cheek and she opens her eyes. "That was awful."

"Sorry. Are you okay?"

"Yeah. Is it safe to get out over here?"

I nod as I throw the door open. "Come with me."

She takes my hand so I can help her down from the car, then she follows me to the back. I sling the strap of the telescope case over my shoulder and grab her hand. It's colder than Raleigh out here, but at least there's no snow. She laughs as I yank her hand and pull her toward the open desert.

"You're laughing now, but we've got a long ways to go, little lady. This is your cardio for the day."

"I was hoping to get my cardio *after* the wedding, not before."

"You'd better stop talking like that or I'm going to bend you over one of these tumbleweeds and give you a workout you'll never forget."

Twenty minutes later, we finally find the spot where Irlina set up the blanket and guitar. Claire shakes her head in disbelief, unable to speak, as she sits on the blanket and watches me while I set up the telescope. I pull a piece of paper out of my pocket and unfold it to read the instructions and coordinates for the telescope.

"It's not dark enough yet," I say once the telescope is set up. "So we're just going to sit here for a while."

She smiles as I sit down next to her on the blanket. "What do you want to do?"

"I'm sure you can take a few guesses, but I have some things I need to say first." She gazes into my eyes, giving me her full attention, as I begin. "I know the past year hasn't been easy on either one of us, but I want you to know that I'm going to try my best to make every day of the rest of our lives better than the last. I promise that I will try to make you smile every day. But I also know that with the good times come the bad times. Fuck, there will probably be *miserable* times, but I wouldn't want to be miserable with anyone else."

"Chris? What is this? Are you dying or something?" I laugh so hard I almost choke. "It's not funny! You're scaring me."

"I'm not dying. I'm trying to tell you that I can't wait to start our life together… as a married couple."

I pull up the sleeve of my hoodie and hold out my left wrist so she can watch as I peel off the gauze. She doesn't blink as I reveal the tattoo slowly. Finally, I remove the dressing and she covers her mouth. The tattoo reads, "To love is to destroy pain. I love your heart," followed by tomorrow's date.

"Why is there a date?" she whispers.

I lift her chin so I can look her in the eye. "That's our wedding date. We're getting married at midnight."

She lets out a deep breath and her lip trembles as the tears fill her eyes then roll down her cheeks.

"Is that okay?" I ask and she nods vigorously though she doesn't speak. She just curls her arms around my neck and I pull her close to me so I can give her some of my warmth.

I give her a few minutes to compose herself before I whisper in her ear. "Can I play a few songs for you?"

She releases me and wipes her face. "Of course."

I kiss her cheek before I grab my guitar. The first two songs I sing aren't my own, but I know they're songs that she loves: "First Day of My Life" by Bright Eyes (she laughs when I sing the last line) and "I Won't Give Up" by Jason Mraz.

When I finish, I close my eyes and take a deep breath as I prepare to sing the song I tucked behind the last page of the songbook I gave her for Christmas. I always get nervous the first time I perform a song, especially when it's a song that means so much to me.

I open my eyes and she smiles, and that's enough to get

me through the first line.

"Bring Me Home"

The sunlight followed you in, but you never saw it coming,
Held the rain clouds like a blanket, and took off running,
Then I grabbed your hand and slowly pointed at the sun,
Closed your eyes and dropped it all just to feel the warmth,

Step inside, it's cold outside
Girl, you're not alone
You waited long, you cried
But, girl, you're still my home
My home

"Love is not the only thing we share," you whispered here,
We let her in, then let her go, never knew such tears,
The morning came, I paid you my heart, you paid me your life,
Won't ever forget my purpose, long as you're my wife.

Step inside, it's cold outside
Girl, you're not alone
You waited long, you cried
But, girl, you're still my home
My home

When the stars fall down upon us
And the last flame flickers out
I'll be there to whisper in your ear
I love your heart, babe, bring me home.

I finish the song and she takes my guitar from me, then gently places it on the blanket behind her. She takes my face in her hands and looks me in the eye. "I want you to make love to me right here."

"It's pretty cold out here and you'll mess up your hair."

"You'll keep me warm and *fuck* my hair."

I chuckle as I grab her face. "I'd rather fuck you."

Crushing my lips against hers, I slide my tongue into her mouth. Her tongue is warm and sweet and she whimpers softly as I pull back to lightly suck on her top lip.

She puts her hands on my shoulders and gently pushes me away, then she proceeds to slowly peel off each layer of clothing. First her coat and sweater, then the rest of her clothing. She instantly begins to shiver and I quickly undress so I can hold her against me to warm her up.

She lies back on one end of the blanket and I fold it in half over us as I settle myself between her legs. She wraps her arms around my shoulders and her legs around my hips. I rub the tip of my cock over her clit and she gasps as she closes her eyes and leans her head back.

"Look at me," I whisper, and she quickly obeys.

She whimpers as she gets closer to coming. I keep my eyes locked on hers as I slide into her.

"Chris?"

"Yes?"

I dip in and out of her slowly, trying to keep time with every beat of her heart. One beat, in. Two beats, out. With every stroke, our bodies get hotter and closer to climax. I feel myself getting ready to explode, so I pull out and slide my hand between us to lightly caress her clit. Her mouth drops open and she begins to close her eyes again, but I shake my head.

"Keep your eyes on me."

"Oh, God."

"I love you," I whisper.

"I love you, too."

When her legs begin to quiver, I ease off and she gasps as I slide back into her. I imagine the beat of our hearts as a song I've yet to write. The soft cries she makes every time I hit her core are the music.

Suddenly, she shakes her head. "I'm gonna come."

I pull out of her again and kiss her hard as I grind my pelvic bone against hers. She moans into my mouth and her entire body begins to tremble. I keep my mouth over hers, kissing her deeply as I swallow her cries of ecstasy. She curls into me and that's when I slide into her again. I groan as I finally release myself inside.

I brush her hair away from her face, my cock still

twitching inside her, as I gaze into her eyes.

"Can't we just stay here all night and get married another day?" she asks.

"There are over a hundred people waiting for us," I whisper as I lean down to kiss her neck and I taste salt. "You're sweating."

"So are you."

"Get dressed. I have something to show you."

CHAPTER THIRTY-SIX

Claire

"ARE YOU READY?" he asks once we're both dressed. "It's the bright star to the right of the cluster of four stars. Right in the center of the star field."

We never took a telescope when we went stargazing at Jordan Lake. I sidle up next to him and bring my eye to the eyepiece. There are thousands, or millions, of stars in this field, but right in the center there is a cluster of four bright stars. To the right of those is an especially bright star. It twinkles and makes me think of my mother and her smile.

"What is it?" I ask.

"It's not really a star. It's an asteroid called Vesta, named after the Roman goddess of home." He smiles warmly as he fixes a piece of my hair that's out of place. "I don't know what happens when we die, but I know that if your mom is looking down on us, she's looking down from there. And she's proud of you."

I wrap my arms around his waist and squeeze him as tight as I can. "Thank you for being my knight in shining armor."

"We'd better get going. It's past nine. We still have to get there and change before Jake and Rachel's ceremony. Then ours comes right after. If we miss their wedding, we can pretty much count on Rachel never planning another wedding for us again."

He packs up the telescope and I fold up the blanket. He slings the telescope case over his shoulder and grabs the blanket while I sling the guitar strap over my shoulder and pretend to play as we walk back to the car.

"You don't remember how to play anything I taught you?"

He grabs my arm and pulls me sideways so I don't step into a craggily bush, since I'm too busy looking at the frets, trying to position my fingers.

"I don't know. I'm pretty sure I could play "I Will Follow You Into the Dark" if you gave me a refresher course."

Once my fingers are positioned in what I think may be the correct placement, I brush my fingers over the strings and the sound that fills the cold desert air sounds nothing like a real song.

Chris shakes his head in dismay. "That's shameful."

"Whatever."

When we reach the SUV, Chris throws the guitar, telescope, and blanket into the trunk and the driver sets off back toward the highway. Chris pulls a bit of brush from my hair and attempts to smooth down the wildness. I brush a bit of dirt off his cheek and he attempts to bite my hand.

Finally, the car begins to slow and my stomach drops as I see, in the middle of the desert, a collection of white tents illuminated from within with golden light. A makeshift parking lot has been cordoned off to the right where at least thirty cars are parked. Lighted pathways intersect from the parking lot and between the tents. On the far left, there appears to be a reception area enclosed with white linen and the top open to the stars.

"I thought the wedding was taking place at the hotel."

"Change of plans," Chris replies with a smirk.

"You did this?" I whisper.

"Rachel and I did this, with some help from Senia and my mom."

"Senia knew!"

"Well, there's no one, besides me, who knows you better. Leaving the reception area open was her idea, but I picked out your dress."

I look at him, my eyes wide, unable to contain my surprise. "You picked my dress."

"Don't look so scared. I picked it from a selection of dresses that Rachel gave me."

"I'm only kidding," I say, punching him in the arm. "I

know you wouldn't pick anything bad."

He rolls his eyes then instructs the driver to take us around the reception tent and toward a couple of tents where the silhouettes of people scurrying about inside look like agitated ghosts. We get out of the car and Chris leads me to the entrance of the nearest tent, but he doesn't go inside. He stands just outside with his back to the entrance.

"Mom, are you in there?"

Two high-pitched squeals erupt through the glowing fabric, followed by the sound of frantic footsteps. Senia emerges from the tent first and she's wearing a beautiful black dress that's cut just above the knee to show off her long legs. The sleeves are made of a thin, slightly transparent material that covers her entire arm. I'm assuming that's because it's freezing out here, but she still looks stunning.

Senia grabs my arm. "Come on, we have to get you ready. Go away!" she shouts at Chris.

Chris reaches for my other hand before I step inside the tent. "See you later, babe."

He kisses my hand and I sigh as Senia yanks me into the tent and around a wall of folding partitions that I suppose are meant to keep people outside from seeing the silhouettes of our naked bodies.

"There's my girl," Jackie says as soon as she sees me.

She gives me a loud kiss on the cheek and I don't bother wiping off the lipstick because I know Senia is going to make me look perfect before I go out there tonight.

I look past Jackie and Rachel is standing in the corner of the boxed-off changing area in front of a full-length mirror.

"Rachel," I whisper, stunned by the sight of her. "You look beautiful."

She turns around to face me and she's smiling. "Do you really like it?"

The dress looks vintage; with a lacy bodice and heart-shaped neckline. The skirt reaches down to her feet and is made of layers of creamy, almost transparent silk. Her ivory skin and red lips combined with her dark curls make her a picture-perfect bride from a long-forgotten era.

"I love it." I try not to show the disappointment in my face as I think to myself that there is no way my dress will be that pretty.

"Oh, just wait until you see your dress, honey," Jackie gushes.

"Yeah, your dress is way prettier," Rachel says. "You're going to flip when you see it."

"Thank you for helping Chris with everything. I don't know how I'm going to repay you. I hardly helped at all with your wedding."

"Well, there's not much you could have helped with, without figuring out what we were up to. And you don't have to repay me, but if you must, you can always name your first born after me."

It dawns on me that Chris has been asking me not to tell anyone about the pregnancy until after the wedding so I don't ruin Rachel's big day, but this is both my and Rachel's wedding days. Why would he tell me to keep it a secret? I shake my head because I have a feeling Chris has yet another surprise planned for tonight.

"Come on. You need to get dressed," Senia says, pulling me toward the other corner of the dressing area.

A dress covered in multiple layers of plastic hangs on a hook next to another full-length mirror. Senia and Jackie begin peeling off the layers of plastic until they unveil what can only be described as the most beautiful wedding dress I have ever seen.

The fitted bodice has a straight neckline that curves down to the waistline. Layers of silky chiffon gather at the waist then tumble quietly to the floor, looking almost dreamlike in their softness. The entire bodice is covered in a delicate lacy pattern, but it's not actually lace. When I run my fingers over the bodice, it feels smooth and cool under my fingertips.

"Do you like it?" Rachel asks nervously.

"I love it."

"All right. You make her look beautiful and I'm going to go see if the wedding planner needs anything," Jackie says as she steps out of the changing area.

After I change into my dress, Senia drapes a smock over me so she can do my hair and makeup. She smiles as she works quietly.

"Wow… This is it. I'm getting married to Chris."

"Are you having second thoughts?" Senia says, cocking an eyebrow as she shades in my eyebrows.

I laugh at this. "What a cliché? Of course, I'm not having second thoughts, but I'm definitely having a moment. This feels surreal. Just six months ago I was… Well, I was convinced that Chris and I were over, and so was my life."

Rachel grabs my shoulders as she stands behind me so I can see her in the mirror. "Sometimes you don't know how much you love someone until you lose them. Jake and I broke up for a couple of months while you and Chris were broken up."

"You didn't tell me that."

"Well, it's not something I like to talk about. But he was on tour with Chris. Tristan was still being an ass and refusing to talk to them. And… I know Jake would never cheat on me, but I had never been away from him for longer than a couple of weeks. It drove me a little crazy and I broke up with him." She sighs as she stares off into the distance at whatever memory she's recalling. "He texted me every single day and sent me a postcard from every city they went to. He talked about Chris in some of those texts and, man, he was not doing well after you changed your number."

I grit my teeth together to keep my eyes from tearing

up. I don't know why Rachel feels the need to tell me this right before the wedding. I guess it's just her need to always be honest.

Senia winks at me as she begins dusting a fine translucent powder all over my face and neckline. "This is to make your skin "glow." Not that you need it."

Finally, she applies my lipstick in a sheer nude color, just a shade darker than my lips. I rise carefully from the stool and scoot over a few feet to stand in front of the full-length mirror. In the reflection, I see the moment Jackie walks in and her eyes lock on my face. I turn around and she presses her lips together, but this does nothing to stop the tears.

"See you later, Mrs. Knight," Senia whispers to me before she and Rachel make a hasty exit.

Jackie tilts her head as she looks at me. "Could you be any more beautiful?"

"You're not allowed to make me cry. I just had my makeup done."

"I don't want to make you cry. I just want to look at you." She walks around to examine me from all angles with a wistful expression. "I need you to promise me something." She grabs both my hands and looks me in the eye. "When you go out there and promise to love Chris for the rest of your life, look him in the eye. He is no longer mine, so please take care of him."

"I will."

"I know."

She blows me a kiss so she doesn't mess up my makeup then she leaves me alone in the tent with no idea when I'm supposed to make my big entrance. I turn back to the mirror to make sure everything is in place and my heart jumps when I see Chris.

CHAPTER THIRTY-SEVEN

CHRIS

"WOW," I WHISPER breathlessly as I attempt to take in the sight of her, but I don't think beauty this exquisite can ever be fully appreciated. "If your beauty were a song, you'd sell out a million stadiums."

The left side of her mouth curls up in a bashful half-smile as she looks at the floor. I walk slowly toward her so I can take in every inch of her. Her face is serious now as she watches me come closer.

"You look incredible," she says. "I love the dark gray shirt with the black suit and tie. I hate tuxedos."

"Don't forget my makeup. I think Senia did a pretty good job." She smiles then suddenly her lips quivers as if she's going to cry. "Are you okay?"

She snatches a tissue off the vanity and dabs her eyes to catch the tears before they fall. "I'm just happy. And... I wish Abigail were here with us."

I want to take her in my arms and tell her I wished the same thing about twenty minutes ago, but I don't want to upset her even more or ruin her dress. We'll have plenty of time to talk about Abigail over the next seventy years, or until she turns eighteen and decides to meet us after she gets all the pictures we'll be sending the Jensens. Right now, I need to give her the one thing I know will get her out from under this dark cloud of grief.

"Claire, when I first met Abby in the hospital, I sang to her. I sang a lullaby as she lay sleeping under the heavy sedation." I grab another tissue for her and continue. "She never so much as twitched when I sang her the lullaby, but as soon as I started singing "Sleepyhead" her tiny hand jerked up and I put my finger in her hand. She held my finger through the whole song. That's when I realized that there's something inside her that has nothing to do with DNA that is connected to us. She will come back. I know that like I know you're the love of my life. One day, she'll come home."

"That's why she stopped crying when you sang to her at the lawyer's office?" I nod and she nods. "She'll come back," she whispers. She takes a moment to compose herself then she tosses her tissue onto the vanity and takes a deep breath. "Let's get married."

"Rachel and Jake are about to say their vows. I linked my phone to the video camera so we can watch from in here." We huddle together and watch as Rachel and Jake stand on the altar.

"Oh, my God! Joel is the minister!" she cries.

"Yeah, he got ordained for the ceremony. I didn't even know until today." I grab her chin to turn her face toward me. "He wants to walk you down the aisle. Are you okay with that? Because if you don't feel comfortable with that, I'll walk you down the aisle."

She grabs some more tissue for her eyes. "I feel so naïve. I actually fantasized about… *Phil* walking me down the aisle."

"Fuck Phil. You have Joel and his mighty beard to give you strength now." She laughs and I grab her arm. "Shh! They're going to say their vows."

She composes herself and we listen as Jake and Rachel speak words that make me feel a little self-conscious about my vows.

"I didn't know myself until I met you," Rachel says and Jake appears to be on the verge of tears.

I hope I don't cry on the altar. Tristan will never let me live it down.

After they kiss, I tuck my phone into my pocket and Claire is covering her mouth. "What's wrong?"

"I don't have any vows written."

"That's okay. Just stand up there and promise you'll never leave me again and I'll be happy with that."

"Well, I only have one thing I've been planning to say

to you."

"What's that? Get lost?"

"Well, other than that. It's something I've been practicing for a couple of years."

"*Practicing*? Is it a song?"

"Nope," she says with a sly grin. "You'll see."

I shake my head. "So you have a surprise of your own. I can't wait to find out what it is." I plant a soft kiss on her forehead. "The wedding planner will come here to call you in a few minutes. I have to go now. I love you."

She blows me a kiss as I leave the tent and I immediately start writing a song in my head about today. I pull my phone out of my pocket to type the lyrics into my notes app as I follow the lighted path toward the tent nearest to the parking lot.

"Hey!"

I look up and to my left. Tristan is bounding toward me with an excited look on his face. He's pulling double-duty as best man for both Jake and me.

"What's up?" I ask as I finish typing and stuff my phone back into my pocket.

"I want to give you and Claire your wedding present before everything gets crazy. Do you mind? It's in there," he says as he nods toward the tent where I just changed into my suit.

"You just *can't* wait to give me that blowjob until later, can you?"

"Nah, that can wait until later. And this present is much better since I'm not nearly as good at sucking dick as you are."

We enter the tent and Tristan digs into one of the many bags Senia brought with all her hair and makeup tools. He pulls a thick envelope out of the bag and hands it to me. The envelope is addressed to Tristan Pollock with a return address from the County Assessor's office.

"What the fuck is this?"

"It's the deed to my house. I don't want it anymore. Senia and I are moving to Chapel Hill so she doesn't have to commute to school next semester."

"Are you fucking kidding me? I don't want your house."

I try to hand the envelope back to him, but he steps back. "It's done. I already gifted it to you. I already put a deposit on an apartment off campus. The house is yours." He runs his fingers through his hair as he stares at the envelope in my hand. "I know you and Claire wanted a house with a good piece of land."

I shake my head as I begin to see all the pieces of our lives falling into place. "You can have my condo. There's still eleven months on the lease."

"Are you serious?"

"As serious as I am that this is the craziest fucking day of my life." I fold the envelope and tuck it into my back pocket. "What about the tour? Are you bailing on me?"

He shrugs at first then he nods. "Yeah, I gotta stay here. My grandma will kill me if I let Senia have the baby alone."

"Doing it for Grandma, huh?"

"Yeah, let's just stick with that story for now. I'm not used to this relationship bullshit."

"Thanks, man," I say as I pat him on the arm.

"Congratulations," he says, and I can tell his mind has wandered off to somewhere else; probably worries about the baby.

I can't even imagine how nervous he must be about having a baby with Senia, having to meet all her family and try to be good enough. I'm nervous as shit about Claire being pregnant and I don't have anyone to impress except for her.

"Hey, Claire is pregnant. Don't tell anyone. I'm going to tell everyone at the reception."

He smiles as he slowly nods his head. "You just had to outdo me, didn't you? Now what? I'm gonna have to get married on a fucking tightrope?"

"I'll be there to cut the rope."

The wedding planner storms into the tent, her black hair flying behind her and a frenzied look on her face. "What are you guys doing? The song has been playing for ten minutes!"

I try not to laugh as I follow her and Tristan out to the other tent. Tristan walks in ahead of me and I smile and nod at all the people I recognize. Most of these people are here for Rachel and Jake. I didn't want to invite a bunch of people; didn't want to risk the location leaking to reporters. I think we did well.

I take my place on the altar and, of course, Joel is not standing there. The music stops and a hush falls over the crowd. The anticipation builds with every passing second, until a new song begins to play. I picked this song especially for Claire and made extravagant promises to Rachel to get her to record the piano and vocals: "In Your Eyes." The first song I ever played for Claire.

Joel enters first and waits as Claire enters behind him. The smile on her face as she slips her arm through his arm just about does me in.

She bites her lips as she walks down the aisle with Joel. She's nervous. Every step she takes feels like an hour. I just want to get married and get on with our lives together.

She finally makes it to the altar and Joel kisses her on the cheek before he takes his place atop the altar. I glance at the front row of guests to see my mom's reaction and she's a blubbering mess. I take Claire's hand to help her up the two steps onto the altar and she alternates between smiling and chewing on her bottom lip.

Joel launches into his opening, but I have no idea what he's saying. All I can hear is the thrumming of my heartbeat in my ears. All I see is Claire as our eyes are locked on each other. A moment later, Joel taps my arm and nods his head.

Jake's nephew, Grayson, steps forward and hands us our rings. Claire shakes her head as I hand her the ring I picked for myself. The ring I pulled out of a Capri-Sun box a few days ago has been turned back into a wedding ring with the words "My Everything" engraved on the inside. We each slide the rings onto each other's fingers, both of our hands shaking with nerves.

Joel nods at me again. It's my turn. I take a deep breath as I prepare to bare my soul to Claire in front of a hundred people.

"I've been waiting for this moment for a long time," I begin. "Writing and rewriting these vows until my fingers were numb."

Claire squeezes my fingers and I block out everything and everyone else except for her.

"I can't believe we're here. I spent so many months thinking this would never happen. So many nights afraid that I had lost you forever. But I think that deep down I always knew this would happen for us.

"The day you walked into our house almost six years ago was the day my world changed. Since that day, I have come to know every piece of you and I've loved every inch of you. I've counted the stars with you and I've counted the days, hours, and seconds I was away from you. And after everything we've been through, I have no doubt that I will love you, every bit of you, until the day I die. When the skies collapse and the Earth ceases to exist, I will still love you."

I bring her hand to my lips and she smiles. "To love is to destroy pain. I love your heart."

Chapter Thirty-Eight

Claire

MY ENTIRE BODY begins to tremble with nervous energy. Chris rubs his thumbs over the tops of my hands and I close my eyes as I take a few deep, calming breaths. When I open my eyes, the air in the tent is completely still and quiet. Chris mouths, *I love you*, and I begin.

"Well, I did not expect this." A few chuckles from the crowd don't distract me as I continue. "So, obviously, I don't have any vows prepared." I squeeze Chris's hands and look him in the eye. "But the more I think of it, the more I know that there is only one thing I want to say to you right now, and that is… thank you.

"Thank you for giving me a home. Thank you for being so patient with me. Thank you for loving me when I didn't think I deserved it. Thank you for being my friend, my love, my home, and my hope."

I swallow the lump in my throat and try to blink away the tears.

"There is actually only one line I've had prepared for this day. I've had it tucked away in the back of my mind for a couple of years. But you can't make fun of me, 'cause it's in French."

Chris chuckles and the sound of his laughter sends a chill over my skin. I love that sound. I let go of his hand and bring my hands up to gently cradle his face.

"*Au milieu de l'hiver, j'ai découvert en moi un invincible été...* In the depths of winter, I discovered in me an invincible summer. That's you. Thank you for being my invincible summer."

I kiss him as if nobody is watching, slowly and tenderly. And the way he kisses me back makes me wonder if Chris invented the kiss. When we pull away from each other, I finally hear the applause and the cheering as Chris rests his forehead against mine.

"Forever," he whispers, then he lays a soft kiss on the tip of my nose and I can hear cameras flashing all around us.

"Happy New Year," I whisper.

BY THE TIME we give hugs and say thanks for all the well wishes, it's almost one in the morning. Half the wedding party has left, but the other half is alive and enjoying the open bar in the reception area. Chris and I sit on the edge of the stage, off to the far left so we're not sitting in front of the gigantic speakers. He holds my hand as I remember the moment just ten minutes ago when we danced to "Bring Me Home."

My fingers are laced through his as I lay my head on his shoulder. Immediately, Chris gently pushes my head off his shoulder.

"Nope. No falling asleep right now. We still have one more piece of news to deliver. Remember?"

"And how are we going to do that?"

"How else? We're gonna sing."

I laugh as he gets to his feet and holds his hand out to me as he stands on the edge of the stage. I take his hand and allow him to pull me up.

"I'll kill you if you make me sing something corny."

He laughs as he approaches the DJ. I was very glad to see that they didn't hire a wedding singer or band for the reception, but the collection of instruments on the stage next to the DJ equipment did draw some suspicions. As soon as the DJ fades out the music, Rachel and Jake begin to climb the steps onto the stage.

Chris smiles as he walks back toward me, his coat gone, shirtsleeves pushed up, his guitar slung across his body, and two wireless microphones in his hand. He hands me one of the microphones and my heart feels as if it's going to explode.

"What the hell is going on?"

"Do you remember the lyrics for 'Your Song'?"

I think back to the night Chris sang "Your Song" to help me fall asleep. I had never heard the song before and he was so disappointed in my lack of musical culture that he insisted I learn the lyrics to sing along with him.

He flashes me a devilish grin as he hands me the microphone. "You take the first verse."

"I know."

"Just making sure," he says as he tucks his microphone into the stand and adjusts the height.

Rachel winks at me as she positions her fingers over the piano keys and I cover my mouth as I giggle nervously. I look out across the crowd of people staring at us; most of their eyes, and cameras, are fixed on me. Chris is the performer. There's no chance he's going to mess this up. They're all going to watch me so they don't miss the exact moment my voice cracks or I flub the lyrics.

Chris grabs my hand and looks me in the eye. "Relax. It's just you and me and the rest of our lives."

A deep hush settles over everyone before Rachel plays the first notes, a soft and golden tapping, a melody that burrows into my chest.

My voice cracks slightly on the last note of the first line, but no one seems to notice or care. Throughout the entire first verse, my throat constricts painfully as I think of how all the dreams Chris and I had are coming true. He smiles softly as he strums his guitar. He's gushing with pride as he watches me sing, but it only makes me more nervous.

Chris's eyes are glossy as he begins the second verse. We harmonize on the beginning of the second chorus, and Rachel pounds the keys to drive us toward the finish. Once the tears begin, I have to stop halfway through the chorus, but Chris continues for both of us.

He lets go of his guitar and slowly kneels before me as he sings the last two lines to my belly. He lays a soft kiss on my belly and looks up at me with a joyful gleam in his eyes.

The sound of sobbing gets our attention and we look out to see Jackie crouched down about ten feet away from the stage, her hands covering her mouth and Joel at her side. He helps her stand up and Chris and I make our way down to the dance floor.

"I knew it," she says as we approach.

Chris hugs her as he whispers in her ear. "Congratulations, Grandma."

She smacks his arm and he laughs as he lets her go. "She's going to call me Grandma."

"We don't know if it's a *she* yet," Chris corrects her.

"It's a girl. I can see it in your face," she says to me, and I think of all the times people said that to me when I was pregnant with Abby. "And she's going to be the luckiest girl in the world."

Jackie wraps her arms around me and, in that moment,

I know that everything will be okay.

In that moment, I am home.

Epilogue #1

Adam

My FINGERS WHISPER over the velvety skin on Lindsay's belly and she smiles as she opens her eyes. I kiss her hipbone and she grabs my hair to pull me on top of her. Her arms curl around my shoulders as she buries her face in my neck. I slide my arms under her back to squeeze her and she wraps her legs around my hips to return the favor.

"Good morning," she whispers.

"I don't want to go to the beach," I reply as I tilt my head back so I can study her face. "Let's stay in today and I'll make you breakfast."

She laughs, a hearty, sexy laugh that never ceases to make my heart race. "I'll pass."

"You'll pass the honey after I make you some tea to go with your delicious breakfast." I kiss her neck and she rakes her nails softly over my back. "Why are you always wearing panties? I told you to stop wearing panties to bed."

"If you insist," she murmurs as she removes her panties. I laugh as she awkwardly uses her feet to push my boxers down. "I guess you'll have to check on the baby *every* time she wakes up."

I slide into her and she moans as she throws her head back. "Fine, you can wear panties every other day."

I suck on her throat and she whimpers as I thrust deeper with each stroke. She squeezes her thighs tighter around my hips and grinds into me. I lick the hollow of her neck and she smiles as she grabs my ears to pull my mouth against hers.

"How hard do you want it today?" I ask.

She sinks her teeth into my bottom lip just hard enough to make me wince. "Very hard." Then she kisses me slowly. "Then very slow."

I move in and out of her slowly as I kiss her, then I tilt my head back to watch her face as I lift her left leg and drive into her hard. She moans louder and I clamp my hand over her mouth so she doesn't wake the kids.

The vibration of her screams against my fingers spurs me on as I pound into her. Just when I'm about to come, I ease off and take my hand off her mouth. She laughs softly as I reach down to stroke her clit.

"God, you're so fucking sexy," I whisper into her ear as I caress her until she begins to tremble beneath me.

I keep my finger pressed against her clit as I dig into her

slowly, carefully unearthing each soft whimper of pleasure as if it were a diamond. When she begins to shake her head, I know it's because she's past the point of orgasm. Taking my finger out from between her legs, I lean down to kiss her slowly as I come inside of her.

"I love coming inside of you."

I kiss her again because I can never get enough of her lips. She pants softly into my mouth and my cock begins to harden again, filling her.

"Enjoy it while you can."

We've been trying for one more baby for over six months. It's totally ridiculous, but I want a son. I love Kaia and Mila more than air, but I feel like a boy would complete us. Lindsay sometimes gets upset. She thinks I want a son because I'm trying to fill a hole in our marriage, but that's not it; not at all. I want a son to teach him all the things I've learned about appreciating the right girl when she comes along.

After a slow and steady round two, I roll off of her and smack her hip. "Go make me some eggs, woman."

She uses both her feet to push me off the bed. "You make *me* some eggs!"

I scramble to my feet and lunge for her, but she rolls off the bed and out of my reach. Giggling like a fucking schoolgirl, she dashes into the bathroom and locks the door.

"Go feed your daughters!" she shouts from the other

side of the door.

Shaking my head, I scoop my boxers off the edge of the bed. Pulling on a T-shirt and shorts, I head for Mila's room, which is right next door to ours for convenience. Mila is the light in every one of my darkest days, but she is also ten times fussier than Kaia was at her age. I slowly push open her bedroom door and she's still asleep. Not surprising since she's usually making noise when she's awake.

Lindsay would probably tell me to wake her so she can sleep at the beach, but I can't bear to disturb her when she's sleeping so peacefully. Her dark blonde hair is plastered to the left side of her head and every once in a while her lips pucker up as if she's sucking on something.

"Daddy?"

I turn around and Kaia is standing in the doorway in her baby-blue pajama shirt and shorts with the pink Care Bear on the front. Her blonde curls are inherited from Nathan's father, but her green eyes and pouty lips are all Lindsay. My love for Kaia surpasses any love I've ever felt. Kaia is more like me than Mila is and somehow, at seven years old, she understands all my jokes and laughs louder than anyone.

"Come on, baby," I whisper, ushering her out of the room so we don't wake Mila.

As soon as I close the bedroom door, Kaia reaches for me so I can pick her up. Lindsay can't carry her anymore, but she knows I'll never refuse.

I pick her up and she immediately rests her head on my shoulder as I carry her down the stairs to the kitchen. "Want to help me make breakfast?"

"Can we have pancakes?" she asks, her eyebrows shooting up as she knows she's asking a lot, but she just has to try.

"Chocolate-chip pancakes?"

"Yes!"

"Okay, but you have to help me because Mommy likes your pancakes better than mine."

"No, she doesn't. She likes the pancakes at Grandma's house."

I laugh as I set her down on the counter and open the refrigerator. "Everybody loves Grandma's pancakes." I grab some eggs and milk then I grab the other ingredients from the pantry and set everything on the counter next to her. "Can you crack the eggs for me?" She nods and I reach for the cupboard. "Watch your head." I grab a couple of bowls and she takes a couple of eggs out of the carton. "Remember what I taught you: crack the eggs on the counter then break them into the bowl."

She taps the egg against the countertop and it doesn't crack. She tries again with a little more gumption and some of the white spills on the counter.

"It's okay. Mommy will clean it up later."

Her eyes widen because she knows how mad Lindsay gets whenever I say that.

"It's okay. Mommy's not here to hear that. Go ahead. Open the egg over the bowl."

She digs her thumbs into the crack of the egg and pulls the shell apart. The eggs plops into the bowl completely intact.

"High five." I raise my hand and she slaps it hard. "Ouch! Have you been lifting weights?"

"No!" she says angrily, as if I've offended her.

"Are you sure?" I ask as she reaches for another egg.

"Lifting weights is for boys."

"Lifting weights is for girls, too. Mommy lifts weights."

She taps the second egg against the countertop and this one splits open easily and sloshes out of its shell and onto the counter. I grab some paper towels and quickly wipe it up.

"Mommy will never know." I grab another egg and hand it to her. "You want to hear a joke?"

"I want to hear the one about the giraffe."

She cracks the egg against the counter and manages to get this one safely into the bowl.

"But you've heard that one about nine thousand times. You haven't heard my dinosaur joke." I close the carton of eggs and set it aside. "Why can't a Tyrannosaurus clap?"

She squints her eyes as if I'm speaking another language. "Duh! Their arms are too little," she replies as she wiggles her hands.

"No, because they're extinct."

She scrunches up her nose, then she giggles so loud I'm afraid she's going to wake Mila.

"Shh! Your sister's sleeping." She covers her mouth apologetically. "You liked that joke?" She nods as I move to the other side of the kitchen to grab the measuring cup. "Here. You measure the pancake mix and I'll tell you another joke."

By the time we have all the ingredients mixed together, Lindsay comes down in her white bikini and a peach sundress. Her hair is still damp and a little messy, the way we both like it.

"Help her with the pancakes and I'll go wake Mila."

"You didn't wake her up?"

I smile sheepishly and she shakes her head. "I couldn't do it. But I'm going right now."

She immediately forgets about me when she looks at Kaia. "Good morning, pumpkin."

"Mommy, I mixed everything myself."

"You *did?* I'll bet these pancakes are better than Grandma's."

I tear my eyes away from them and race up the stairs to Mila's room. When I walk in, she's awake in her crib; a rare occurrence. I scoop her up and she immediately begins to cry. I gently tap her bottom lip because this always seems to calm her, even when there's no promise of food. Instantly, she stops fussing and curls her tiny fists around my finger. She tries to pull my finger back into her mouth, then she gets frustrated when I resist.

"Come on. Mommy's boobs are downstairs."

I love that Lindsay insists on breastfeeding, even when we're busy traveling. And we're almost always traveling these days. It's nice to be in the beach house for the next three weeks. Kaia hates flying and Mila has to be starved of food and sleep before a flight or we become "that couple" on the plane that everyone hates because they can't quiet their screaming baby.

Hey, sometimes people with babies have to travel. If I could legally give her a tranquilizer, I'd be all over that shit.

When I enter the kitchen, Kaia is standing on a chair in front of the stove as Lindsay pours pancake batter into a skillet.

"That's too big!" Kaia squeals.

"That's because that pancake is for Daddy."

"I like big pancakes and I cannot lie."

Lindsay looks over her shoulder at the sound of my voice and she rolls her eyes when she sees Mila sucking on my finger. "Stop letting her do that."

"She's hungry. Give me the spatula." I kiss her cheek as we trade the tiny human for the kitchen utensil. Kaia looks up at me, bubbling over with excitement as I hand her the spatula. "Flip it, girl."

She carefully slides the spatula under the pancake and lifts it up, but a small piece sticks to the skillet and she ends up folding the pancake in half.

"Oh, shit," she curses, and Lindsay and I look at each other in horror. Kaia immediately covers her mouth. "Sorry."

I cup my hand over my mouth so she doesn't see my smile. "It's okay, just don't let it happen again."

"Sorry," she apologizes again.

"It's okay, baby. It's just a word. You're not in trouble."

Lindsay sits down in a dining chair, so she can cradle Mila as she feeds. I watch her for a moment as she strokes Mila's head and I marvel at how lucky we are to have fate on our side. If Lindsay had never cheated on me with Nathan, our relationship probably would have fizzled out the more I tried to push her away. If I had never met Claire, I may never have learned the power of forgiveness. If Nathan hadn't taken that trip to California, I would never have had the opportunity to fall in love with Kaia and to fall back in love with Lindsay.

I have this realization almost once a day because I still can't believe how fucking lucky I am.

"Daddy! It's burning!"

"Oh, shit!" I say and Kaia giggles. "Oops!" I say as I flip the burnt pancake onto the plate.

"You said it, too!"

"That's okay because Mommy's going to put Daddy in timeout later," Lindsay says from across the room.

I can't help but grin. "Yes, and Daddy is going to hate it."

"Ha, ha! You're going in timeout," Kaia teases me.

"You think that's funny," I say as I pour more batter into the skillet.

"Yes."

"Is it funnier than my dinosaur joke?"

"Yes."

"Oh, that hurts. You really hurt my feelings."

"No, I didn't. You're smiling." I frown dramatically and she laughs. "Tell Mommy the joke."

I hand Kaia the spatula again and cross my fingers that this time she'll flip it correctly.

"Mommy already knows the dinosaur joke, but I have another one. It's a surfing joke." Kaia groans and Lindsay laughs. "Hey, you have to brush up on your surfing jokes for when we go to the beach today."

"Surfing is boring," she complains.

"Flip that pancake."

She slides the spatula under the pancake less carefully this time, but she flips it successfully.

"High five."

She smacks my hand and I take the spatula from her. "Surfing is not boring. You'll see when I teach you to surf. You'll never want to stop."

"I don't want to learn to surf. I want to dance."

"You can do both. Okay, here's the joke. How do two surfers say hi to each other?"

"They wave," she says automatically.

"Have I told you that one before?"

"Only a million times!"

"That's because it's so good."

"No, it's not!" her and Lindsay shout at the same time.

I take the pancake out of the skillet and grab the ladle to pour some more batter in. "Yes, it is. And Daddy knows best."

We eat breakfast as quick as we can, which is never really fast at all because Kaia loves to talk while we're sitting at the table. Finally, we get everyone dressed and slathered in sunblock and I grab both mine and Lindsay's boards. We drive the block and a half to Carolina Beach because it's too damn hard to walk with two surfboards and two kids.

We set up our blanket and umbrella far enough down the beach that the crowds that are here for the music festival can't smother us. Lindsay sits on a beach chair under the umbrella with Mila in her arms. Mila's sunhat flops over her face so all I see is her chubby cheeks and it takes everything in me not to grab her face and bite those cheeks.

I stand Lindsay's board up so the sand doesn't rub off the wax. Then I tuck my board under my right arm and hold out my hand to Kaia.

"Come on. It's time for your first surfing lesson."

Kaia slowly reaches for my hand and we set off through the warm sand toward the water.

"Be careful!" Lindsay shouts.

When we reach the water's edge, we both stop. "You know what Grandpa Jim used to tell me about going in the water?"

"What?"

"He used to say, "The water isn't afraid of you. You have to show the water the same respect."" I don't know if she knows what this means, but she smiles. "Are you ready?" She nods and I crouch down so she can climb onto my back. "I love you, baby."

"I love you, Daddy."

EPILOGUE #2

CHRIS

JIMI'S ROOM STILL smells like the lilac paint we slathered on the walls four days ago. Claire insisted we paint her room with the non-toxic paint, but I swear they gave us the wrong kind because this smells worse than the stuff we used on our bedroom. Jimi's sleeping under her white comforter, on her belly, as usual. Ever since she used to fall asleep on my chest, she never really broke the habit of sleeping on her belly.

Her light-brown hair falls in wisps around her face as the soft morning light caresses the tops of her cheeks. Other than her hair color, she looks just like Claire: same eye color, same dip in the tip of her nose, the same pouty top lip. I could watch her sleep for hours, but today is beach day and it's one of Junior's favorite places to go.

I crouch next to Jimi's bed and softly brush the back of

my finger against her cheek until she groggily opens her eyes. "Good morning, princess." She closes her eyes as if she's going back to sleep, but she grabs my hand to make sure I don't leave. "It's time to wake up, sweetheart. We're going to the beach, remember?" She keeps her eyes closed, but she smiles. I brush her hair away from her forehead and kiss her before I stand up. "Come on, baby. Let's go wake up your mom."

I pull the comforter back and she opens her eyes as she reaches her arms out. "Mommy's a sleepyhead."

"Yes, she is." I lift her off the bed and she curls her arms and legs around me. "Mommy loves to sleep."

"Mommy loves you?"

I chuckle at the beautiful intonation in her question. "Yes, Mommy loves me, and you and Junior."

"And the baby?" she asks as I carry her down the second-floor hallway past the years of memories captured in family photos.

The pictures hanging on the wall are one of my favorite things about the beach house, and also one of my least favorites because it's still so incomplete. Abigail is nowhere on this wall. Claire and I haven't decided yet when we will tell Jimi and Chris, Jr. about their big sister. Jimi will be six years old in September. Three months and my princess will be in first grade. It makes my chest ache just to think about it.

"Yes, Mommy loves the baby, too."

The baby growing inside Claire right now will be our last, according to Claire. But I have a feeling I may be able to convince her to give me one more.

I push the bedroom door open and Claire isn't in bed. Jimi's mouth drops open and I push her chin up with my finger.

She laughs as she pushes my hand away. "Mommy's not here."

"Do you think she's in Junior's room?" She nods enthusiastically, as if we've solved a complex mystery. "Let's see if we're right."

When I open Junior's door, I'm not at all surprised to see Claire curled up with my three-year-old mini-me in his twin bed. He has the same light-brown hair as Jimi, but everything about his face is mine. Claire acts like she's a little disappointed with this, but she's not. She's forever smothering him with affection and I can never get enough of watching them together.

Claire opens her eyes then whispers something in Junior's ear. He laughs as he wiggles in her arms and she squeezes him tighter to hold him still.

"Get up, Junior!" Jimi shouts.

She can be a little bossy with her brother, but it's so hard for me not to encourage her when it's so fucking adorable.

"Be nice, princess." She pouts and hangs her head. "You have to be gentle when you wake someone up.

Remember how I woke you up?"

She doesn't nod or say anything. She tends to shut down when I correct her, which is why I hardly do it. Of course, this only makes her more of a daddy's girl.

"You want bubbles in your bath when we get home from the beach?" I ask Jimi and Claire laughs.

She knows I'm trying to make up for admonishing her. I don't care because Jimi's eyes light up as she nods.

Claire sits up and Junior crawls under his blanket toward the foot of the bed to get away from her. "Did Jake call?" she asks as she grabs the blanket and throws it off the bed.

"Still haven't heard from him. I'll call him again." I poke Junior in his ribs and he squeals. "Get up, baby bear. Momma has to get you dressed." I grab Jimi's hand and look her in the eye as I sway side to side. She loves when I dance with her. "I'll get this one ready," I say to Claire as I carry Jimi back to her room.

Once we're all dressed, I call Jake again to make sure he and Rachel are coming over to our house in Cary when we get back from the beach. Claire's been planning an outing for the twentieth anniversary of her mom's death, so we're driving almost three hours to Cary from the summer house, just so Rachel and Jake can babysit Junior. Besides my mom and Joel—and Senia and Tristan—they're the only ones she trusts to babysit her precious monster.

Claire hasn't wanted to go stargazing since the last time

we went on our wedding night. She doesn't want anything to overshadow that memory. This will be the first time we will acknowledge the significance of June 7th in a long time.

Now that Jimi is older and she loves her Grandma Jackie, Claire thinks it's time to introduce her to the grandma she never got to know. She's afraid of the kinds of questions Jimi will ask about her Grandma Kelly, but I've reassured her that there's nothing she could ask that would require anything but the truth: Kelly Nixon loved her daughter more than she loved herself, and she'll always be a powerful presence in our lives.

Jake still doesn't answer my call and I'm beginning to get more than a little pissed. Both he and Rachel know how much this means to Claire. I try not to let Jimi see that I'm upset, but she catches on quick. She's a lot like Abigail. She can sense things inside me.

"Are you mad, Daddy?" she asks as she looks up at me from where she stands in front of the closet at the bottom of the stairs.

I grab Claire's beach bag off a hook in the closet just as Claire comes bounding down the steps with Junior bouncing on her hip and a white dress draped over her baby bump.

"No, princess, I'm not mad," I say, rubbing her head.

"Can I wear my Barbie skates?" she asks, her squeaky voice full of hope.

"To the *beach*? How are you going to roll in the sand?"

"Let her wear the skates," Claire says as she passes us on her way to the kitchen.

"Babe, take this." I hold her beach bag out to her and she snatches it out of my hand as she keeps walking.

"Okay, you can wear your skates, but only if you promise to be extra good tonight when you go to dinner with Mommy and Daddy."

"I already promised!"

"Baby, what did I tell you about yelling?"

She narrows her eyes. "I promise."

I try not to shake my head in dismay. This girl is going to give me a heart attack by the time I'm forty.

Grabbing her skates from the shelf in the closet, I glimpse the clear, plastic box where Claire and I used to keep our photos of Abigail until we had a small kitchen fire a couple of years ago and we moved the pictures into a fire safe in our bedroom. The plastic box is now stuffed with foam letters, pipe cleaner, glitter glue, and a bunch of other craft supplies. It used to be too simple for Claire to take the box down and stare at the pictures for hours. Now that she needs a key and a code to get to them, she looks at the pictures less often, but she still talks about Abigail just as much.

We both still strongly believe that she will come back to us, if only just to meet us once in her lifetime. I refuse to believe that she can't feel how much I love her from hundreds or even thousands of miles away.

Thirty minutes later, we're packed up and seated in the car and Claire puts on a playlist of pop songs she made for Jimi—with a few of my songs mixed in because Jimi gets so excited every time she hears one of Daddy's songs in the car. I steal glances at her in the rearview mirror as I drive. Her eyes are closed as she nods her head to the beat. I don't think I could have asked for a more perfect girl than the one who wants nothing more than to dance to my music.

I look away from the rearview mirror and I catch Claire staring at me. "What are you looking at?"

She shakes her head and sighs. "Nothing."

I grab her hand and bring it to my lips. "We're teaching Junior to swim today."

"No. He's staying with me in the shallow waves. I'm not feeling well."

"Why didn't you tell me? We could have skipped this."

"No, we can't. Jimi's getting her time with us tonight." She reaches into the back and jiggles Junior's knee. The sound of his laughter is too sweet for words. "My monster is getting a day at the beach."

Claire is always putting our needs before her own. Sometimes, I worry that she's forgetting to do the things that make her happy. But one look at the smile on her face as she gazes at Junior and I know that it's her family that makes her happier than anything.

I grab her hand and give it a soft squeeze to get her attention. "Did you call Wendy yesterday?"

"Yeah, she got a couple of offers. She's trying to decide whether she wants to auction it off."

After we got married, Claire decided that the best path for her to help others while still being able to take care of her family—and herself—would be to write about her experience in the foster care system. It took her four and a half years to write the book, but it took less than four months for her to find a literary agent who believed in her story. I've always known that she would become the kind of person that my children would be proud to call "Mom."

"Are you going to tell everyone?" I ask.

"Not yet. I want to have a signed contract before I tell them."

"Always playing it cool," I say, as I turn right onto Lake Park Boulevard.

"I learned from the best."

When we were trying to decide where to buy a summer home on the coast, Claire insisted on having something right on the beach. Unfortunately, there was nothing available in Carolina Beach at the time. But I think it worked out to our advantage. Wrightsville Beach is much cleaner than Carolina Beach, which makes it much healthier for the kids. The only reason we're making the drive to Carolina Beach today is because of the music festival. I promised a local radio station that I would be there to sign autographs for half an hour.

I find a spot to park and pull on my baseball cap and

some sunglasses before I exit the car. Claire gets the kids out of the backseat while I grab the cooler and the beach bag.

"Do you want to go check in with Pete right now or can you just call him?" Claire asks.

"I'll call him once we find somewhere to sit. This place is a fucking madhouse."

The sand and water are packed with bodies and I don't like the idea of walking through this with my kids.

"Let's go further down away from this. This is crazy."

"But then you'll be so far from the booths," Claire replies.

"I'm not taking the kids in there."

A girl in a bikini bumps into the cooler I'm carrying as she passes us and I nearly lose my grip on it. "Sorry," she says, her gaze lingering on my face for a moment before she continues.

Why the fuck did I agree to come here?

"Let's just go to the booth and we can go back to the house for a little while after that."

"You're not supposed to sign for another two hours."

"Plans change. I'm not staying here or we're going to get mobbed."

I stuff everything back into the trunk and we each carry one of the kids as we head for the booths.

"You're going to feel guilty about this later," Claire says.

I can't see her eyes under the sunglasses or the floppy

hat, but the smirk she's wearing makes me want to smack her ass. She knows me too well.

"Are you going to help me sign autographs?" I ask Jimi and she nods as she adjusts her pink sunglasses. "Make sure you sign Princess Jimi. Okay?"

"I don't know how to write cursive."

"That's okay, baby. You can print your name like your teacher taught you and everyone will love it."

Claire sits a few feet behind us in the booth and Jimi sits on my lap as I sign autographs for nearly an hour to make up for the time change. Jimi is too embarrassed to sign anything, so she just clings to my neck like a little monkey as I work. I'm about to call it a day, when a blonde girl about Jimi's age, maybe a year or two older wanders over to our booth.

"Do you want an autograph?" Pete says from where he sits next to me.

The little girl stares at Jimi, like she can't believe I'm letting this little girl hug me.

"Hey, princess, I think somebody wants your autograph." I pry Jimi's arms from my neck and she faces forward as she sits on my lap. I put my black marker in her hand and grab one of the promo pictures the station brought.

"Can I put a heart?" Jimi whispers to me.

"Of course you can," I reply, then I look at the girl standing before us. "What's your name, sweetheart?"

She looks up at me and smiles. "Kaia. K-A-I-A."

I whip my head around to see if Claire heard that and she's staring at me with her mouth hanging open.

Jimi concentrates hard as she draws a shaky heart then begins to print her name next to it. When she finishes, she puts down the marker and turns her face into my chest again, too embarrassed to see what Kaia thinks of her autograph.

"It's beautiful, princess," I assure her. "Do you like it, Kaia?"

"Kaia, what are you doing?"

The relief on the blonde woman's face when she finds Kaia is palpable. I've never seen Lindsay, but this must be her, because her face goes a little pale when she sees me— and not because I'm Chris Knight. It's because I'm Claire's husband.

Jimi takes her face out of my chest to look at Kaia again, as if she can sense that the energy has shifted. "Daddy, did she like it?"

There are moments in life, and they happen so infrequently that they tend to really stand out, when life hands you the gift of perspective. Sometimes, we forget to show our appreciation. Sometimes, we get our priorities mixed up. And, sometimes, we forget how far we've come. But life always has a way of nudging you to remind you about these important things.

"Yes, baby. She liked it," I reply.

And as Kaia hugs the picture to her chest, I realize the number of things that had to happen for my daughter to give Adam's daughter this small token of affection: a shaky heart and a longing for her approval.

"I'm proud of you," I whisper in Jimi's ear.

"Can I go skating now?" she asks as Lindsay stands behind Kaia with her arms wrapped around her shoulders.

"Just a minute, baby."

Looking over my shoulder, I nod at Claire for her to join me at the table. I hold my hand out to Lindsay and she glances at Claire before she takes it.

"I'm Chris."

"Lindsay."

Claire stands next to me with Junior in one arm as she holds out her hand. "Hi, Lindsay. It's good to see you again."

They shake hands then Lindsay looks over her shoulder, presumably searching for Adam. There are too many people for me to pick him out, but Lindsay quickly squeezes through the river of bodies flowing behind her. He's standing at the booth across from us; another radio station.

I look up at Claire and I don't know why I'm surprised to find her looking at me. "Crazy," I whisper. "Did you see my princess give Kaia her autograph?"

Claire runs her fingers through Jimi's hair and I can feel her body instantly relax. "My beautiful girl," Claire says.

"She learned from the best."

EPILOGUE #3

Claire

CHRIS'S HAND LANDS on the back of my thigh as I stroke Jimi's hair. When you're with someone as long as Chris and I have been together; when you've shared so many things that there are no boundaries, physically or emotionally, a simple touch on the back of the leg can go unnoticed because it's second nature. Chris's body is as much mine as it is his. And my body is as much his as it is mine. The same way it is with every part of him and every aspect of the lives we share. I try to remind myself of this every day. I hope I never take his touch, his kiss, his words, or his love for granted.

The baby kicks inside me, as if he can sense that his daddy is near. Chris didn't want to know the sex of this baby. He said, "I have my princess and my monster. Anything that comes out next will be a Knight, which will complete the set." But I had to know. Because of the complications Abigail had with her heart, I've obsessed over all three pregnancies. So I cherish every kick and every roll I feel inside of me.

I grab Chris's hand off the back of my leg and move it onto my belly so he can feel it, too. He smiles as he waits for it.

"Claire?"

Chris and I look up at the same time and Adam is standing there with Lindsay and Kaia. There's a sleeping baby strapped to his chest and a gleam in his eyes as he grabs the back of Lindsay's neck. Chris stands up and switches Jimi to his other arm so he can hold out his right hand.

The handshake happens in slow motion. Chris's hand reaches forward and Adam looks a bit surprised as he removes his hand from Lindsay's neck to shake Chris's hand. They're both smiling and they nod at each other and say something I can't quite hear. *How's it going*, or something like that. As their hands come apart, Adam's hand moves right back to where it was before, on the back of Lindsay's neck.

A simple touch.

Adam's face is the same, except for a few new crinkles at the corners of his eyes. He must be thirty or thirty-one now. I look down at Junior's head where it rests on my shoulder. My monster is bored out of his mind and dying to get into the water.

"Are you hungry, baby?" I ask him, and he nods as I switch him to my other hip.

My boy is getting too big for me to carry him for long periods of time.

Chris sets Jimi down on the sand and takes Junior from me as he steps away from the chair. "Sit down, babe." As soon as I sit down, Jimi immediately tries to climb into my lap. "Give Mommy a break, princess," Chris says, taking her hand to pull her away.

"It's okay," I say, grabbing her and sitting her on my knee so she's facing the crowd.

"How have you been?" Adam asks as he flashes Jimi a smile.

I can't see Jimi's face, so I don't know if she returns the smile.

When she's home, Jimi is so outgoing, and even a terror. But she tends to get shy around strangers. I'm happy she wants to take dance lessons. I'm hoping this will help her come out of her shell. She's a lot like me. She's sensitive. She experiences the world with her emotional volume turned all the way up. This is why she's daddy's princess.

Junior, on the other hand, is the most easy-going three-year-old boy ever to grace this Earth. He is his father. He's fearless and loving and he can be quite protective of his big sister. I only call him my monster because he thinks it's so funny. A more accurate nickname for him would be my sunshine.

"We're good," I reply as I brush Jimi's hair over her ear and resist the urge to ask Adam why he wasn't at Cora's funeral three years ago. "Just expecting our third in six weeks and enjoying some time off before Chris starts the promo stuff for the new album. How are you two doing?"

I look at Lindsay when I say this and she smiles, the same mildly uncomfortable smile I remember from the last day I saw her six and a half years ago.

"We're doing well," Lindsay replies and she looks to Adam to finish filling us in.

"When we're not traveling, we're living here in Carolina Beach to be close to our families, but we still make the drive out to Durham every so often so Kaia can see her Grandma and Grandpa Jennings."

I would never guess that Kaia was not his. Except for the fact that her blonde hair is curly and her lips are a bit fuller than Adam's, she looks like Adam and Lindsay's biological daughter. It makes me insanely happy to know that Kaia still has Nathan's family in her life. I wish my mother's family had been there for me after her death.

"Hormones," I say with a smile as I wipe a tear from my eye. "She's beautiful."

Chris kisses the top of my head and whispers, "Are you okay, babe?"

I nod as Jimi looks back at me over her shoulder.

Suddenly, I'm reminded of why I was advised to quit the caseworker position I was offered straight out of UNC. It was impossible for me not to become emotionally involved when everything still reminds me of my mother.

I'm hoping that tonight's outing with Chris and Jimi will ease some of that latent heartache. My therapist thinks sharing my love for my mother with my baby girl is important for me to feel close to Jimi. I took that advice to mean that the love shared between a parent and child can transcend and heal generations the more it is shared.

With Rachel and Jake not answering their phones, we may not even get to go stargazing. But we'll still get to spend the night in Cary in our house, with all the memories we've created. My mom would be happy if she could see us.

I grab Jimi's chubby cheeks and plant a loud kiss on her forehead, which she quickly wipes away.

"Well, we should let you get back to work," Lindsay says and Adam nods in agreement. "It was so nice seeing you all."

"You, too," I reply as an irresistible impulse bubbles up inside me. "If you guys ever get the urge to visit Wrightsville, we're in the yellow beach house, three houses south of the pier. We'll be there for another three weeks."

"Yeah, we're having a kid-friendly dinner thing next Saturday. You all should come," Chris says, and my heart swells with pride.

Adam looks a little confused by this hospitality coming

from Chris, but I'm not. Chris has never been the type of person to hold a grudge. I think of the tattoo on the back of his neck: *What we think, we become.* Chris always chooses to see the goodness in others and, in turn, his goodness shines through.

Adam and Lindsay look to each other, silently communicating, and I can't help but smile. In the years following the breakup, I would remember things that made me realize that he never got over Lindsay. We were both using each other as bandages to cover our wounds. Somehow, we still found our way home. This is evident by the way Adam and Lindsay communicate so effortlessly—like Chris and me.

"Sounds great," Adam says, addressing Chris. "I guess we'll see you guys later. Enjoy the festival."

"You, too," I reply. "Bye, Kaia."

She smiles shyly then they all walk away, disappearing into the stream of people moving through the maze of booths. I look up at Chris and his expression is serious.

"That was hard."

"But you did exactly what you always said you'd do," I reply as I think back on all the conversations Chris and I have had about the time he almost lost me.

He always said that if we ever ran into Adam, he would invite him over for dinner as a way of thanking him for bringing us back together. I've always been skeptical of this, but Chris proved himself today.

"Because I love you more than this."

And by "this" he means *everything*.

The End.

Turn the page for a scorching hot preview of

TRISTAN & SENIA'S STORY

http://bit.ly/abandonbook

A Shattered Hearts Series Novel

ABANDON

NEW YORK TIMES BESTSELLING AUTHOR
CASSIA LEO

CHAPTER ONE

SHE WALKS INTO Yogurtland with her cell phone pressed to her ear and a scowl on her face. Behind the scowl, her vulnerability shines like a fucking nuclear explosion in a dark closet. Whoever she's talking to has stripped her bare. I find myself wishing it were me who affected her that way.

She's digging inside her purse while balancing the phone between her shoulder and her ear; probably searching for money to get her frozen yogurt fix. What is it about frozen yogurt that makes us feel better? Maybe it reminds us of being kids, and how something as simple as a trip to the yogurt shop could turn a bad day into a great one. Whatever it is, I can see that she desperately needs some frozen yogurt. But with each passing moment that she's unable to locate her money, I see the hope draining from her face.

"I told you to stop calling me. I don't care if your car is in the shop. I'm not picking you up!"

She drops her purse and cell phone onto the checkered tile floor and curses loudly. "What the fuck are you staring at?!" she barks at the man who's ogling her ass while ushering his small child out of the shop. "You've never seen a girl in a skirt bend over?"

She falls to her knees as she reaches for the cell phone first. She presses it to her ear and says hello a few times before she realizes there's no one there. I walk over to her, coolly taking my time, then I kneel next to her and reach for the lipstick tube that rolled behind her left foot. I hold it out in front of her. She looks sideways at me and her mouth drops as she's stunned into silence. Most girls are stunned when they see me. I'm used to that. But Senia has seen me plenty of times. She's not amazed by my good looks. She's stupefied by my impeccable timing.

Her gaze immediately falls to my lips, which are just inches from her own. Then she begins to sob as she drops her purse and throws her arms around my neck.

I can't help but chuckle. "Hey, it's okay," I whisper into her ear as I breathe in her scent. She smells like strawberries or pineapple. Something fruity. It's intoxicating.

I reach up and grab her face to pull her away, so I can look her in the eye. "What flavor do you want?"

A tear rolls down her face and I wipe it away as she stares at me, still dumbfounded. "Cheesecake, with strawberries."

"Perfect."

I help her gather the rest of her belongings into her purse then I order her yogurt as she watches me from where she stands next to the trash bin. Her gaze follows me as I approach her with her bowl of frozen yogurt, one of her perfect eyebrows cocked skeptically.

"Don't look at me like that," I say as I pass her the bowl of yogurt.

"Why?" she says as she pops the first spoon of creamy yogurt into her mouth.

She licks the spoon clean and I find myself wondering what it would feel like to have those full, red lips wrapped around my cock. I lean in and whisper in her ear, "Because you're turning me on and I can't fuck you in Yogurtland."

She continues to cock her eyebrow as she takes another spoonful of yogurt into her mouth. "Then maybe we should get the fuck out of Yogurtland."

IN THE THREE years I've known Senia, we've almost fucked three times. The first time happened the day I met her, after a show we played in Durham. We were interrupted backstage by Xander, the band's manager, just as Senia was about to get on her knees. The second time was at a Memorial Day picnic. We were both pretty shitfaced and she ended up tossing her cookies all over me as I was sliding her panties off. The third time happened less than three months ago, in a pub restroom stall. She started crying and couldn't go through with it; she was too heartbroken over her ex. I think the fourth time may be the charm for us. For some reason, this makes me really fucking nervous.

I'm not afraid I won't be able to satisfy her. There's no doubt I'll make her come harder than she's ever come before. But for the first time in my life, I'm afraid of what will come after the sex.

Senia is Claire's best friend. Even if Claire and Chris never get back together, I know Claire will always be around. Chris is my best friend. I can't avoid Claire and, therefore, I can't avoid Senia. Something about this terrifies me and intrigues me; like I'm flirting with danger or, more accurately, fucking with danger.

I grab the door handle on the passenger side of my silver Audi and pause as I look her in the eye and pull the door open. "Get in."

She smiles and shakes her head as she slinks into the passenger seat. "Please don't bother using your manners."

"I won't."

I slam the door shut and walk around to the driver's side, tapping the trunk as I note my surroundings. It's eight in the evening. There are only three other cars in the parking lot and at least one of those belongs to the guy working behind the counter in Yogurtland. I look up at the lamppost in front of the car illuminating the hood and shining through the windshield.

I open the door and slide into the driver's seat. Gazing into her eyes, for a moment I'm reminded of the last time my mom took me to get ice cream, when I was nine years old. I clench my jaw against the visceral nature of this memory and Senia takes this as an invitation.

She climbs into my lap and takes my face in her hands as she crushes her lips to mine. I thread my fingers into her hair and roughly grab a fistful of her dark locks. She whimpers as I thrust my tongue into her mouth and squeeze my fist around her hair, intermittently tightening my grip then easing up. Finally, I pull her head back by her hair and her eyes widen with shock and excitement. That's when I notice her styrofoam bowl of yogurt upended between us, the cold stickiness seeping through both of our shirts.

She smiles as she swipes her finger through the cool, sticky substance and slowly eases her finger into her mouth. "Creamy," she purrs.

"Fuck," I whisper as my dick jumps, trying to escape my jeans.

I grab the bowl and toss it into the backseat and she smiles as I swipe my finger through the yogurt on her shirt then shove my hand under her skirt. Her thighs are smooth and warm against the back of my fingers as I move straight for her panties. She holds my gaze as I slip my fingers under the fabric and find her clit. She swallows hard as her smile melts into an expression of pure ecstasy.

"Oh, my God," she breathes as I stroke her gently.

I grab the back of her neck and pull her mouth against mine, swallowing her moans as if they were the air keeping me alive. I shove two fingers inside her and she gasps as I curl my fingers to reach her spot. Her body folds into me as I lick the soft skin below her earlobe. Abruptly, I remove my hand from her panties. Her face is incredulous as I grab her shoulders and push her away.

"Get in the back."

For a moment, it seems as if she's questioning this abrupt request. "This better be good," she says as she slithers between the two front seats to get into the backseat.

I reach under her skirt as she crawls into the back and yank down on her panties. "Jesus Christ, Tristan!"

"Make up your mind," I say as I place my hand on her ass and push her into the backseat. "Am I Jesus Christ or Tristan?"

She laughs as I scramble into the backseat after her, holding onto her panties so she's forced to leave them behind. I quickly position myself between her legs as she lies on her back and smiles. "You can be whoever the fuck you want."

I slide my arm under her waist and lift her up so I can place her back against the passenger side window. Pushing her skirt up, I spread her legs wide open and marvel at the sight of her. She perfectly shaved with a small landing strip of dark hair that ends at the top of her slit.

"I prefer Tristan," I say as I flash her my crowd smile.

She whimpers like a kitten in pain, her hips writhing against me as I devour her slowly and methodically. She tastes like the frozen yogurt I smeared all over her.

"Oh, Tristan," she moans and I hook my arms tightly around her thighs to steady her as her legs begins to tremble. "Oh, my fucking God!"

I suck gently as her clit pulsates against my tongue. She lets out a loud cry that sounds like a sigh mixed with a scream. I can't help but smile as I continue to stimulate her until she grabs chunks of my shoulder-length hair and yanks me up.

"Holy shit," she breathes as she wraps her arms around my neck and pulls me on top of her.

But she doesn't kiss me. She just holds me there and I quickly begin to feel uncomfortable with this closeness. I begin to push away, but she tightens her grip.

"Please don't move," she begs, and I can hear something strange in her voice—she's crying.

I lie still with her for a while until I no longer hear her sniffling. I slowly pull my head back to look her in the eye and she quickly wipes at the moisture on her cheeks.

"I'm sorry," she whispers.

I grab her hand and pull it away from her face. "It's okay," I murmur as I brush my thumb over her cheekbone.

"No, it's not," she says, a hard edge to her voice as her

hands reach down to undo the button and zipper on my jeans. "But it will be."

She pushes my boxers down until my dick springs free and I suck in a sharp breath as it comes in contact with her.

"I don't have a condom."

My hair hangs around my face as I hover over her. She reaches up and pushes my hair back as she pulls my mouth to hers. I groan as I try to resist making such a stupid mistake. Despite the rumors, I don't have unprotected sex. I may be a whore like my mother, but I'm not as reckless as she is.

I try to pull my face back, but Senia holds my head still. Suddenly, I'm royally pissed off. I tear myself from her grasp and glare at her.

"This is just a fuck. Nothing more," I insist and her eyebrows scrunch together. A sharp pang of regret twists inside my chest. "I'm sorry."

Why the fuck am I apologizing?

"Then shut up and fuck me," she says as she tightens her legs around my hips and the tip of my cock presses against her opening.

I slide in slowly, watching as she closes her eyes and tilts her head back. Leaning forward, I suck on her throat as I gradually ease myself further inside her with each stroke.

"You're tight as fuck," I whisper as I carefully work my way deeper inside.

She doesn't respond, so I keep thrusting, slowly at first

then working my way up to a steady pace. I pull my head back to see her face and her eyes are still closed. I don't know why, but I want to see her eyes.

"Look at me," I command, and she opens her eyes instantly, her gaze finding mine.

Her eyes are slightly red and that's when I notice the tear tracks running from the corners of her eyes, down her temple, and disappearing into her dark hair. A strange urge overcomes me and I lean down and kiss her temple. Licking my lips, the saltiness of her tears turn me on even more. I ease my hand behind her knee and lift her leg higher so I can thrust deeper.

She whimpers as she threads her fingers through my hair and pulls my mouth to hers. I kiss her slowly, matching the rhythm of my hips to the movement of our tongues. She bites my top lip and I feel myself getting so close to blowing my load.

"Holy shit," I whisper as I try to pull my head back, but she holds my head still and kisses me deeply as I let go inside her.

My dick twitches as I fill her with my gushing warmth. I grunt into her mouth and she continues to kiss me, swallowing my cries the way I did hers. Finally, I tilt my head back and look her in the eye. Then I ask her a question I haven't asked anyone since I broke up with Ashley four years ago.

"Who was that on the phone?"

"BRING ME HOME"

The sunlight followed you in, but you never saw it coming,
Held the rain clouds like a blanket, and took off running,
Then I grabbed your hand and slowly pointed at the sun,
Closed your eyes and dropped it all just to feel the warmth,

Step inside, it's cold outside
Girl, you're not alone
You waited long, you cried
But, girl, you're still my home
My home

"Love is not the only thing we share," you whispered here,
We let her in, then let her go, never knew such tears,
The morning came, I paid you my heart, you paid me your life,
Won't ever forget my purpose, long as you're my wife.

Step inside, it's cold outside
Girl, you're not alone
You waited long, you cried
But, girl, you're still my home
My home

When the stars fall down upon us
And the last flame flickers out
I'll be there to whisper in your ear
I love your heart, babe, bring me home.

Bring me Home Playlist

"You Could Be Happy" by Snow Patrol
"Slow Dancing in a Burning Room" by John Mayer
"Just Say Yes" by Snow Patrol
"I Will Follow You Into the Dark" by Death Cab for Cutie
"Lullabies" by Yuna (Adventure Club Mix)
"Heal Over" by KT Tunstall
"Lego House" by Ed Sheeran
"Blank Page" by Christina Aguilera
"Talk" by Kodaline
"Kiss Me" by Ed Sheeran
"Hear You Me" by Jimmy Eat World
"A Thousand Years" (Part 2) by Christina Perri feat. Steve Kazee
"Already Gone" by Kelly Clarkson
"Falling Slowly" by Kris Allen
"Ordinary People" by Mathai with Chris Cauley
"Oh Father" by Sia
"Count On Me" by Bruno Mars

"First Day of My Life" by Bright Eyes

"I Won't Give Up" by Jason Mraz

"How Long Will I Love You" by Ellie Goulding

"In Your Eyes" (Acoustic) by Sara Bareilles

"Your Song" by Ellie Goulding

"Halo" (Acoustic) by Beyonce

"She Is Love" (Acoustic) by Parachute

"Anchor" by Mindy Gledhill

Listen to the playlist on YouTube.

http://bit.ly/bmhplaylist

Listen to the playlist on Spotify.

http://bit.ly/bmhplaylists

Acknowledgements

I have so much thanks to give to my old and new beta readers: Jordana Rodriguez, Christine Estevez, Deborah Meissner, Jennifer Mirabelli, Sam Stettner, Jodie Stipetich, Haley Douglas, Shannon Ramsey, Kristin Shaw, Carrie Raasch, Sarah Schwartz, Vilma Gonzalez, Michael Finn, Trisha Rai, and Sarah Rabe. You all have been so generous with your time and feedback. Thank you so much for taking time away from your families and from your to-read lists for me. I am so glad to have been on this journey with you all.

Thanks again to Sarah Hansen at Okay Creations. Thanks for finding the photographer of the image I so desperately wanted. I'm very grateful for your patience and expertise.

Huge thank-you to all the book bloggers who have shared *Relentless* and *Pieces of You* with your friends, families, and readers. Thank you for sharing the teasers and cover reveal. Thank you for supporting me and my books. You all work tirelessly for the love of books, and for that, I love you.

My family, especially my daughter, for encouraging me to continue writing when I was ready to give up.

And, last but not least, a huge thank-you to my street team and all the readers who have shared my books and cheered me on the past three months. Even the ones who challenged me and drove me up the wall. You make my job not feel like a job at all.

Other books by Cassia Leo

CONTEMPORARY ROMANCE
Relentless **(Shattered Hearts #1)**
Pieces of You **(Shattered Hearts #2)**
Bring Me Home **(Shattered Hearts #3)**
Abandon **(Shattered Hearts #3.5)**
Black Box **(stand-alone novel)**

PARANORMAL ROMANCE
Parallel Spirits **(Carrier Spirits #1)**

EROTIC ROMANCE
Unmasked Series
KNOX Series
LUKE Series
CHASE Series

Get Involved

RATE IT: If you enjoyed this book, please consider leaving a review wherever you purchased it or at *Goodreads* (http://bit.ly/XHTv1L).

DISCUSS IT: Discuss the books with us on *Facebook* (http://bit.ly/shatteredhearts).

JOIN US: Follow Cassia on *Facebook* (http://on.fb.me/XrRo0c) and *Twitter* (http://bit.ly/cassialeoTWT). Sign up for email updates on *Cassia's blog* (http://bit.ly/cassianews) or become part of her *street team* (http://bit.ly/cassiateam) to get inside information on new releases, exclusive street team giveaways, and more.

About the Author

New York Times and *USA Today* bestselling author Cassia Leo loves her coffee, chocolate, and margaritas with salt. When she's not writing, she spends way too much time watching old reruns of *Friends* and *Sex and the City*. When she's not watching reruns, she's usually enjoying the California sunshine or reading—sometimes both.

Made in the USA
Middletown, DE
24 March 2015